ALRIN

by
Kyle King

For my loving wife Jennifer.

CONTENTS

CHAPTER ONE

ALRIN'S PUZZLE BOX

T *wo-thirteen.* To everyone in Everglen, that was his name.

It wasn't his actual name, of course. His name was Alrin Turner, but the 2-1-3 on the back of his hand made them care about little else, least of all his name.

Staring up from his bed, he listened to the wind's one-note melody whistle through the branches and followed the two-step dance of their shadows across his ceiling. His mind gripped him, for something incredible had happened that day. The trouble was, the last thing he could remember was falling.

He and his older brother, Thrain, had spent a generous part of that day tracking a large whitetail deer deep into one of their favorite parts of the Tatra Mountains. Throughout much of the year, melting snow from the surrounding peaks funneled into a small hidden-away valley, gifting it with sparkling waterfalls that misted down into crystal-clear pools below. During the warmer months, Alrin and Thrain often dove from the hundred-foot cliffs into the safety of their brisk depths. But with winter already making its yearly descent back into the valley, the ground below had been nothing but a blanket of stone such as you would find at the bottom of a dried-up creek bed.

Alrin had no memory of landing, nor any clue how he'd survived, but however he'd managed it, it had to have been nothing less than magical. And that was the problem. Alrin couldn't use magic. No one could at level one.

Searching the ceiling for answers was only making falling asleep harder when, from across the room, the silence was dampened by a light tap against Thrain's wall.

Thump-thump. Thump-thump.

They often did this when one of them couldn't sleep and wanted to see if the other was still awake. And the tap always came in twos. Like a heartbeat.

"Can't sleep either?" Alrin called out into the darkness of their room, relieved to hear something other than the pounding in his ears.

"Nope," came an airy breath.

Silence filled the next several moments, but it was a different kind of silence now.

"What happened today?" Thrain finally asked.

Alrin took a deep breath and watched his words rise to join the dancing shadows across his ceiling. "No idea…"

Each waited for the other to speak again, but neither of them did.

Alrin rose just before the sun the next morning. Flashing images from the day before had consumed his dreams until he woke with a jolt as if falling out of a nightmare. He looked out of his frost-glazed window and saw the faithful border of the Tatra Mountains beginning to part from the horizon just as the stars were starting to turn out their lights. There was rarely an uninspiring view from that window. It never mattered what greeted him from the other side. It was home.

They lived just outside the border of Everglen in a small three-room cabin, only a ten-minute walk from town. "Close enough, but far enough," their mother, Aurora, would say. Their cabin was dug into the side of a hill, making three of the walls and much of the roof obscured from view by the surrounding embankment. There was a single solid-oak door and one much-too-small window—the one next to Alrin's bed.

Alrin and Thrain shared the smallest of the rooms. Aurora's was on the opposite end of the house, and between the two was the family room. Alrin always rolled his eyes when someone actually called it that—as if being in another room would somehow magically make them less of a family. He had always wondered if its being called a "family room" was a constant reminder to those who lived alone that they didn't have one. *How terribly insensitive*, Alrin always thought to himself. He often daydreamed about such things, possessed by the uncontrollable need to defend those who didn't need defending (more often than not when they didn't need defending because they didn't even exist).

A faint glow from the dwindling embers in the fireplace joined the growing light from his window, allowing Alrin to make out his brother as he lay in bed. Alrin turned over and knocked their secret heartbeat pattern against the wall, but when Thrain didn't answer, he decided not to rouse him and instead reached up to his windowsill where he kept a small wooden puzzle box. His mother had had it specially made one year for his birthday by someone in town. Jorund Ashcroft was his name—he was Everglen's guild leader of wisdom, and among his many talents was the ability to craft nearly anything requested of him. Wooden toys, ax handles, rocking chairs…you name it. But by far his favorite thing to make was *puzzle boxes*.

They were strange little trinkets, no larger than Alrin's fist, and nearly impossible to open. Each one Jorund made came with several hidden prongs or intricate grooves that needed to be maneuvered or aligned into just the right position for the lid to unlatch. It took Alrin weeks to figure his out, but once he did he was finally able to open it and find the prize that each of the boxes came with—one of Jorund's infamous riddles etched under the lid.

Like the boxes themselves, the riddles were all different, but each one Jorund chose was undeniably placed for a reason. A sort of hidden meaning within its hidden meaning.

Alrin twisted the lid clockwise a quarter turn and slid a few pieces that jutted out along the sides to the positions that only he knew, and the box clicked open. He raised the lid and read the inscription beneath it just as he had so many times before.

At the end of a blade, I shall be found. Through halls of stone, I grandly resound.

His was about glory, of course. Not too difficult to figure out once you realized that it was all anyone cared about.

Alrin didn't actually keep much inside the puzzle box, mostly just ordinary rocks that happened to out-sparkle their neighbors as he walked through the woods, but it was the one thing in their tiny cabin that he didn't have to share with anyone else. It was his.

He spun the box over in his hand and listened to its contents tumble softly against one another. Something about it had always fascinated him. It wasn't what he kept inside, or even the riddle under the lid; it was the box itself. Every part was intricately crafted and flawlessly smooth. All except for a tiny bored-out hole that made it seem as though a knot in the wood had fallen out. At first that's precisely what Alrin had thought, until the day he learned that everything Jorund made came with the same tiny hole. Another hidden meaning, no doubt.

After several forcibly patient minutes of waiting, and not sensing any end to Thrain's snoring, Alrin worked up the nerve to leave the cocoon of warmth that he'd carefully concealed with him under the blankets and set the puzzle box back on the windowsill.

The room was frozen. The fire must have died out earlier than usual in the night.

Reaching down by the foot of his bed, Alrin fumbled blindly for his jacket. He usually tried to keep it over his legs as he slept because its added weight was comforting and it helped to combat the chilled air that easily found its way through his single-paned window. Somehow or another it always seemed to end up on the ground, which was right where he found it. Slinging it over his shoulders, he tiptoed into the family room and over to a large lumber pile stacked neatly in the corner. With a few handfuls of kindling and two quick breaths, the wood began to crackle, instantly warming his face and hands.

There, Alrin thought. *Hopefully that keeps them warm.* He made his way to the door, quietly unlatched it, and slipped outside into the darkness.

The morning's chill covered the valley, and a thin layer of frost coated the ground, creating a strangely satisfying crunch as it gave way under his feet. He took the dirt path away from their cabin and went over to sit on an old moss-covered stump. When he and Thrain were younger, they had both taken turns chopping at the immovable nuisance, but had been unsuccessful—which was fortunate, because it now served as the perfect place to watch the sunrise. A light fog flowed out of the trees and over the glasslike surface of a pond, making it seem as if even the forest itself had woken up and joined him in watching their breath plume out into the cold mountain air.

Alrin knew every ridge and every peak of the Tatras from that stump. He'd never been more than a few miles outside of town, but he was certain that even if he traveled the entire world, there would be nothing else like them.

He'd always found comfort in living in the shadow of the mighty giants. At any moment he could close his eyes and paint them in his mind—each peak a softer shade of bluish purple than the one before it, until the last finally blended into the color of the crisp morning sky. They almost felt like blankets wrapping themselves around Everglen, protecting it from the outside world.

Alrin brought his knees to his chest and tucked his feet up under his jacket to keep warm. But even though each breath of the mountain air awakened his senses, he couldn't remember much from the day before. It was worse than trying to remember a dream. He removed his arm from his jacket and stared down at his ensignis as if they somehow held the answers.

His stomach turned a little every time he looked at them. Most people were obsessed with their ensignis. Alrin hated them.

He'd first learned their meaning when he was younger, from Halvdan, Everglen's guild leader of magic. Of course his father would have been the one to teach him, had he not died shortly after Alrin was born. Halvdan had once been a close friend of his father's, though he rarely spoke of it (despite Alrin's incessant prying), and Alrin would visit his guild as often as he could to hear of their great adventures. And, if he was lucky, to see Halvdan use magic.

Every town had three guilds and three guild leaders—one for each of the three ensignis. Whoever held the highest level in each skill was appointed the town's guild leader, so being one was an extremely prestigious position, and competition was stiff. Being in Halvdan's presence, let alone asking him questions, was a rare privilege. Alrin looked up to him like family, and visiting him never failed to be both enlightening and inspiring.

One morning at the age of six or seven, Alrin visited the guild in hopes of seeing the students practice their magic, as on any other day. But this time was different. This time he finally worked up the courage to ask Halvdan the one question he knew he should already know the answer to.

The magic guild was a magnificent stone building at the northeast corner of town. At its center was a large, uncovered courtyard that opened up to the sky, where many of Halvdan's students studied or practiced their spells. Making his way down several long corridors and past countless unwelcoming stares, Alrin came to the small wing of the guild where Halvdan always worked.

It was there that he sat, his back turned at his desk. The air smelled of thick pipe smoke and old parchment. Every time Alrin stepped into that room, he was inspired and intimidated. Shelves upon shelves crammed full of books lined every wall, but the good stuff was always behind Halvdan's desk. There were the oddest-looking stones with strange glyphs on them, countless vials of spell components, and even stranger plants that Alrin swore would turn toward him as he walked by. It was organized chaos to Alrin's eyes, but he loved it.

"What are you working on?" Alrin asked, announcing his presence.

"Ah, Alrin…just sharpening the tools in the ol' noggin, really. What trouble are you getting into today, I wonder?" Halvdan smirked as he glanced at Alrin out of the corner of his eye.

"None yet," Alrin answered. "That's why I came here, of course."

"Bah! Quick-witted, I see—very quick indeed." Halvdan continued to write feverishly. "I admire that in you, Alrin. Don't ever lose it."

Alrin paced slowly around the room, admiring scrolls and old maps of distant places that he'd heard of only in very old tales. "Can I ask you something?" Alrin finally asked, lowering his eyes to the ground.

"Of course, my boy. Ask away." The pace of Halvdan's work was unbroken. The smoke from his long wooden pipe billowed around him. He had a gentle face, small beady eyes, and a thin beard that was beginning to turn gray. Alrin could always tell that he wished it were longer, because he tugged on it incessantly with the tips of his fingers.

"What do the numbers on my hand mean?" Alrin asked.

Halvdan choked back a burst of laughter, trying his best to disguise it as a sudden cough, as if he'd accidentally inhaled too much smoke. "I do suppose you were too young for your father to teach you that before he…" Halvdan paused. "What do you know about them?"

"Nothing, really," Alrin said, somewhat embarrassed.

"Mmm." Turning around in his chair, Halvdan looked Alrin over and combed his hand through his scraggly beard. Alrin knew he was choosing his words carefully. As a guild leader, he knew the importance of the question, and the deep impact his response would have.

"Sit, won't you?" he requested, sliding several stacks of books off a bench beside his desk. He pushed back into his chair and filled several moments of silence with deep drafts from his pipe.

"I will tell you only what it means to others," he finally said. "What it means to you is for you alone to decide."

Alrin hung on every word as Halvdan reached out and took Alrin's right hand.

"The numbers on your hand…or your *ensignis*," Halvdan explained, "show how powerful you are. Every person on Dalroth, myself included, bears the markings of the three ensignis." Halvdan pointed to each number on Alrin's hand, starting closest to his knuckles and moving in a triangle. "They are read in this order, and in none other, so listen well: *strength, magic,* and *intellect.*

"Strength, as I'm sure you know, represents your physical power. The swiftness of your sword, how deadly your arrow, your endurance, and, yes—even the strength of your body. Your *magic* level, or mana as some would call it, shows how proficient you are in the wondrous arts of magic. Every potion, spell, and magical ability you attempt requires you to reach a high-enough level to successfully cast or master it. Even King Abaddon, the most powerful man in all of Dalroth, is limited to the extent of his magic level.

"And finally *intellect*," Halvdan said, pointing to the final number on Alrin's hand. "Although I am Everglen's leader of magic, intellect, in my not-so-humble opinion, can be the most useful level to advance. It measures what others cannot see— wisdom, perseverance, and determination. This ensigni is not to be taken lightly, you see, because no matter how powerful one may be in strength and magic, one is limited to the extent of one's cleverness and mental swiftness.

"Your ensignis are your legacy, your pride, and if you let them, they can lead to your downfall. What you do as your profession, down to the very people you can associate with, is all decided by the levels of your ensignis. From the moment you are born, they track your every move. Every ounce of energy used, every spell that you cast, and any knowledge you obtain, your ensignis remember.

"As you become more powerful, your ensignis reflect it. They start with the ones you are born with and go all the way up to ninety-nine. Some keep them visible at all times, some choose to keep them hidden. But be warned, for many regard hidden ensignis as a sign of weakness or deceit...but to each his own, I suppose."

Sparked by a sudden curiosity, Alrin shifted his gaze to Halvdan's right hand and saw that his ensignis were concealed under a brown leather glove. Remembering why his attention had moved there to begin with, he looked up to find Halvdan's eyes meeting his own.

"Ah, see what I mean? Having access to the strengths and weaknesses of those around you rouses curiosity, doesn't it? Being privy to an individual's most cherished possessions can be dangerous, so be ever cautious with how you use it. You are forever bound to your ensignis, Alrin, and they to you. Leveling their ensignis is what drives people. From the moment they wake up until sleep subdues the obsession, it is all everyone thinks about..."

Hearing the latch of his front door shook Alrin from his memory. He glanced back to the cabin and saw Thrain slowly making his way over. Seeing him awake heartened him, for the longer Alrin had to sit and think by himself, the more uneasy he became.

Thrain wore nothing more than what he slept in, and as usual was remarkably unaffected by the frigid morning air. He had always been more tolerant of cold weather than Alrin, likely because he nearly doubled Alrin in size.

Alrin was seventeen, only two years younger than his brother, and despite being the same height, he felt like a child next to him. Thrain had that type of athletic and brawny build that can be achieved only through tireless years of dedication. On the very day he turned ten years old (the earliest age at which guild masters would accept new students), Thrain had been invited to be a part of the strength guild by its leader, Bogdan Blackwell. The relentless training over the last nine years had chiseled him into the fine-tuned machine he currently was.

Alrin had always been proud of the commitment his brother put into his training. The 12-1-4 on his hand was very well deserved, and Alrin shared in his excitement every time Thrain came home having increased another level after several months of training.

Except for their difference in size, Alrin and Thrain looked remarkably similar. Each had shaggy blond hair that often shadowed his deep, emerald-green eyes. Alrin's hair was slightly longer and extended down past his shoulders, which definitely did not help in making him look any older. From what their mother always said, they'd inherited several of their father's warriorlike features. Two of these were their prominent cheekbones, and eyebrows that always made them look far more stern and unapproachable than they actually intended.

Without a word or even a nod, Thrain joined him on the tree stump and breathed in the serenity of the surroundings just as the first edge of brilliant orange cracked over the mountaintop, bringing a hint of warmth to the valley.

"How's the arm?" Alrin asked.

"Almost healed, actually. Whatever you did yesterday, it seems to be working."

"About that...," Alrin said. "What did I do exactly?"

"You don't remember anything?"

Alrin shrugged. "Only pieces."

Thrain drooped his head and let out a muted sigh. Reliving what had happened the day before seemed like the last thing he wanted to do. "We tracked that stag all the way to Batara," Thrain said. "Do you remember that at least?"

"Yeah," Alrin said, looking down at his hand. "But that's about it. After that, only a weird symbol on my hand and feeling...unstoppable."

"Have your levels changed at all?"

"No. Still 2-1-3," Alrin replied, slowly rubbing the numbers with his thumb as if he were massaging a scar, and hoping they would change. "But how did I go from hunting at the top of the cliffs to suddenly healing your arm at the bottom? I must have busted my head on something."

"The deer was right below us," Thrain said, exhaling heavily. "You walked up to the edge and strung your last arrow…"

"And that's when I fell?" Alrin asked.

"I wish…," Thrain answered, but then cracked a smile and shook his head as if trying to take back what had just come out of his mouth. "Well, I mean that would've been better than what actually happened," he said. "You were out of arrows and the deer didn't run off, so I thought I could drop a stone on him and knock him out." He suddenly clenched his jaw. "We never would've got that big of a deer home anyway. I don't know what I was thinking. Of course I had to choose the biggest rock I could find. Right when I was about to drop it over the edge I guess I just lost my footing. Somehow the weight of the rock landed on my arm and pinned me to the ground."

He reached over and gripped his shoulder with the opposite hand, exploring the extent of the damage. "And that's when you rushed over." He looked over and saw Alrin hanging on his every word. "Man, I wish you could remember. It was more weight than I've ever seen you lift. I thought surely you would've leveled just from that alone. Once I was able to slip free, I rolled out of the way…and I guess the weight must have toppled you over the edge."

Alrin could hear a knot form in his brother's throat.

"It felt like the world was in slow motion. I remember you looking back up and I'll never forget the look on your face. It's what kept me up all night. You seemed…at peace. Like you chose me instead of you. Then, just as you were about to hit the ground, a flash of light shot out of your hand and you just…stopped. You were still floating by the time I made it down." Thrain paused and stared ahead. "But that's not even the weirdest part. When you finally woke up, you said something."

Alrin could feel his heart pounding.

"'The sun rises and the sun falls, then hurries back to where it rises…'"

Alrin breathed in deep and focused his eyes on the nothingness in front of them. The calmness of the morning was starting to give way to the sights and sounds of the forest's coming alive. Alrin wrapped his jacket around him tighter, and the intoxicating scent of the smoldering pine from their chimney entered his nostrils.

"Maybe we should go speak with Halvdan today?" Alrin offered finally.

"Yeah, you had me at *maybe*."

They both let out a nervous but much-needed laugh.

Aurora hollered at them from the cabin doorway, "Thrain! Alrin! Breakfast is ready!"

They quickly hopped to their feet and headed back down the dirt path toward their cabin.

"How 'bout we don't tell Mom any of this?" Thrain said.

"Agreed."

CHAPTER TWO

EVERGLEN

Y ou two were up early," Aurora said, setting their breakfast down and joining them at the table.

"Couldn't sleep," Alrin answered. "Too much on my mind."

Thrain sent a sharp kick under the table, then, after making sure their mother wasn't looking, threw him a reminding glare.

"Oh. Why's that?" Aurora asked compassionately.

Alrin's eyes met Thrain's nervously, and each waited for the other to redirect the conversation.

"It was just really cold this morning," Thrain blurted out just in time. "Once we were up, it was really hard falling back to sleep."

Alrin shot him an annoyed look and subtly rolled his eyes. Both statements were perfectly true, he noticed, but their reason for having lost sleep was definitely not the cold. "Where did we get these?" Thrain continued, reaching for a bowl of ripe berries and giving Alrin a reassuring wink. "They're delicious."

"Sirena brought them over yesterday while you two were out hunting," Aurora answered. "And nice try changing the subject…" The boys froze. "You know, it wouldn't be so cold in here if you two would finish splitting that wood like I've asked you a thousand times."

Alrin breathed a sigh of relief. But only a short one. Despite Thrain's best intentions, he'd inadvertently brought up something they had been putting off for weeks, and he could tell that Aurora meant business. Any time their mother was on the verge of another very long lecture, she had this peculiar habit of inserting *a thousand times* into everything she said. Then that certain look would creep up on her face—the one that somehow only mothers had the ability to summon when they were about to bring up the topic of unfinished chores.

"Winter isn't too far off and it isn't going to chop itself," she said sternly. "I figured you of all people would jump at the opportunity to show off your strength," she said, looking to Thrain.

Thrain groaned. "Even if I chopped wood for a month, I probably still wouldn't level," he said, darting his eyes to his ensignis as if they were sworn enemies. "Besides, Alrin should be the one to do it. He could use the experience more than I could."

"There it is," Aurora exclaimed, dropping her fork to the table. "Experience this. Experience that. Ever since you were accepted into that infernal guild, all you ever think about is leveling!"

"This is the only family in Everglen where that's a bad thing," Thrain muttered under his breath.

Alrin lowered his head and braced himself for what he was sure would be at least a week's grounding. But miraculously, Aurora didn't hear Thrain.

"If I've told you once, I've told you..." but she stopped herself and took a deep breath instead.

Thrain must have completed the sentence in his head as Alrin had, because their eyes met and it took nearly everything they had not to burst out laughing.

"There is more to life than your ensignis," she continued. "That is why I've worn this since the two of you were born." She lifted her arm and revealed a dark leather glove very similar to the one Halvdan always wore. Intricate patterns spiraled throughout the leather, separating shades of slightly different browns and golds. "I've kept this on so that the two of you might one day realize that there is more to people than just the numbers on our hands." She lowered her arm back down to her side. "All your father ever cared about was his ensignis, and look where that got him," she said, her voice hardening. "It crept into everything he did until eventually there was nothing left. It consumed him—and took him away."

She rose from her chair and carried what she could with her to the sink, which unfortunately included a nice hunk of ham and flake of biscuit that Alrin was still delicately eyeing. It was there that she paused, her eyes unintentionally fixed on one of the dishes that she rested on the counter, as if suddenly lost in a deep and painful memory.

Aurora rarely allowed any emotion to appear on her face that she didn't intend to be there. There were only two people in the world who knew the difference between when she was upset and when she was genuinely saddened, and they both watched her very carefully from either side of the table. The difference was subtle. She would turn very quiet and then the kind and gentle smile that she wore would dim ever so slightly. There was only one thing Alrin knew of that would make this happen, and it was talking about their father.

"If the only thing a person develops in themselves is what is shown on their hand," she muttered, "their life will be filled with emptiness. Remember that while you train. The both of you."

"We will," Alrin assured her. "And the wood will be finished today. We promise."

Alrin's voice seemed to bring her back. The concern on her face washed away and her smile returned. "Thank you, my dears," she said, walking up to Thrain, brushing the hair out of his eyes, and kissing him lightly on the forehead. She then turned to Alrin, likely to do the exact same thing, but he jerked away before she could reach him, bashfully guarding his forehead with the back of his hand.

She did this quite often, but in truth, Alrin pretended to care only when Thrain was around.

"I don't mind that you want to improve yourselves," she continued, grinning at the sight of Alrin trying desperately to wipe away a kiss that had never been planted. "And don't think I'm trying to keep you from doing what you enjoy. I just want your interests to stay simply that—interests. If you are to train, then you must train for no other reason than yourselves. The moment you become focused on beating someone else is the moment you begin to lose yourself."

"Yes, ma'am," they both answered.

"So," she said, turning again to the dishes in the sink. "Enough of that. What will you both do today, I wonder?"

"Thrain and I were thinking about going into town," Alrin said in the most ordinary way he could manage. "Maybe even go see Halvdan."

"Oh? Has he invited you into his guild?"

"No, not yet," Alrin answered, making his disappointment clearly known. "He only invites those who show the most promise...but his guild would be the only one I would consider. Watching what they can do is fascinating."

Alrin went to the counter where Aurora was setting the dishes after washing them and began to dry them with a hand towel.

"Yeah," Thrain snorted. "Tell her about the time Iarund hit you in the back of the head with that ball of water," he said, laughing to himself. He took the plates Alrin had dried and returned them to their proper place in the cabinet.

"Well, that wasn't particularly fascinating," Alrin admitted, "but being able to summon an orb of water from a fountain and control it in the air certainly is."

"That Iarund is a menace," Aurora sharply interrupted. "You two need to avoid him as best you can."

"Well, that's a pretty difficult thing to do in a town like this," Alrin said, rolling his eyes. "I can't even go a day without bumping into him or at least hearing about his *wondrous* achievements. He is the top student of both the strength *and* magic guilds, after all."

"Soon to be the second highest in strength if I have anything to say about it," Thrain said, overly flexing one of his bulging arms in Alrin's direction.

"Now, what did I just finish telling you!" Aurora hollered.

Thrain looked at his mother and quickly relaxed his pose. "Oh, I'm only joking, Mother," he said, grinning. "You of all people know I'm the most humble person in all of Everglen."

At this, her expression turned from anger to irritated amusement. "There's that bragging about being humble again."

Thrain grinned wildly. "Well, at least I'm the best at *something*."

Aurora tried her best to fight the smile that was forming across her face, but she quickly gave in and smacked him on the arm. "Oh, get out of here already," she said, shaking her head hopelessly.

Once Thrain and Alrin were finished helping her, they grabbed their jackets from a small coat closet by the front door.

"Need anything while we're out?" Thrain paused to ask. Alrin wasn't quite as successful in concealing his eagerness to leave as he nearly crashed into Thrain at the doorway.

"Not that I can think of," she said, eyeing Alrin suspiciously, "but Sirena will be along any minute. You should wait to thank her for the berries. You know, she really looks up to you, Alrin. She's always talking about how you're the only one in Everglen that is nice to her."

"Her father's archery range is on the way," Thrain offered impatiently. "We'll stop to thank her if we don't see her beforehand."

"All right, then. Send my regards to Halvdan, won't you? And be careful today!" Aurora watched as they bolted out the front door, Thrain first, and Alrin tailing close behind. "And don't forget about the wood!" she hollered after them, to which the only reply was the slamming of the front door.

Outside, Alrin followed Thrain south to the main road. The sun was well above the horizon and was glistening off the surface of the pond next to their cabin. He was excited to finally talk to Halvdan about what had happened. He had more questions than he knew what to do with, but about halfway to the road, a nervous pit grew in his stomach and he stopped. To his left was a small trail that split off down a hill and into a neighboring field. This was his normal path into town.

It wasn't faster by any means. In fact, it was completely out of the way, but the trail wound next to the Narew River and cut through some of the nicest parts of the valley. The best part about it, however, was simply that it wasn't the main road, and this meant that Alrin could avoid the mocking and insults that his ensignis would most assuredly earn from anyone passing by.

"Come on, Alrin," Thrain hollered back at him. "If anyone says something today, they're gonna have to answer to me."

Alrin hurried up next to his brother, trying to nonchalantly shrug off the remark as if that weren't what he had been thinking about, although both of them knew that it was. Together they followed the main road north a mile or so, beyond Mrs. Rider's sea of cornfields, until the road split around a large oak tree. Many years ago (before Alrin knew the implications of his ensignis), they would each choose a different path around the tree and race to reach the other side. But that was a long time ago. Now Alrin wouldn't dare to leave his brother's side.

Surprisingly, their stroll into town turned out to be rather uneventful. As far as he knew, Alrin made it the entire way without even a scowl. Not that he would have noticed, since he watched his feet the entire way and quietly rehearsed what he was going to say to Halvdan. Then, just before the magic guild came into view, a small voice stopped them in their tracks.

"Hi, Alrin!"

He turned around to see a small girl, no higher than his elbow, run up and hug him around the waist. She peered up at him through a disheveled mess of tangled brown curls and gave him the biggest freckle-cheeked smile.

"Hi, Sirena!" Alrin said, hunching over and returning her embrace. "What do you have there?" he asked, noticing a dazzling new bow slung over her shoulder. "Did Sagittari make it for you?"

"For my birthday." She nodded excitedly. "I've been practicing all week like you showed me, but I haven't hit nothing yet. Did you like the berries I picked for you? I found them growing in some bushes by the back fence when I was trying to find my arrows." She said it all very quickly and barely paused for a breath.

"They were delicious," Alrin answered. "We were on our way to thank you right now, in fact." It was hard not to smile at the energetic mumblings and slurred pronunciations of the little six-year-old. Also, he couldn't help but feel responsible for some of her missing arrows.

Sirena's previous bow could have likely been outshot by a similar-size toy. The actual bow was made from a switch off a tree and the string itself was about as useful as a shoelace. When Alrin had last helped her, he'd tightened the bowstring as best he could and showed her the greatly exaggerated angle she would need to even come close to one of her father's targets.

Equipped with Alrin's well-intentioned advice and her new masterfully crafted bow of ash wood and tautly spun flax, there was no telling how far she was now oversailing her mark. Alrin's only hope was that Sagittari, the master of archery himself (who also happened to be Sirena's father), hadn't already witnessed the repercussions of his advice.

"If you would like," Alrin offered, "I would be happy to come by the range sometime to help you with your new bow."

"I would love that," she said, lowering her head bashfully. "That's so nice." She began fumbling with the edge of her jacket and kicked around a few rocks at her feet.

Thrain suddenly cleared his throat. Hiding impatience had never been one of his strong suits.

Alrin nodded. "Well, I think Aurora is expecting you," he said politely. "She may start to worry if we keep you much longer."

"You're right. I don't want her to worry. We're supposed to be picking some more berries today. Good-bye, Alrin! Good-bye, Thrain!"

"Good-bye," they said together, and watched her skip off toward their house, singing a playful little tune as she went:

Under the willow where the grass shines green;
Beyond the veil of golden gleam.
Twinkling bright, shine their candlelight,
To all below in sleepless dream.
Under the willow where the grass shines green…

Everglen was so simple at her age, Alrin thought jealously as her voice trailed off around the corner. But very soon that all would sadly change. The bow that she was cheerfully toting around was far more than just a gift for her birthday. It signified that her father now deemed her old enough to begin her training, and knowing Sagittari, her path had long been chosen for her.

Any day now she will be plunged into the arduous crafts of fletching, bow-making, and relentless target practice. Then in a few years, at the ripe age of ten, being the daughter of a prominent leader of Everglen, she will likely be accepted into any guild of her father's choosing. From there her ensignis will sink their teeth into every part of her life until, very slowly, her song will end.

"Good morning, Alrin," came an alarmingly close voice from directly behind them. "Might I have a minute of your time?"

Alrin and Thrain spun around to see Sagittari himself standing no more than an arm's length away.

"Sa-Sagittari, how good to see you," said Thrain, "without hearing you coming...as usual."

"Trick of the trade," Sagittari said vacantly. He always spoke very slowly, as if every word had been meticulously chosen, and even a syllable beyond that would have been an unimaginable inconvenience. "You just missed Sirena," he muttered listlessly. "I believe she was looking for you."

"We just saw her," Alrin said reassuringly. "She couldn't have left more than a moment ago."

"I see...but now that we're on the topic of *missing* something. Sirena seems to be missing a few arrows of late."

Alrin could feel the blood rush to his face. "Sir, if I had only known about her new bow, I promise I never would have—"

"Not necessary," he sharply interrupted. "It has been...corrected. She did, however, mention you are quite proficient with a bow yourself."

"Oh, I don't know about that," Alrin said, shying from the compliment. "Only good enough to help put food on the table, I suppose."

Sagittari squinted down at him, then glanced at his ensignis. "I find modesty is used by those who are either being truthful about their incompetence, or lying about their skill. So which is it, Alrin? Are you incompetent…or simply a liar?"

"Umm." Alrin gulped.

The way Sagittari uttered his name made it sound like an insult. "Never mind," he said sourly. "The real reason I stopped you today is because I have something for you."

"For me?" Alrin asked.

Sagittari glared at him, making it abundantly clear that he had no intention of repeating himself. "Your father and I go way back—any son of the great Meldun Turner deserves a proper weapon, to be sure."

Alrin was speechless. There was no better weapon in all of Everglen than one of Sagitarri's coveted bows. They were made from some of the rarest and most hard-to-find items in all of Dalroth. The horn and sinew were from a powerful beast known as the stonetusk mammoth, and the tree that supplied the wood didn't have a name other than *ax-breaker* because the bark was that difficult to get through. Each and every bow that Sagittari decided to make came out to be a thing of beauty.

"I…I don't know what to say," Alrin stuttered. "That would be incredible! I've heard the bow you use has never missed its target."

"It hasn't," Sagittari snapped. "Perhaps the two of you should stop by before the Trials. I'm setting up a little archery range of sorts. If you're lucky, you might just be able to see it in action."

"Um, Trials, sir?" Thrain chimed in.

Sagittari studied them carefully. "You haven't heard?" he asked blankly. "Well, don't let me spoil it. You will find out soon enough." He began to turn, but stopped. "Oh, one more thing. I wanted to thank you for helping Sirena with her shooting." From the look on his face, he seemed just as shocked by the words coming out of his mouth as Alrin and Thrain were.

"Thank me?" Alrin said, quite unsure whether he was serious or not. "Err, it's nothing, really. But I'd understand if you wanted me to stop—seeing how anything I know pales in comparison to what you could teach her."

"Her training will begin soon enough," said Sagittari. "If that were indeed my intention, I wouldn't be thanking you, now would I?"

Alrin shook his head.

"I do, however, need something from you in return. As you know, Sirena shows incredible promise in archery, but I can already see her following in the footsteps of her sister. Despite my best efforts to steer her where she belongs, Trishna has crippled her fate by joining Halvdan's magic guild instead. And now, just as I feared, Sirena is showing interest in it as well."

"So…you want me to *continue* helping her?"

"Yes," he said with a frighteningly forced calmness. "Nothing sparked her interest in archery until you came along. For whatever reason, she looks up to you, it would seem. If she sees you devote your time to archery, it may once again draw her back to the path for which she was destined. Can you do that for me?"

Alrin wasn't sure what to say. Helping Sirena was something he actually enjoyed doing, but now he suddenly didn't feel right about it. He wasn't about to let Sagittari twist something he enjoyed into another plot to manipulate Sirena.

"I suppose so..."

"Good. Do this for me, and the bow is yours. See you before the Trials, yes?"

Alrin nodded hesitantly.

Once Sagittari was gone, Alrin and Thrain continued toward the heart of the city—toward the guilds. They were arranged in the same triangular pattern as the ensignis. Strength. Magic. Intellect. Such was the norm in every town, Alrin had learned, in reverence of the fallen heroes who had dedicated their entire lives to them.

The guilds had never felt so alive. The air itself was charged from the robust clamor of activity. Everywhere they looked, students were honing their skills as if their lives depended on it.

"What's gotten into everyone?" Alrin asked, gazing back and forth in awe of the madness.

"No idea," Thrain answered, then began making his way toward the strength guild, which was at the top of a very steep hill. Its leader, Bogdan Blackwell, was overseeing some of his students as they practiced intense sword routines. One of whom, to Alrin's great dismay, was Iarund Lucas. *So much for avoiding him today*, Alrin thought, as he tried to mentally prepare himself in case Iarund happened to look down and notice him watching.

He hated to admit it, but from where Alrin stood, Iarund's form was flawless. Each stab and pouncing strike of his two-handed sword was charged with even more grace and power than the last. Thrain had once explained to him that by using a heavier weapon, one could increase one's strength much faster than by using any ordinary weapon. So it was no wonder that Iarund was the star pupil.

"Keep your blade up!" Bogdan shouted suddenly. "I didn't train you to practice getting yourself killed."

Bogdan must have sensed someone watching, because he glanced over to see Thrain and Alrin standing along the edge of the fence and immediately began making his way down the stairs toward them. "Again," he shouted back to Iarund, "but this time use a heavier sword!"

Iarund's face sank, and he lumbered back into the guild to change out his weapon.

Alrin felt himself move behind his brother as the leader of the strength guild bounded toward them, taking the stairs by threes. Bogdan was utterly ruthless. Without a doubt, he was one of the top five reasons that Alrin went out of his way to avoid the main road. His being Everglen's guild leader of strength meant that he was the strongest, and it was quite obvious that it had gone to his head a long time ago. He hated weakness, and wouldn't hesitate to let you know about it. And of course, in his book, that meant Alrin.

"So where have *you* been all week?" Bogdan asked Thrain as he skipped the last five steps and landed with a graceful thud next to the fence.

"Sorry," said Thrain uneasily. "I got a little tied up at home. What's all the commotion about?"

Bogdan looked disgusted. "Tell me you're joking," he said. Then, seeing that Thrain was indeed clueless, he motioned toward a sign posted nearby.

At the center of the three guilds was a large triangular bulletin board fastened to wooden stakes buried deep in the ground. One of the boards faced each of the guilds, and it was here that Everglen's quests were posted. The guild leaders always had some incredibly difficult and dangerous task posted for their students to complete. Like everything else, the quests were designed to inspire competition, and, of course, to advance the students' ensignis.

Alrin had once seen a quest facing the magic guild that required thirty-two wings of the zephyr wisps in order to be completed. These large, dragonflyish creatures could be found only near the very peaks of the highest mountains in the Tatras and cast powerful enchantments on anyone approaching. The reward was one of Halvdan's famed Hero Drafts, which, when drunk, would increase each of your ensignis by one. Of course, Alrin had no desire venturing to such a place, but when Thrain asked if he could try to complete the quest, Aurora was passionately against it, saying, "You have no business venturing to a place where even trees refuse to go." To their dismay, the brave winner of the potion ended up being Iarund, of course, and they had to hear him gloat about it for nearly a month.

Draped over the quest boards today, however, were elaborately inscribed banners, one facing each of the guilds. The ornamented lettering was difficult to make out, yet it read:

Verindi Trials:
King Abaddon Graciously Extends the
Invitation to Train as Part of the Verindi.
Present your Strongest Warriors on the
Third Morn of September. Only One
Shall Be Chosen, and Never Forgotten.

*Verindi…*Alrin repeated the word again and again in his mind. He knew he'd heard it before, but couldn't for the life of him remember where. Despite the fear of asking Bogdan a question, Alrin asked, "Forgive me, sir, but who are the Verindi again?"

Bogdan glared at him almost as though he were speaking another language, and then stared down at his ensignis. A slew of undecipherable words came rushing out of his mouth, of which Alrin managed to catch only *ignorant* and *lurker* before quickly hiding his hand behind his back.

"The Verindi," Bogdan spit, "are King Abaddon's army. They are the highest of the elite in all of Dalroth. Their power is unmatched and their authority untested…save for Abaddon himself. Every year the king sends his men to the strongest towns in Dalroth to hold competitions for the most powerful warriors. The winners are granted the opportunity to live among them in Dunblane, and train under their guidance. This is the seventeenth year the trials have been held, but the first time that Everglen has been given the chance to compete. It's the opportunity of a lifetime."

"Why now?" Thrain asked curiously.

"No one knows. Everglen has always been overlooked for not requiring an ensigni level to live within our borders. However, as of yesterday, it appears the king has extended his invitation to the entire realm."

Alrin and Thrain turned to each other and their eyes met nervously. It had to just be a coincidence.

"Why is everyone acting like they have a chance of winning?" Alrin asked. "Everyone knows the guild leaders are the strongest ones in Everglen."

"We are unable to enter," Bogdan said, gritting his teeth at yet another ignorant question. "Only those fifteen to twenty years old are allowed to enter." He finally moved his attention back to Thrain. "I expect Iarund, or Thrain here, to take the victory for our strength guild."

Thrain suddenly looked as if he would burst with pride. "I would be honored sir, but…" And then he fell silent.

Alrin knew what was running through his mind, for it was the same thing running through his. There was no way around it. He would have to ask Aurora. And after their discussion that morning, asking for her permission to enter a competition in which the victor would be whisked off into the presence of everything she was vehemently against seemed like a frivolous pursuit at best.

"*But* nothing." Bogdan scowled. "Now get up there. The Trials are tomorrow, and Iarund needs a sparring partner."

Thrain looked over at Alrin. "Come by after and tell me what Halvdan says," he said quickly. Then he hoisted himself over the fence and hustled up the stairs to join Iarund.

CHAPTER THREE

THE MAGIC GUILD

B ogdan's commands blended into the background as Alrin crossed the courtyard toward the magic guild. Even on a normal day, Alrin felt he was in the way, but today he quite literally was. People scrambled back and forth setting up for the competition, many of whom shoved him out of the way or cursed him for even being there.

Several people were setting up a small circular arena where the competition was to be held, while others were setting up tables and benches, apparently in preparation for a very large banquet. With every step toward Halvdan's guild, a growing pit in Alrin's stomach filled with the realization of just how unwelcome he actually was. He had been to the guild dozens of times before, but once he finally made it to the gate, his nerves got the best of him and he started to turn for home. Maybe it would be best to wait until all the excitement of the Trials blew over to talk to Halvdan.

Then, just as he was turning to leave, Halvdan emerged from the doorway, and following closely behind him was Sirena's older sister Trishna.

"There is room enough out here," Halvdan said, leading her onto the grass and over to a small pond. "It's easier to see over water."

Before she reached the grass, Trishna kicked off her shoes so she could step barefoot into it.

"Now, I want you to focus," Halvdan said softly. He stood off to the side with his arms crossed firmly over his chest.

Trishna approached the water's edge and stood very still. Her long brown hair moved gently in the breeze before resting again across her back. She wore a faded-gray robe with a belt clasped comfortably around her waist. She had that sort of olive glow that only happens to those who spend countless hours in the sun. She was inarguably beautiful.

Even from the way she moved, Alrin could tell she was strong and powerfully graceful. But the most fascinating thing about her was how little the surrounding commotion seemed to affect her concentration. Her breath seemed harmoniously deepened by each gust of wind that glanced across her face.

"Block everything out," Halvdan continued. "Focus only on the flow of the wind…Memorize how it breaks around you. When you're ready, focus it and push it out as hard as you can."

Except for a small wrinkle of concentration across her brow, Trishna remained perfectly still. But then, almost as calmly as she exhaled her next breath, she thrust her arms out in front of her as a pulsing wave of energy shot from them. Just as Halvdan had suggested, the wave was hardly visible at all until it reached the water, and when it did, it sent white-capped waves and spraying foam all the way to the opposite side of the pond.

"I did it!" Trishna exclaimed, as she watched the waves rock back and forth, splashing over her feet.

Halvdan bellowed a deep and cheerful laugh. "Well done, Trishna. Well done! You have just successfully cast your first wind wave."

A huge smile spread across her face as she struggled to catch her breath.

"That *was* pretty impressive," Alrin said, stepping through the gate and walking over.

Trishna glanced at Alrin's ensignis, and her smile disappeared. "It was nothing," she said as she reached up and brushed her hair away. Alrin couldn't help but feel his compliment was even more bothersome than the wind that was persistently blowing it back into her face.

"First try, even," Halvdan added. "And to hear Sagittari say, you have no business in magic."

At the mention of her father's name, her focus narrowed even more. "I want to go again," she muttered sharply.

"All right, all right," Halvdan said, chuckling, "but don't overdo it." He then turned to Alrin. "Now, what can I do for you, my boy?"

"I was hoping to ask you about something that happened yesterday. Do you have a minute?"

Halvdan looked back to his guild at several other students who were waiting for him. "Err…I suppose I could spare a minute or two. But you'll have to walk with me."

Alrin hurried along as Halvdan made his way to the entrance of his guild, and once Trishna was far enough away, Alrin said in almost a whisper, "I fell off Batara Falls yesterday."

Halvdan tried to shoot him a most sincere look of concern, but he was terribly distracted, so it more closely conveyed, "And why does this concern me?" "Well that could've turned ugly," he said, motioning to another student that it wouldn't be much longer. "You were lucky there was water enough to land in this time of year."

"That's the thing," Alrin said quietly. "There wasn't any."

Halvdan stopped and folded his arms impatiently into his cloak. "I'm not sure I follow." For a moment, Alrin's eyes caught a glimpse of the brown glove over his ensignis.

"I don't either," Alrin stammered. "Everything is still pretty fuzzy, but I remember waking up at the bottom of the cliff, and my hand was glowing."

"Glowing?" Halvdan snorted skeptically, raising his hand again toward the student, who was now staring at Alrin as if he were his next meal. "Perhaps you hit your head and it just appeared to be glowing?" He phrased it in the form of a question, which Alrin knew was purely out of courtesy. He had spent that entire morning trying to figure out how to explain what had happened in the least outlandish way possible. Hearing himself say it out loud, however, he quickly realized that he had failed miserably.

"Thrain was there," Alrin added. "He mentioned that I made something from bistort and wormwood leaves?"

And that's when Halvdan's face changed. "Who was injured?" he asked abruptly, turning to Alrin with his full attention.

"Thrain was—a boulder landed on his shoulder," Alrin answered. "But wait. How did you know someone was injured?"

"Just a moment," he said quietly. "We will continue in private. Follow me."

Through the main entrance of the guild, students lined each and every hallway, studying at long tables. Stacks upon stacks of very old books were scattered just about everywhere Alrin looked as those preparing for the competition stampeded through their pages. Upon the walls were intricate maps of the most enchanting places in Dalroth and endless lists of magical abilities, which the younger students were committing to memory.

Alrin followed closely behind, until finally they came to a large, open courtyard at the center of the guild. Before they entered it, however, an inscription above the doorway caught Alrin's eye:

Those who strive to progress their tracks are but fools if they fail to track their progress.

Every part of this place stirred up butterflies from somewhere deep in Alrin's stomach. Even he couldn't help but wonder what it would be like to know what they knew and to be able to do the things they could do—to be pushed to the boundary of his ability, and feel the excitement of seeing what lay beyond.

But then, as quickly as it had come, the desire faded. For Alrin, not knowing had always been part of the intrigue.

The courtyard opened up to a bright, cloudless sky. A large statue, inscribed with the name Gondor Dinivus, stood at its center, several feet of sand surrounding it on every side. Rocks of various sizes were spread across the sand; some small, some very large, and others even larger than the statue itself.

Two girls, no older than Alrin, stood with their toes buried in the sand. They were levitating an impressively large boulder back and forth through the air. *That would have come in handy*, Alrin said to himself as he watched them float it effortlessly above the ground, thinking of Thrain trapped under the boulder. That's when one of the girls noticed him watching.

Like a bird falling from the sky, the stone fell instantly to the ground with a thud. The other student whipped around to see what had distracted the first. Their glares almost looked synchronized. Both pairs of eyes flashed to Alrin's ensignis and then quickly back to him. From the looks on their faces, it was abundantly clear that he wasn't welcome in their guild.

Once they were on the opposite side of the courtyard, Halvdan led him through several more doors, until finally they approached a sturdy oak door trimmed in black iron. Instead of reaching for the handle, Halvdan raised his hand toward a stone beside it and his finger disappeared through the wall.

Alrin stared in amazement as a portion of the wall began to move, sending small ripples out from Halvdan's finger as if he had dipped it in a pool of water. Halvdan watched Alrin closely as he scribbled something secretively into the haze. The lock clicked and the door creaked open. "If you don't mind closing that behind you," Halvdan said, walking in and sitting at his desk.

As Alrin closed it behind him, he was still struggling to unravel whatever it was that he'd just seen.

As usual, everything around Halvdan's office was precisely as he remembered it. Frightfully overwhelming. Halvdan had about five times as much on his desk as anyone should own in a lifetime, yet Alrin knew that everything had a proper place (even if its proper place was in one of the precarious piles strewn across the floor).

Then Alrin saw something lying in the corner. It was an animal he had never seen before. At first glance he thought it was a large cat, but as he looked closer, it looked more like a miniature tiger. It had bright-red fur and three tails that were tucked up under its chin as it slept in a warm patch of sunlight coming in from a window.

"Her name's Moltrix," Halvdan said, noticing Alrin staring.

At the mention of her name, Moltrix opened her eyes and yawned. As soon as she noticed Alrin, she jumped to her feet and a thin layer of fire spread over her fur.

"What is she?" Alrin asked.

"She's an elemental," Halvdan answered. "Part beast, part flame. It seems we weren't the only ones able to use magic when Gondor Dinivus imparted his gift to the world. You can pet her if you'd like. Don't worry, her bark is worse than her burn," he said, chuckling.

Alrin reached down and began rubbing his fingers together. Almost immediately Moltrix bounded over. She stopped only briefly to sniff his hand and then nuzzled against the side of his leg.

"She's warm," said Alrin.

"Of course she is," Halvdan said, smirking, "And don't be surprised to learn that water elementals have wet noses." He suddenly laughed to himself as if what he'd said had been remarkably clever.

"I've never even heard of them," said Alrin, scratching under her chin.

"Fascinating creatures. Incredibly rare too. Moltrix here has many properties of a phoenix—grows incredibly fast, then is reborn from her ashes. Can't fly, though, as far as I can tell." Halvdan pursed his lips together and let out a soft whistle, at which Moltrix waddled over and curled into a tiny ball by his feet.

"Now," Halvdan said, changing his tone dramatically. "Who showed you how to use herb amalgamation?"

The seriousness in his voice caught Alrin horribly off guard. "H-herb…what?" he asked.

"This is no time for games, Alrin. That spell is dangerously beyond the capabilities of your ensignis. Was it Trishna who showed it to you? Or Iarund perhaps?"

"Neither," Alrin said almost fearfully. "I don't know how I did it. Honestly."

"I see," Halvdan said, watching him carefully. "Well, the particular spell you performed heals wounds much faster than ordinary." He then looked down at Alrin's hand. "If what you say is true, and I sense that it is…surviving the fall at Batara wasn't the only way you cheated death."

"How do you mean?" Alrin asked nervously.

"At level one, that spell alone should have killed you. But before we get to that, tell me what you remember. There are many gaps we must fill before we jump to conclusions."

Alrin took a nervous breath. "We were hunting on top of the cliffs when Thrain slipped next to the edge. When I went to help him, I fell over." Halvdan listened carefully, examining his every word. "One thing I do remember was the ground. When I fell, it caused some sort of clearing. Boulders that I wouldn't even dream of lifting were cast aside like pebbles." Halvdan's eyes narrowed ever so slightly. "Thrain mentioned something about seeing a bright light, and then just before hitting the ground…I stopped."

This sparked something in Halvdan. He rose from his chair and moved over to one of his many bookshelves. Moltrix lifted her head and began wagging her three tails, but she quickly stopped once she realized that they weren't going outside.

Halvdan began searching the numerous book spines on a shelf until he finally found the one he was looking for.

"Aha!" he exclaimed. "Here we are. *The Ever-Unfinished Guide to Magic and Mystery,* by Darius Glade." He pulled it off the shelf and began thumbing his way through several pages toward the back. "You know, I actually met him once, this Darius," said Halvdan. "Crazy as a loon, but beyond brilliant."

After flipping through several pages, he placed the book back on the shelf and continued searching. Then his eyes landed on a book that looked incredibly old and incredibly fragile.

"I wonder," he whispered, pulling at the hairs coming from his chin.

Alrin tried his best to read the title, but it was far too smudged to make out.

"Who else have you spoken to about this?" Halvdan asked him suddenly.

"Only Thrain," Alrin said quickly. "Honest."

"For now, let us keep it as such." Halvdan grabbed the book from the shelf, walked to his desk, and began working to light his pipe.

Alrin looked back and forth between the book and Halvdan for several moments, until finally the silence got the best of him. "What is it?" he yelled. "What happened to me?"

Halvdan looked up and seemed just as surprised as Alrin at his uncharacteristic outburst. Before he answered, Halvdan lit his pipe and tried to seem completely ordinary. "I'm sure it was nothing more than fate bestowing a random sympathy to a kind and well deserving young man," he said calmly. "Now run along. I have much to do before tomorrow."

"Yes, sir," Alrin said cautiously. "I promised I would be home soon anyway."

"There's a good lad," Halvdan said with a reassuring smile.

As Alrin closed the door behind him, he turned to catch a glimpse of Halvdan as he opened the book and began turning through its brittle pages.

CHAPTER FOUR

VERINDI TRIALS

Thrain…," Alrin whispered, jostling his brother and trying to wake him. His arms throbbed with soreness from the several hours of wood splitting the night before. He'd finished the remaining logs just as he'd promised he would, and fallen asleep before Thrain returned from the strength guild. "Thrain," he repeated, much louder this time. "Get up. I have to show you something."

Thrain let out a soft but obviously fake snore as if he had no intention of waking up.

Alrin reached over his brother's face and lightly flicked him on the nose.

"What?" Thrain groaned, barely peeking an eye open.

"I leveled!" Alrin exclaimed, holding his hand right in front of Thrain's face so that the dazzling new 3 of his strength ensigni was in clear view.

Thrain tried to mumble, "Congratulations," but it trailed off behind the thick blanket that he pulled up over his head. It was definitely not the reaction Alrin had been hoping for, but he wasn't about to let it ruin his moment. Leveling wasn't as big a deal to Thrain, since he had done it so many times before, but to Alrin it came about less often than his birthday.

He sat at the edge of Thrain's bed and began bouncing up and down to make sure Thrain had no chance of falling back to sleep. "The trials are about to start. Aren't you competing?"

A very annoyed "No" came out from under the blankets. "And you can stop. I'm awake."

"Didn't go over too well, I take it?" Alrin said. "Asking Mom?" Alrin fought the urge to keep bouncing just to annoy him.

Thrain kept the blanket over his head as he spoke. "She actually seemed OK with it at first. Until I mentioned the word *Verindi* and she 'bout tore my head off."

The hope of watching his brother compete instantly faded into thin air. "Maybe she just doesn't like words that start with *V*," Alrin offered sarcastically. "Maybe the Verindi are nothing but vacuous vagrants, void of any virtue or valor."

Thrain cracked a smile, albeit a small one. "Maybe so," he said. It was obvious he wasn't interested in being in a better mood just yet.

"At least go watch them with me," Alrin begged. "It looked like there was going to be a huge festival after."

Thrain pulled the covers up higher over his head.

"There's gonna be tons of food," Alrin said enticingly. "And I saw Mrs. Rider making a maze in her cornfields last night. Now, even you can't say no to that."

"The only thing I hate more than corn," Thrain grumbled from under his blanket, "is being lost in it."

"Suit yourself," said Alrin. "I'm going. I have to see how powerful these Verindi characters are." Alrin turned to leave, but that's when he noticed the small jacket closet by the front door was open.

"Where is she, by the way?" Alrin asked.

"Probably went to go talk to Halvdan. After I mentioned the *V*-word, the only thing she managed to say other than no was that Halvdan was likely up to something."

Alrin felt his insides twist into knots. What in the world did she have to talk to Halvdan about?

"Well, speaking of Halvdan," he said nervously. "I have loads to tell you. If you come to the Trials, I can tell you what happened…" Alrin looked back, hoping to see his brother jump out of bed and get dressed. He waited in their doorway for a moment, but he could tell that nothing he could say was going to persuade him, so he gave up and headed out.

The outskirts of Everglen were uncommonly quiet as Alrin took his hidden river path leading into town. The vibrant colors of the autumn birches and maples were already beginning to sprinkle their way through the contrasting evergreens that spread over the valley. He walked with his hands tucked warmly in his pockets, admiring the specks of reds and yellows flaking from their branches as each gust of wind wrestled them to the ground.

The changing of the seasons always brought Alrin a sense of peace and serenity. Whenever his mind was burdened or he simply wanted to be alone, he would leave his troubles at the forest's edge, and upon returning, he would find them much smaller than he had left them. It was as though being in the woods somehow answered questions he never even needed to ask.

He replayed the conversation with Halvdan over and over again in his mind. The more he did, the more troubled he became. It was obvious that Halvdan had more information than he was letting on, but it was even more obvious that there were things Halvdan didn't know, and that was what troubled him most. The memory of Halvdan's pulling the book from the shelf receded in his mind when he heard the sounds of cheering and laughter up ahead.

As he reached Everglen's market square, he was hit by a delicious wave of yeasty odor from the nearby bakery. It too was in full swing and, although the odor was mouthwatering, it felt like a punch to the stomach because his lack of breakfast was suddenly all he could think about. The marketplace had been completely revamped overnight for the competition. For the first time since Alrin could remember, it was free from the countless merchants and the overwhelming noise they brought to the heart of the city. In their place was a large white circle staked into the ground for the main competition, and decorations of the brightest colors hung from every corner, stretching the entire length of the courtyard.

Along the bank of the Narew River was a dark tent covered in black flags bearing emblems of a fierce dragon crouching and baring its razor-sharp teeth. Small groups of onlookers gathered at inconspicuous distances, sharing whispers and curious glances, trying to see who or what might be concealed within. Alrin knew it had to be the Verindi.

He wasn't sure why he was so curious to see them. He was kind of ashamed to admit it, but he couldn't wait to see their ensignis. If they were indeed King Abaddon's own personal army, they had to be unthinkably powerful. And as he looked around, he could tell that was exactly what everyone was excited about as well.

In an effort to restrain his own curiosity, Alrin decided to occupy the time before the competition with the entertainment provided. Throughout the market square, several exhibitions were under way that allowed the townspeople to showcase their different ensignis and abilities. It didn't surprise Alrin that he saw very little that enticed him.

The first exhibition he came to was an arm-wrestling match. Two men, Haldor and Fargus (as Alrin learned from the boisterous cheers), were locked over a wooden crate, each refusing to give in. It looked more like a battle of wills, or better yet a staring contest, for even though each man boasted an 18 in strength, they looked equally matched in pride as well. Their arms shook and sweat poured off their faces. Each man looked poised to forfeit life and limb rather than risk the embarrassment of losing in front of their growing swarm of witnesses.

It wouldn't have surprised Alrin in the least to come back a day or two later and still see them there. *Pathetic,* Alrin said to himself. He rolled his eyes and was suddenly quite thankful he hadn't eaten breakfast that morning. He could have very easily lost it just from the sheer ridiculousness of it all.

Then, across the courtyard, a much larger crowd erupted in laughter. Once Alrin found a place to stand while making sure he was still out of the way, he saw two sets of stones lying on the ground in front of a long wooden platform. Each set had four stones apiece and each one was much larger than the one before. As Alrin looked on, a man suddenly emerged from the crowd and began explaining the rules of the contest. Unsurprisingly, that man was Bogdan Blackwell, the leader of the strength guild.

"The rules are simple!" Bogdan shouted, dragging his boot into the dirt to create a starting line. The noise of the crowd hushed to a dull roar. "Each person will have four stones. When I say, you will start with the smallest stone on the left and place it on top of the platform, then move on to the next. Whoever succeeds in getting the final stone on top first is the winner. Now then, who are my first two challengers?"

The crowd grew deathly still. They all looked around, trying their best to avoid eye contact with him...Alrin most of all.

"I'll go," came a deeply confident voice from somewhere in the crowd. Several of those around him began grinning and patting him on the back as the intimidatingly large man stepped forward. From the look on his face, he was already certain of victory.

"Ahh...Kael Morag," announced Bogdan, less than surprised to see him volunteer. They grasped one another's forearms while making sure their ensignis were in clear view. This was the customary greeting in Dalroth, for revealing your ensignis was the only true sign of trust and honor.

"Now who here dares to face the 32-12-22 of the great Kael Morag?" shouted Bogdan, extending the challenge to anyone foolish enough to try. Everyone smiled and looked uneasily down at the ground. Kael was next in line to be the leader of the strength guild, being only a few levels behind Bogdan himself. Even though the two never spoke of it, the competition between them was legendary.

"Not everyone at once," Kael chuckled to himself as he began stretching his arms very flamboyantly to either side.

Alrin knew it was more for intimidation than actual preparation, but suffice it to say, it was working. It was as if every muscle in his body were showing off. No one dared to move.

That's when Alrin heard someone walking up from directly behind him. "What did I miss?" came the familiar voice.

"Thrain! You made it!" Alrin tried his best to hide his I-told-you-so smile. He knew Thrain wouldn't have missed the competition for anything. "Kael is waiting for a challenger," he said.

"Bah." Thrain snorted. "There's no way. That guy is a monster. Whoever challenges him has a death wish."

But no sooner had he said that than someone did step forward…and it was a woman. A forest-green robe concealed her face, but from where Alrin and Thrain stood, they could see dark-brown curls peeking out from her hood.

A mixture of laughter and applause rose from the crowd as the unknown challenger approached Kael and Bogdan. The closer she got, the more they towered over her tiny stature. Even Alrin couldn't help but snicker at how tiny she looked standing next to them.

Once Bogdan successfully composed himself, he raised his hand to silence the crowd. "It seems we have our second competitor," he yelled. Another round of laughter rang out. "And who is our courageous volunteer?" Bogdan roared. He seemed to be directing the words more to the crowd than to the woman.

Suddenly Thrain stopped laughing as his hand slowly rose in the direction of the cloaked woman. "Look at her hand," he whispered.

Peeking out from the length of her robe was a dark leather glove, spirals of brown and gold concealing her hand and ensignis.

"No." Alrin nearly choked. "It can't be."

They watched together as the woman raised her hand and slipped her fingers under the loose fringe of her hood and slowly removed it.

Their gasps were immediately drowned out by everyone else's. Just as they'd feared, it was their mother. "What is she doing?" Thrain asked as he started toward her, but he was stopped when someone grabbed him by the shoulder.

They turned around to see Halvdan standing right beside them, a cryptic grin playing at the corner of his mouth. "You're going to want to watch this," he said. Then, when he loosened his grip, they all turned toward Aurora.

Kael looked positively enraged that this was his only challenger. "You cannot be serious!" he hollered, turning angrily to Bogdan.

Bogdan only shrugged. He looked just as confused. It was known throughout Everglen that Aurora wanted very little to do with anything related to power or competition.

"She won't allow her son to compete," Bogdan said loud enough for the crowd to hear, "and yet…here she is."

The crowd laughed and turned to where Thrain stood, looking utterly mortified, with his face turning bright red.

"I am only here to prove a point," said Aurora calmly. "Then I will be on my way."

"Oh, really?" Bogdan laughed. "Pray tell. What is this point of yours exactly?"

Aurora fell silent. She folded her hands in front of her and fixed her gaze straight ahead of her on the waist-high boulders.

"As you wish," Bogdan said, moving to the side and motioning sarcastically to the line he had dragged into the ground.

Kael moved first, chuckling and shaking his head the entire way. "You sure you want to do this, sweetheart?" he turned and asked condescendingly as he paused at the starting line.

"I am," Aurora said softly.

"All right, then." The look on his face dissolved to an intense stare before he turned to Bogdan to give a quick nod. He wasn't the sort of person to show any kind of sportsmanship. From the looks of it, he didn't hope to only beat her; he was going to annihilate the course in the fastest time possible.

"Challengers ready," Bogdan's voice rang out. "Three...two...one...go!"

With every step that Kael took as he sprinted toward the first stone a cloud of dust rose into the air. He hoisted the stone to his shoulder with relative ease and dropped it on the platform before dashing to the next. Everyone in the crowd, Alrin and Thrain included, watched in amazement at the unveiling of his incredible strength and blinding speed. After placing the second stone atop the platform with a little difficulty, he glanced back and saw that Aurora hadn't even moved.

The third stone was significantly larger. Kael squatted down, wrapped his giant arms around it, and heaved. It took a considerable effort, but somehow he managed to get to a standing position without his knees or back buckling underneath the colossal weight of the stone. Pinning it against the platform, he quickly repositioned himself under it, and then he forced it on top.

The strain took its toll. He doubled over gasping for air and hardly looked up even when the crowd cheered his name.

"Three down!" Bogdan shouted. "Now if he's able to get this last one, he will be only the *second* person in all of Everglen to have ever finished the course."

Alrin rolled his eyes. Even now Bogdan couldn't pass up the opportunity to draw even a little attention back to himself.

"Why is she just standing there?" Thrain whispered. All he could do was shake his head. "I'll never be able to show my face at the guild again."

"Keep watching," Halvdan said from behind them. "It's not over yet."

The final stone stood as high as Kael's waist. But in the same manner as before, he reached down and locked his arms around the monstrosity. Finally, with a deafening yell and sweat pouring off his face, he heaved with all his might. Inch by inch the stone rose into the air. He managed to rest it on his knees while he paused for a few deep breaths and prepared for his last great effort.

The crowd began chanting his name, and every cheer seemed to awaken a new spark of energy inside him. He repositioned his grip and cracked his neck to either side. With a last deep breath and boisterous cry, he channeled everything he had into one last explosive effort. The boulder inched higher and higher, until right at the edge of the platform, it paused.

An anxious silence swept over the crowd as even its cheers stood poised on the brink of Kael's near victory. Bogdan had never seemed so nervous in his life. No one had ever come this close to matching his achievement.

The veins in Kael's neck looked as if they could explode at any moment. He fought with an unrelenting madness, but it appeared as though a small groove in the stone was lodged against the corner of the platform, preventing it from sliding on top. Kael fought with remarkable endurance, until at last, once his stamina had been spent, he jumped out of the way and the boulder crashed to the ground.

He collapsed against the platform and threw an arm on top to brace himself and keep from hitting the ground. "One more level," he heaved, staring down at his ensignis, "Just one more."

Kael finally rose to his feet. "If you can even get the first stone off the ground," he said to Aurora between labored breaths, "I will admit defeat." He stepped out of the way and motioned his arms toward her set of stones.

"Yes, show us this lesson you have prepared," Bogdan said, laughing.

All eyes turned to Aurora, who remained perfectly quiet at the starting line, somehow remarkably unaffected by everything that had just taken place. Without a word she bowed her head and glanced over to her to sons. For the briefest moment her eyes met Alrin's and Thrain's. Her face hardly changed at all, but it was that look again. The one that they alone could recognize. It was a mixture of love and sadness, as if she were wishing a loved one good-bye. Then she turned her attention promptly back to the stones.

And as she did, a rush of wind shot out in every direction from where she stood. The tail of her robe flapped behind her like a scourged flag in a thunderstorm.

Her power was incredible.

The only sound Alrin could hear was the pounding drum of his heartbeat pulsing in his ears. He shielded his face with an arm, but lowered it just in time to see his mother raising her hand toward her set of stones. Then, suddenly, all four of them rose into the air.

The force of her magic sprayed the crowd with wave after wave of dust, forcing many of them to turn and even run for cover. But not Alrin and Thrain. Despite the sand stinging their faces, they couldn't turn away. They hardly even blinked. As Aurora lowered her arm back to her side, the boulders crashed down on top of the platform and the gale of wind subsided.

No one cheered. No one moved. They were shocked into silence, frightened even. Everyone, that is, but Kael Morag, who looked gloweringly defeated. "I didn't realize deception was allowed in our friendly competition," he grumbled, looking nervously at the glove that covered her hand.

Aurora didn't say a word. Not to him or even the crowd. She didn't gloat or relish the victory. She simply turned and walked away, leaving Kael standing there shouting unintelligible excuses in exchange for his pride. As she reached Alrin and Thrain, she raised an arm and brushed the hair out of their eyes. "Strength isn't heightened by the number of people who know of it," she said softly. "There is more to life than this."

With that, she kissed them both on the forehead and headed for home.

Halvdan exploded with laughter. "Didn't see that coming, did you?" he bellowed.

As the crowd slowly dispersed, whispering among themselves, Kael continued working hard to collect what remnants of dignity he could find among his dwindling admirers.

Still struggling to wipe the smile from his face, Halvdan walked up to Bogdan and relayed a message that all guild leaders were needed for the final preparations for the Trials.

They found Jorund Ashcroft not too far away, and together they headed toward the Verindi's tent.

Alrin still couldn't fully grasp what he had just seen. He searched every memory he could find of his mother. Surely there was something in his past, something she'd done, that might have clued him in to their mother's phenomenal power. But there was nothing. Not even once. How she had concealed it from them this long was beyond him. What discipline...what control. *Halvdan knew*, Alrin thought to himself. *He knew all along.*

Thrain obviously didn't share in his enthusiasm. He stood, fists clenched, riving with anger. "After all the lectures about my training...," he muttered.

"Maybe she's right," Alrin offered. "Maybe she's just trying to protect us."

"Protect us from what?" Thrain yelled. "My power has been stifled my entire life by someone who is secretly the most powerful person we know...Everything she ever told us was a lie!"

Alrin reached an arm out consolingly, but Thrain quickly evaded it. "I don't care what she says, I'm competing in the Trials," he said, and then promptly stormed off.

Alrin wanted to go after him, but thought it would be best to let him cool down first. He knew from extensive experience that there was no use reasoning with him if it meant bringing down a wall that had no desire to be brought down. Besides, the same questions that likely fueled Thrain's anger were running through his own mind. Just how powerful was she, and why had she kept it from them for so long?

Then something exciting hit him. *I wonder if she should be the guild leader*, he asked himself, but then laughed at the thought of it. *There's no way. No one is stronger than Halvdan.* As the crowd continued to thin out, and Kael's complaining grew even louder, Alrin thought it best not to stick around, for fear that being Aurora's son would make him the perfect target for Kael's retribution.

It took several moments for the person waving him over to come into focus. Oftentimes, when he was deep in thought, Alrin's eyes got fixated on an object. Usually, much to his embarrassment, this object was the ground or some other equally inanimate object that happened to be close by.

Across the market square, Sagittari had set up a few targets for his makeshift archery range, and he was beckoning Alrin to come over. "Who was winning?" Sagittari asked in nearly a whisper once Alrin made it to him.

"Winning?" Alrin said, echoing the word in the same hushed manner. He desperately hoped Sagittari hadn't seen what had just happened. He was in no way prepared to explain his own ignorance of his mother's astounding power.

"Your staring contest with the ground," Sagittari said blankly. "Who was winning?"

"Oh." Alrin breathed a sigh of relief. "Sorry, I just had the stares. Umm, why are we whispering?"

"I thought maybe you would want to take a few shots at my targets," he said softly, motioning to a small crate that rested out of sight of anyone who passed by. Peeking out from around it were two small feet, bouncing playfully back and forth. Hiding behind the crate and fumbling with something in her hands was little Sirena. She was sitting on the ground making piles out of the rocks that were within her tiny reach, and humming a soft little tune to herself.

Alrin tried his best to hide his aggravation but then nodded understandingly. He walked over to several longbows leaning against a fence post. There were dozens of them—all different lengths and styles. He looked them over carefully until he found the one that most closely resembled his own.

The targets that Sagittari had set up were arranged so that you shot with your back facing the city, which meant that any arrow that missed its target would sail straight into the Narew. For a moment Alrin wondered just how many heads Sagittari had nearly torn off that morning for sinking an arrow in the river.

Picking up a medium-size longbow, Alrin nocked an arrow and smoothly drew it back. The other games made him feel vulnerable and completely out of place, but not archery. Archery he was good at.

Even the resistance of the bowstring was nostalgic. It brought him back into the calmness of the woods where Thrain had first taught him how to shoot. The semicircular enclosure of Batara Falls where he had fallen just two days prior served as the perfect range for even the most novice of archers. They would spend countless hours challenging each other to hit certain limbs, small mushrooms clinging to the sides of trees, and, as Alrin improved, even tiny saplings no wider than his thumb. But the best part about Batara Falls was that when he missed a target, the arrow simply stuck in the dirt wall of the cliff behind it, which made quick work of retrieving it. It was here that Alrin could be alone—to practice in peace without the crippling fear of failure that was never in short supply at Sagittari's archery guild.

Since there was no ensigni dedicated to archery in particular, to many, prolonged dedication to it was an incredible waste of time. However, this happened to also be the reason Aurora never minded his spending so much time with it. Over the years Alrin got to the point where he could even split branches as they swayed in the wind.

But this wasn't Batara Falls. Even though Alrin was confident, he was still incredibly nervous.

With his back turned to practically the entire town, it was guaranteed that at least a few passersby would casually be watching. His missing a target now would result in a quiet splash in the river, followed by deafening whispers and insults. The pressure alone would have normally prevented him from even getting close to a bow, but then again—archery he was good at.

With the feathered fletching of the arrow brushing against his cheek, he surveyed the range for a suitable target. His eyes went down the spine of the arrow, locking on to hay bales, clay jars, straw figurines holding wooden shields, and large posts jutting out of the ground.

A few of them may have proven fun to shoot at, but everything was boringly close. If he was going to shoot anything at all, it was going to be something only he could hit.

And then he spotted it. A good ways across the water was a small island. During the spring and summer, it was popular to swim over and lie in its shade, but it was vacant this time of year, except for its only inhabitant—a solitary oak tree.

Halfway up its trunk was a circular nub that had been left over after its limb was struck by lightning and sawn off several years back. Very few people could even get an arrow over to the island, and fewer still could actually strike the tree. But Alrin wasn't aiming just for the tree.

He raised his bow again and took aim just as Thrain had taught him. *Say your levels in your head as you breathe,* Thrain would say. *It steadies your aim.* Oddly enough, Alrin had always found it to be relaxing.

He took a deep breath in, and then exhaled slowly...*3.*

Feet shoulder width apart. Breathe in...1.

Open grip for the distance...trace wind from the left. Breathe out...3.
Release.

The flight of the arrow was short, but the instant it left his knuckles, he already knew.

Dead center. Even with the unfamiliar bow, it came naturally.

"Alrin!" Sirena jumped up upon hearing the arrow's thud across the water to see who had caused it. "That was amazing! Can you teach me how to do that?" she asked, running up to him.

"Of course," said Alrin, returning her hug and excited greeting.

"Excellent shot!" yelled Sagittari from where he casually watched. Alrin looked over to see him grinning from ear to ear at Sirena's reaction. It was the most emotion Alrin had ever seen him express.

"Do you have your bow with you?" Alrin asked. "I could help you practice some right now."

"Yes, yes! It's over here." Sirena hurried over to a table where it was lying next to several dozen arrows. She skipped happily back over and stood right next to him, trying to instantly mimic everything he was doing.

"All right, now what you want to do," Alrin explained as he demonstrated, "is hold the arrow right about...*here* on the string." He pointed the bow to the ground and placed the shaft of an arrow along the appropriate rest. "Now pull it back so that your bow arm is as straight and relaxed as possible. Then, when you're ready, you just let go." Alrin released the arrow into a nearby haystack, and precisely when he did, Iarund Lucas walked right behind him.

"Wow, look at that!" Iarund said sarcastically as he went by. "Two-thirteen hit a huge bale of hay!"

Alrin gritted his teeth. "It's three-thirteen now, by the way," he replied. "And I have a name, you know."

Iarund shook his head. "Not with ensignis like that you don't."

Sirena turned and squinted angrily at him, sticking out her tongue as Iarund walked toward the Verindi's tent. Standing outside it now were all the guild leaders and their prize students: Trishna from the magic guild , Edric from intellect, and then, walking pompously over to join them, Iarund, who had chosen to represent the strength guild (since he had his choice between magic and strength).

"Don't pay any mind to him, Sirena," said Alrin, stooping down and whispering in her ear. "He was dropped on his head as a baby."

Sirena giggled.

"Now you try."

She placed the arrow just as he had shown her, and drew it back. "Like this?" she asked, slightly unbalanced.

"Try moving your feet apart some."

She looked at Alrin's stance and mirrored it as closely as she could. After a few moments of her adjusting her feet, Alrin could hear her whisper the words "Straight and balanced" under her breath, just as he had said them.

Alrin smiled. He was starting to realize how much Sirena actually looked up to him and just how mindful he needed to be of what he did and said around her. For some reason he felt protective of and responsible for her, as he would about a younger sister.

Of course, Iarund had to walk behind them again at the exact moment her arrow stuck into the ground just a few feet shy of Alrin's. "Bah! Is that all you got?" he laughed. "I expected more from Sagittari's daughter."

Sirena bowed her head as she fought back the tears that immediately began to well in her eyes.

Something inside Alrin suddenly snapped. It felt searing and involuntary, like pulling his hand out of a blazing fire. He felt the floor of his power suddenly give way to unreachable depths below. It was back—the same power that saved him from his fall at Batara had returned.

He glared at Iarund, his whole body clenched and shaking violently with anger. That's when the ground beneath him started to shake. A bright light shot out from his hand, and Alrin looked down to see the same strange symbol that had taken its place over his ensignis before.

The entire market square scrambled to grab hold of something. He could sense each person darting under a table or away from a building. The whole world seemed to lag behind his accelerated senses. Everything seemed to be in slow motion, including Halvdan, who was in a strange half-speed sprint right in Alrin's direction.

Each startled scream and crash of a clay target to the ground sounded more like an explosion to his heightened senses. Every second felt more like an eternity…yet strangely instantaneous.

"What's happening?" Iarund cried out. "Your ensignis. Th-they're glowing!"

Alrin directed his focus entirely on Iarund, who was cowering under a table, his face filled with terror.

The ground shook harder.

Alrin felt unstoppable.

A thousand variations of Iarund's death flashed into his mind. Somehow he knew that if he focused too hard on any one of these images, it might actually happen. The longer he let his anger fuel them, the more he felt the power slipping out from under him. By the time Halvdan reached him, the power was gone. Just as the symbol dimmed back to his ensignis, Halvdan grabbed Alrin's hand and yanked him behind a nearby building.

Before being dragged out of sight, Alrin looked back to see a cloaked figure watching him from inside the tent. His eyes were hidden under the shadow of his hood, and on his forearm was the symbol of a black dragon.

CHAPTER FIVE

THE TRACE

D id he see you?" Halvdan yelled. He shook Alrin by the shoulders, his brows raised and eyes wide open. It was something Alrin had never seen in him before—fear. "The Verindi! Did he see you?" Halvdan yelled again, pinning Alrin against the building. But before he could answer, someone darted around the corner right behind them.

Halvdan stepped in front of Alrin and turned to face whoever had followed them. "It's just Thrain," he exhaled heavily.

Alrin had never been happier to see him in all his life. As always, he appeared just when Alrin needed him most.

Halvdan yanked Thrain out of sight and held them both firmly against the wall. "Luck, for the moment," Halvdan said, peering around the corner, "seems to be with us." He relaxed his grip.

Once Halvdan was convinced that enough time had passed to guarantee they were alone, he turned to where Thrain and Alrin stood. The panic on his face had slowly washed away, but a lingering uncertainty remained. He glanced back and forth between them, lost in his own thoughts. Every answer that came across his face seemed to be followed by yet another question, until finally his gaze landed on Alrin. "Light of distinction," he whispered.

"Light of what?" Thrain asked. "Wait," he said, taking a step away from Alrin. "That light came from you? It happened again, didn't it?"

"I...I couldn't control it," Alrin said, looking down at his open palms. "I'm just glad it stopped before..."

"Stopped?" Thrain bellowed. "Why would you want to stop it? This is your chance! We need to use this to our advantage while we still can." His eyes suddenly lit up. "You should be in the Trials! "

"No," Halvdan said firmly, finally emerging from his dreamlike trance. "There is far more at stake here than the two of you realize."

"Why not?" Thrain asked a little too bravely. "You just don't want him to win, do you?"

Alrin braced himself for whatever fantastic display of magical retaliation Halvdan had in store. *Just don't turn him into something awful,* Alrin thought. But to his surprise, nothing came. "Know your place, Thrain," Alrin whispered, nudging him in the ribs. Even he knew that you didn't talk back to someone with higher ensignis than you. In Dalroth, age wasn't the deciding factor on who the "elder" was—it was your ensignis. So the fact that Halvdan far exceeded Thrain in both made it a wonder that Halvdan didn't lose his temper. The tendency to avoid confrontation definitely wasn't a trait that Alrin and Thrain shared. Alrin avoided it at all costs, but Thrain always seemed to find his way smack-dab into the middle of it.

"I see your father in you more every day," Halvdan said calmly. "But I'm sorry, Alrin must not enter."

"But he would win!" Thrain insisted. "I've seen it in action. Just get that thing to appear on his hand again and nobody would stand a chance."

"There was a change to the rules," Halvdan explained. "Only one from each guild will be competing. It was made perfectly clear that the Verindi have no intention of staying in Everglen longer than is required. Trishna, Edric, and Iarund have been chosen."

A tirade of objections came hurtling from Thrain's direction, but Alrin was far too preoccupied to hear them. The only words he managed to catch were *unfair* and *only opportunity*, but as soon as Thrain realized that arguing with Halvdan was beyond useless, he left—surely to go plead his case before Bogdan.

"Don't worry about him," Halvdan said once Thrain disappeared around the corner. "He's only trying to ensure a brighter future for himself, and for you. There aren't many lucky enough to have someone looking out for them so...ardently. I see a yearning for greatness in him, though I fear that if he pursues it too vigorously, it may end up far dimmer than he imagined."

Alrin tried his best to hide how conflicted he was about what was happening to him, but he obviously wasn't doing a good-enough job of it. Halvdan raised his arm and put it around Alrin's shoulder. They walked a few steps toward the Narew River, and as they stared into the gently rolling current,

Halvdan began speaking again. "I remember a time when Thrain would…"

But Alrin's thoughts spoke louder. The memory of the hooded figure watching him was still replaying vividly in his mind. He heard enough of what Halvdan was saying to know he was reminiscing about a time, before Alrin was even born, when he and their father would sit and talk, taking long drafts on their pipes, and watch Thrain get into endless amounts of mischief.

"Why are the Verindi really here?" Alrin interrupted suddenly. "I'm sorry," he said when he saw Halvdan's eyes widen, "but I know you're just trying to distract me."

Halvdan's story stopped abruptly. "Not much escapes you, does it?"

Alrin shrugged.

"I do suppose it would be wise for you to know," Halvdan said. "If my suspicions are correct…the Verindi…are here for you."

"For me?" Alrin said. He suddenly felt very nauseated.

"Well, not YOU specifically," said Halvdan. "As luck would have it, I don't think they yet realize that it is you they're searching for. But yes. And they've been searching for quite some time."

Alrin opened his mouth to speak, but no word was brave enough to come out.

"I know you have questions," Halvdan said, "but first, you must trust me when I tell you that you do not want to be found." He then pulled a small notebook from his pocket. Pushing a pencil out from its leather binding, he wrote something on one of its pages and tore it out. "Go to my wing in the guild and wait for me there," he instructed, folding the paper over and handing it to Alrin. "Follow the bank of the river, and speak to no one. I'll come as soon as the Trials are over."

Alrin clenched the piece of paper tightly in his hand. He knew whatever Halvdan had written would be of utmost importance, but he feared that it would only lead to more questions if he opened it without him.

"Wait," Alrin called out, "how do I unlock your door?" But when he turned around, Halvdan had already vanished around the corner.

Off in the distance, he could hear the Trials already under way. A loud voice was announcing each of the competitors, which guild each represented, and each one's teacher. Then, after copious amounts of fluff and flattery had been meticulously applied, Alrin finally learned the names of the Verindi.

"Please join me in welcoming," came Bogdan's gargantuan voice, "King Abaddon's most elite guardians of Dunblane— Nabal and Gywdion!" Boisterous cheers echoed through the town, rattling the panes of glass next to where Alrin stood.

So there are two, he thought. He wondered instantly which one had seen him. For the briefest of moments, he thought seriously about sneaking out to get a better look at them. That's why he had come into Everglen that day in the first place. They were the strongest men in all of Dalroth, sworn protectors of the king; surely they would be wearing their ensignis with pride. Alrin couldn't explain why, but he still found it hard to fight the overwhelming desire to see their levels, though he eventually talked himself out of it and left for the magic guild.

Heeding Halvdan's warning, he retreated to the Narew and followed its bank north. The only person he had to avoid was an older man named Mason Murray as he was closing up his store and rushing to catch the competition. Mason owned a small rune shop, where Everglen's finest collection of mana stones and spell components could be purchased. Alrin had never been inside it, of course, but he had overheard plenty of stories while hanging around the magic guild about the mystical wonders kept inside.

Alrin crouched behind a few bushes while Mason fiddled with the lock; then, once he was around the corner, Alrin dashed into Halvdan's guild.

He knew it would likely be deserted while the Trials were being held, but that didn't keep him from moving cautiously. After what Halvdan had just told him about the Verindi, Alrin wanted nothing more than to just make it to his wing uneventfully. But that was easier said than done. He was so focused on who or what might be around the next corner, Alrin got completely turned around more than a time or two and it took much longer to find Halvdan's office than he would've liked. It wasn't until he recognized the sign about "tracking your progress" etched above a doorway that he again found his way.

Once he finally made it to Halvdan's sturdy iron-trimmed door, Alrin raised his hand into the magical lock just as Halvdan had done the day before. The tips of his fingers disappeared behind the wall and small, waterlike ripples spread out across the stone.

It was cold.

He couldn't keep himself from moving his hand back and forth for a while, watching the wall splash around like the surface of a pond, but then he started to feel a light jolt on the tip of his finger. It wasn't much at first, nothing more than a faint tingle, but the longer he kept his finger submerged in the wall, the stronger it became.

He began to panic and tried to pull his hand away, but wasn't able to move it more than an inch or two before the magic pulled him back in. The tingling grew stronger.

Alrin moved his finger around, searching frantically for anything to grab hold of, or maybe even a hidden lever to press that would open the door from the inside. But there was nothing. He stopped moving again and the shock intensified, sending daggers of pain shooting up his arm.

I bet it needs a password, Alrin said to himself, finally realizing that anyone capable of simply walking up and sticking a hand into a wall could've done exactly what he just had. No, Halvdan was much smarter than that. The only person who would be able to unlock the door was Halvdan himself, or anyone else he…*gave the password to*. "Duh!" Alrin said out loud as he yanked the sheet of paper out of his pocket.

That's when he heard them…footsteps.

Alrin turned his head down the long corridor toward them. They were getting closer.

He quickly unfolded the paper, and when he saw what Halvdan had written, his heart felt as if it jumped into the back of his throat. It was the symbol again. The same symbol that had now appeared twice on his hand and granted him unspeakable power. But Alrin knew that this wasn't the time to dwell on what it could mean. He needed to get inside…and fast.

He had a terrible feeling that the only ones who might be inside the guild during the Trials were the exact people he was afraid of running into. Alrin stared down the hallway and could almost picture the black-hooded warrior turning the corner and staring directly at him. He looked down at the piece of paper and frantically duplicated the strange triangular symbol into the wall.

There was a faint, metallic click and the door creaked open. Whatever strange magic held his finger finally released him, and he darted through the door and closed it behind him as softly as he could.

Once his heart stopped pounding, he finally turned around. Halvdan's office felt even more magical without him in it. Alrin's first instinct was to explore everything he possibly could, which instantly made the necessity of a lock on the door clear. The sun was shining in through the window behind the desk, making tiny specks of dust floating through the air glow like tiny fireflies. Off in the corner, Moltrix was curled up into a warm ball, fast asleep with her three tails covering her face. Halvdan hadn't been kidding about how fast she grew. Even after just a single day, she looked noticeably bigger. Alrin tiptoed across the room so as not to wake her, but the very moment his weight landed on a loose floorboard, her triangular foxlike ears perked up and she cracked open her large, beady eyes. Bright-red flames ignited over her fur, but as soon as she blinked the sleep from her eyes and recognized him, they disappeared and she lowered her head back down again.

"Good girl," Alrin said soothingly. "It's just me." He went over and sat in a chair across the room and immediately began rubbing his hand. The tingling was nearly gone, but massaging it still seemed to help. For the moment, looking around Halvdan's office had taken his mind off whoever had been coming down the hallway. But that panic quickly returned when he heard the footsteps stop directly outside the door. So did the shadow to whom they belonged.

A deep, threatening growl echoed from Moltrix's corner, as she stood up and glared at the door.

There was no use hiding, so Alrin simply shut his eyes and waited. *Where are you, Thrain,* he asked himself as the lock clicked and the door slowly began to open.

The soft squeak of the old hinges was more of a shrieking howl as it sounded the removal of the only barrier separating him and whoever was coming for him.

"Everything all right?" asked a voice.

Alrin opened his eyes to see Halvdan standing in the doorway looking at him quite inquisitively. Moltrix had already made it to the door in a single hop and was rubbing the full length of her body against Halvdan's leg and purring loudly.

"Fine," Alrin said, clearing his throat, and then finally took a deep breath—his first in quite some time.

Latching the door behind him, Halvdan turned to a shelf along the wall and picked up a small stone.

"What's that?" Alrin asked as strongly as he could manage.

"We will get to that," Halvdan said. "How's your hand?"

Alrin didn't realize it, but his hand was clasped firmly around his wrist. "Better," he answered.

Halvdan looked at the stone in his hand and examined it for a moment. "I was glad to not find you unconscious with your arm stuck in the wall," he said with a raspy chuckle. "You must have taken quite a shock, though. There is far less mana in here than when I left it." Halvdan opened his hand and focused on the stone. Almost at once it began to glow a bright blue, but then, just as quickly, it returned to its perfectly ordinary slate gray.

Alrin looked on in wonder as Halvdan placed the stone back on the shelf.

"Are the Trials already over?" Alrin asked.

Halvdan nodded.

Outside the door Alrin heard someone darting around thunderously through the halls. Halvdan glanced over his shoulder, acknowledging that he heard it too, but didn't seem concerned in the least, so Alrin wasn't either. "Trishna," said Halvdan, motioning to the door. "She's not too happy with me at the moment, I'm afraid."

Suddenly a great force of wind blew under the door and sent papers and books flying into the air and all over the floor.

"I take it she lost?" Alrin asked, somewhat dazed. He leaned over in his chair and made a valiant attempt to organize what he could.

"Not exactly," Halvdan answered. "I removed her from the Trials. Without her it was over in a matter of seconds. Edric didn't stand a chance against Iarund's strength, the poor boy."

Alrin gave him a horrified look.

"Oh, he'll be all right," Halvdan reassured him. "Just a little…shaken up. Yes, Iarund has been crowned the champion, garbed in a cloak of the king's black dragon, and hoisted off into the glorious abyss for his training. It was all very…sudden to say the least."

"So the Verindi." Alrin gulped. "They're gone?"

"Yes."

"Sheesh," Alrin sighed. "You weren't lying about them not staying long." Alrin's ears popped as another gust of wind blew past the door and sent papers spewing toward the ceiling again. *Trishna must be training like a lunatic out there*, he thought.

Once the papers had finally settled to the floor, Alrin couldn't help but laugh. Even with papers everywhere, he realized that it didn't look much different than it had before.

But even so, he went about shuffling what he could into reasonable bundles and tried his best to keep his eyes to himself. But as he was stacking several books back onto a shelf, he saw something that made him freeze in his tracks. The cover of one of them jumped out as if his own name had been written across it.

The symbol.

Alrin grabbed the book from the floor, and several loose papers lying over it fluttered to the ground. He recognized the spine immediately; it was the same book he'd seen Halvdan grab before. It was very old, and quite frankly it was a wonder that it was still holding together at all. In faded, cracked lettering the words *Legend of Visarga* were burned into the withering leather spine.

Alrin followed the symbol with his finger. It was the first time he'd actually gotten a good look at it. Then, without even realizing it, he was staring at the back of his hand, where he had seen it moments earlier.

Halvdan watched him closely.

"What is it?" Alrin finally asked.

"It is called the Trace," he answered.

Alrin opened the book to the first page. "'The Tale of the Dinivus Brothers,'" he read aloud.

"Have you heard the story?"

"I don't know," said Alrin. "It sounds familiar. When I was younger, perhaps."

"Go ahead and take that home with you. I think your first lesson would be best spent in those pages."

Alrin felt his stomach disappear. "Lesson?" he said excitedly, then lifted his eyes to see Halvdan smiling back at him.

"As of today, you are officially a member of the magic guild!" Halvdan said triumphantly. "Your training begins in the morning."

CHAPTER SIX

LEGEND OF VISARGA

That night Alrin waited until Aurora and Thrain had fallen asleep to open the book.

And this required far more patience on Alrin's part than he would have liked. It felt like an eternity before Thrain finally stopped bellyaching about how he'd been cheated out of the Trials. "There's no telling what secrets Iarund is learning, even as we speak," Thrain would say, and then as soon as his head hit the pillow, he would bounce right back up, even more upset than before. "Anytime I hear his name now, all I want to do is bang my head against the wall."

Welcome to the club, Alrin wanted to add, but refrained. He figured that if he kept his mouth shut, it might get Thrain to go to sleep faster, but Alrin soon found out this wasn't the case.

Not everything Thrain said turned out to be meaningless ramblings, however. Just as Alrin was about to doze off, Thrain mentioned one Verindi's levels, and it woke him up faster than a bucket of water over his head. "You should have seen them! 83-74-68," Thrain said dramatically from across their bedroom. Alrin refused to believe it until he made Thrain swear up and down that that's what the numbers were. Neither of them had even heard of ensignis that high before—at least not around Everglen. Thrain hadn't gotten a good look at the other Verindi's hand, but he mentioned overhearing someone say that you needed at least one level over eighty to even be considered.

Apparently, once the Trials were over, Iarund's ceremony was even more short-lived than the actual competition. "Just from how impatient they were," Thrain explained, "it didn't even seem like the Trials were the real reason they were there." At this Alrin's stomach turned sour, and his heart didn't stop racing until long after Thrain had fallen asleep.

But eventually he did, and Alrin was finally able to remove the book from its hiding spot between the wall and his bed. Creeping into the family room, he added a few small logs to the fireplace and moved a chair close enough that he could make out the old faded letters as they danced across the pages in the firelight.

Nervousness and excitement swept over him as he ran his hand over the symbol on the front cover. He knew that for the first time ever the hope of finding answers was finally within his reach.

The Tale of the Dinivus Brothers

In the beginning Dalroth was ruled by three brothers, and together they held the secret to unlimited power. Like saplings interwoven to form a mighty tree, their power was rooted within one another and held fast through tumultuous gales of chaos.

There was Draegan—the mightiest of warriors—who, with strength unmatched, forged an unbreakable loyalty among the people. Then there was Gondor—the most powerful wizard in the realm. By sacrificing a portion of his own power, he allowed men and beasts alike to share in his mystical enchantments. Finally there was Oswyn—the wisest among them. It was he who brought order to this land of darkness with an unwavering light of reason. Peace inhabited Dalroth for centuries…but it would not remain.

Hoarding the gifts the brothers bestowed, a man called Beswic amassed a power so great that it rivaled even that of the Three. Though because his power was poured equally into each ability, he saw his cup as empty and therefore always thirsted for more.

A hidden darkness grew within. Beswic began to covet the admiration that the brothers received, attributing it to their heightened power. He established lordships and dominions, hoping that a world raised in the shackles of hierarchy would shine a light upon his greatness—but like all things born into shadow, the people remained blind.

He bestowed one final gift to the land of Dalroth, casting a mighty spell that displayed everyone's strength, magic, and intellect as three numbers on their hands for all the world to see; for surely this would proclaim his transcendent power. Thus the ensignis were spoken into existence.

The spell found its way into the incendiary hearts of men and blazed wildly. As all streams flow into the sea, and yet the sea is never filled, so was their insatiable desire for more. With Dalroth's gaze fixed on them, the gleam in their eyes that Beswic desired only continued to fade. Blinded by a lust for dominance and arrogant about his abilities, he betrayed the brothers, seeking to bend their will to his own. Just as the walls of their minds were about to collapse, Draegan, Gondor, and Oswyn unleashed a power so great that it brought Beswic crumbling to his knees. In what was *now an undeserving world, the brothers concealed the secret to their power within a stone—a mighty rune that would stay hidden away until one who is worthy should rise to possess it. So will shine a light of distinction in an endless sea of similarity. The location of the stone has turned from fact to fable, and is slowly forgotten in the fading pages of time.*

Alrin knew at once where he'd heard the story before. Aurora used to read it to them when they were falling asleep. But it had always just been the story of how they had gotten their ensignis, nothing more. Why it had anything to do with him was beyond baffling—that was, until his eyes came across a particular phrase toward the end.

"'*Light of distinction,*'" he whispered.

Alrin could still hear Halvdan's voice saying it. He read the story over and over again until he likely could have recited it from memory, but even then he wasn't sure what it meant. It made even less sense than when he'd heard it as a child. Surely it didn't speak of him. His whole life, Alrin had been nothing but worthless—less than worthless, even. He was a weakling, an outsider…the lurker too afraid to set foot inside the circle of power. Three-thirteen.

Alrin looked up at the dwindling fireplace and shivered. He could tell the night was going to be a cold one. He reached out in front of him, warming his hands over the sputtering logs as the frigid air crept in around him, and before he knew it, he was staring at his ensignis again. It was harder and harder to turn away.

What a load of nonsense, he thought to himself, closing the book a little louder than he had intended. He looked over to the woodpile against the wall, but decided against it. Rising from the chair, he walked into his room and climbed back into bed. The sheets took forever to warm, but as they did, he was finally able to relax and fall asleep, the book cradled safely in an arm.

Alrin arrived early the next morning at the guild. *His* guild.

Everglen was asleep, still recovering from the festivities the night before. The town was so empty, in fact, that Alrin didn't even feel the need to take his secret path by the Narew. *I'll have to get used to this,* Alrin thought as he walked the empty cobblestone streets. *I am in the magic guild now, after all.*

The first snow had fallen at some point in the night. It had been more of a light dusting than an actual snow, but the highest peaks bordering Everglen were lit up like desert sands by the glistening moon overhead.

As he reached the outer gate of the magic guild, he paused for a moment and stared at the small pond where he had watched Trishna learn the wind wave a few days before. *One more step,* he thought, smiling to himself, *and no one can call me a lurker ever again.*

He couldn't wait to see the look on his brother's face when he told him. He pictured hitting Thrain in the back of the head with an orb of water, just as Iarund had once done to him.

Yes. Alrin smiled. *Perfect way to tell him.* But then he pictured telling his mother, and his smile disappeared. He knew that he would have to find some way to break it to her. There was no turning back now. After what had happened to him, there were just too many questions left unanswered…too many pages left unturned. If Halvdan thought he played a role in the story he'd read the night before, he was determined to find out why.

He took a deep breath and walked in.

He was relieved to see white smoke rising from the chimney above Halvdan's wing. Standing outside his door, Alrin was immediately tempted to recreate the strange symbol of the Trace in the wall. The magical lock intrigued him…as did the password that it required. *I'll have to remember to ask how this thing works*, Alrin told himself as he reached up and knocked on the door.

Knock-knock. Knock-knock.

A small grin spread across his face once he noticed the heartbeat pattern that only he and Thrain would have recognized.

"Good, you're early," Halvdan said, opening the door. "Have you eaten?"

Alrin shook his head and slowly entered. The warmth of the room and the lingering aroma of food immediately enveloped him and made him intensely aware of how empty his stomach was.

Halvdan brought him a plate of roasted ham, blackened potatoes, and fresh fruit. He wasn't exactly sure why, but Alrin always had the urge to decline anything someone offered him. Somehow his paradoxically mixed-up kindness always convinced him that declining politeness was the polite thing to do, but this time he accepted what was offered graciously. It just looked too good to pass up.

"So," Halvdan said, pushing back into his chair and reaching for his pipe. "What did you think of your reading assignment?"

"Er…I didn't get as far as I would've liked," Alrin said, tearing off a juicy hunk of ham.

"I see," Halvdan said, stroking his chin. "How far did you get?"

Alrin gulped. "The first two pages," he said, rather embarrassed. "I couldn't stop thinking about something you said the other day."

"Off to a good start." Halvdan smiled. "The light of distinction...I hoped that you had noticed. But before we get into all of that, I want to start by asking you the same question that I ask every student at the beginning." Halvdan's eyes narrowed as the guild instructor in him started to come out. "What do you wish to gain from being here?"

The question sounded so rehearsed. It was something Alrin knew he had said a hundred times before, but even so, it was the most exciting question Alrin had ever been asked.

"I'm just excited to find out what there is to learn, I guess."

"Interesting," Halvdan said. "You're the first to ever say that." He thought on it a moment as the smoke from his pipe rose toward the ceiling. "Most talk about how they've always dreamed of being the strongest mage in all of Dalroth." Halvdan moved his hand to his chin and eyed him carefully.

At first Alrin was nervous because no one had ever answered like that before. He could tell Halvdan wasn't quite sure what to make of it. But he definitely didn't seem disappointed by Alrin's answer, so maybe it wasn't the wrong one after all.

"You will learn plenty," he said slowly. "That I assure you. But knowledge alone won't awaken your potential. Now that you are a part of my guild, there is no more excuse for weakness. If you ever leave the guild as the same person who entered, then that day was wasted. You will never better yourself by being satisfied with what you already possess—and you, Alrin, have the ability to glimpse perfection."

Alrin gulped. "I'm not even sure what that means."

Halvdan laughed. "Well…that is where I come in. With my guidance—and a considerable amount of effort on your part— you could become the most powerful student in a matter of weeks, and maybe, one day, even stronger than me."

Alrin's eyes widened. "I appreciate the vote of confidence," he said, smiling. "But I fear you might be setting the bar a little high. Some have trained their entire lives…How could I possibly—"

"Yes, but they've only trained with what I've given them," Halvdan interrupted with a wink.

"I don't understand."

"Think about it, Alrin. Whoever has the highest ensigni in Everglen is the guild leader. Why in the world would I equip everyone with abilities that could someday surpass my own?"

Alrin had never thought of it like that before. It made perfect sense, of course, but it disappointed him to see a side of Halvdan that was just like everyone else. Maybe the reason Alrin had never been invited to the guild wasn't his lack of potential, as he'd always thought. He was a Turner, after all…Maybe the reason had been that he had *too much* potential. Perhaps Halvdan's letting him come ask questions had been his way of keeping tabs on his competition. A question entered his mind at the same time it accidentally left his lips: "Why now?"

Halvdan looked at him, quite surprised. "That is a very perceptive question. I assume what you're really wanting to ask is why I would train someone who might reach a power greater than my own. Or better yet…why should you trust me?"

Alrin was too afraid to nod.

"Well, to be honest, it's because you're a clean slate. Before anyone else even sets a foot into my guild, they're already arrogant about what little they actually know. They are blinded by their own motives...by their own desires. Trishna only trains from the desperate need to lash out against her father. Iarund trains just because he couldn't live with himself not being the strongest. Others show a ray of promise, but as soon as they reach whatever goals they had originally set, their desire to improve disappears. But then there is you," he said, looking to Alrin. "I've never come across it before. You are a blank canvas—a beautiful anomaly of indifference. I had to ask you to be a part of the guild, not the other way around...and, I believe, therein lies the difference. If I can trust you to keep your slate clean and follow my every instruction, then you can trust me to not hold back in painting my masterpiece."

"Believe me," said Alrin, "my cup is empty."

"Then so it begins."

Alrin rested his half-eaten plate of food on the table next to him. He didn't want to seem insulting, but he was hardly in the mood to finish it now. The sun cracked over the Tatras and entered the window behind Halvdan's desk. He heard the crow of a rooster ring out from one of Mrs. Rider's chicken coops far in the distance. Another day had dawned over the small town nestled in the valley, but to Alrin it was far from just another day.

"The first thing you must know," Halvdan began, "is that *all magic requires sacrifice*. Great or small, for good or for evil, all magic requires some type of sacrifice. Most commonly, this is your mana. The higher the level of magic you perform, the more mana gets used up. As your level increases, you have more mana at your disposal—and it can be replenished faster. Are you with me so far?"

"I think so," said Alrin. "But you said 'most commonly.' Can something else be used?"

"There is some magic that draws its power from certain items, or spell components. After the spell is complete, these items are destroyed."

"Like bistort and wormwood leaves?" Alrin asked.

"Precisely. Some of these components, like the ones for the healing spell you somehow performed, can simply be found in the wild, if one only knows where to look. Others are extremely rare…and incredibly expensive."

Alrin looked down at his ensignis. "I meant to ask you. What level is needed to cast that healing spell?"

"Herb amalgamation starts at level nine," Halvdan replied. "Which brings me to the most important lesson you can learn. If you only take one thing away from your training today, it must be this. Never attempt any spell or ability beyond your magic level. This much is crucial. I'm not sure how you were even able to use magic at level one, but until we figure that out, you must never try anything above your ensigni. Understood?"

Alrin nodded.

"Think of mana as a magical life-force. You can use it, manipulate it, and even store it. But if you push too hard, or attempt something beyond your level's capabilities, you can very easily die from it."

"How do you know what's safe?" Alrin asked. He wanted to know more about the Trace, and how he had been able to survive using magic at all. Those questions had burned in him ever since Batara Falls. But knowing Halvdan, everything he was saying, as well as avoiding, was chosen deliberately.

Halvdan sprang to one of his shelves littered with books and rummaged though several stacks of papers until he found what he was looking for (which seemed like nothing less than a miracle from where Alrin was sitting).

"Here," he said, handing Alrin a sheet of paper. "Commit these to memory."

"'*The Magical List of Do's, Don'ts and Distant Dreams*,'" Alrin read aloud, "'by Darius Glade.'" He looked down the page at a list of numbers going from two to ninety-nine in two long columns. Beside each number were the names of various spells, very few of which Alrin could have pronounced. His eyes went immediately to level nine, and sure enough, "Herb Amalgamation" was written beside it. Directly below that: "Wind Wave."

So that means Trishna must be level ten, Alrin thought excitedly. He scanned over the rest of the levels, looking for anything that might explain what had happened to him at the cliffs or in the marketplace, but nearly every spell was completely foreign to him.

"What about level one?" Alrin asked, realizing his level wasn't on Glade's list.

"Well, normally, you aren't able to access magic at level one. It has to be awoken first."

"How do we do that?" Alrin asked curiously.

Halvdan fiddled with his beard. There was much more gray in it than Alrin remembered.

"Do you remember the first thing I taught you?"

Alrin thought for a moment. "All magic requires sacrifice?"

Halvdan raised both hands into the air. "Well done, Alrin, well done. That is rule number one. In the same manner, reaching level two also requires sacrifice."

"A sacrifice of what exactly?"

"The only thing that you have to give," Halvdan said, looking to Alrin's right hand. "One level from each of your other two ensignis."

Alrin's heart sank. He had worked so hard to earn his new level three in strength. The result of endless hours of chopping wood, simply disappearing in a flash—Alrin nearly groaned at the thought of it. "What would happen if you tried to awaken someone with all level ones?"

"That person would die," Halvdan answered sharply. "But magic isn't simply woken by mistake. Someone has to do it for you. And if anyone were to use their power in such a way, it would be by no accident, I assure you."

Alrin gulped. The only person he knew with all level ones was Sirena, but he knew Sagittari wasn't about to let anything happen to her—especially if it had anything to do with magic.

"Before we awaken yours, however," said Halvdan, "there is another piece to the puzzle that we must first discuss…and that is the *Void*. Now, I realize everything you know about magic must seem like nothing but fantasy and fairy tales, but I assure you, the Void is as real as you and I. Once you are awakened, it becomes an integral part of who you are. It is the realm of power within us that acts as the source of our magic."

Alrin scrunched his face. "So it's like an internal mana bank?"

Halvdan laughed. "That and so much more. You can tap into it not only for magic, but also for memories, thoughts, and emotions. It's linked directly to your ensignis, so with every spell you cast, you can actually feel the boundaries of your power growing. In time you'll even be able to know how far you are from leveling—and know when you've leveled without even looking."

Alrin listened excitedly.

"It is so vitally linked to you, in fact, that the first thing I will teach you is how to protect it. If left unguarded, others could access it as well." The seriousness in his voice suddenly changed. "Once you decide to awaken it, Alrin, it can never be undone."

Alrin looked down at the embarrassing numbers staring back at him. What did he have to lose? Maybe when he walked around Everglen, people wouldn't mock him anymore because of his weakness. Who knew, maybe now that he was in the magic guild, Trishna would even start talking to him. Perhaps they could even start training together.

Alrin barely hesitated. "I'm ready."

"All right, then," Halvdan said. "Give me your hand."

Alrin stuck out his right arm and Halvdan closed his hands around his ensignis.

"Close your eyes and clear your mind," he said. After a few moments, he uttered the words of the spell. "*Devovi excitāre.*"

Alrin immediately felt it. It was as if something had been lying dormant in him all along, just waiting to be woken up. And Halvdan was right about its being an internal realm. It was as if the essence of everything he was, everything he thought, felt, and remembered, was stored inside him. Then, even with his eyes closed, he sensed a light growing brighter and brighter, forcing him to open them. As he did, he saw beams of light shooting out between Halvdan's fingers, which were curled around his ensignis.

Halvdan let go and the light suddenly vanished.

CHAPTER SEVEN

INTO THE VOID

W hat? What is it?" Alrin said nervously. Seeing Halvdan as surprised as he was made him very uneasy.

Halvdan peered down at Alrin's ensignis. "Nothing," he said casually. "That's just never happened before, but everything seems as it should be."

"Nothing?" Alrin nearly shouted. "That didn't seem like nothing." But when he looked down and saw the numbers on his hand, he almost couldn't believe it. 2-2-2.

The disappointment of losing a level each of strength and intellect quickly faded. For the first time in his life, there wasn't a 1 staring back at him to remind him of his weakness at every turn.

"I dare say that you're the first level two purist I've ever seen," Halvdan said with a chuckle.

"Purist?" Alrin asked, feeling strangely proud of the accomplishment that, until now, he'd never even known existed.

"A purist has all of their levels the same, and they do everything in their power to keep them that way. You see, there are those out there who believe that by keeping all three ensignis equal, they are somehow stronger. Superstitious hogwash if you ask me. Of course, Iarund is one of those people, so the fact that he won the Trials sure hasn't helped the ongoing myth around here. You're just the first I've seen at level two, because, as you can imagine, most students have their levels trained up much higher when their magic is awoken."

Alrin's excitement vanished. It suddenly didn't feel like an accomplishment anymore. Being compared to Iarund, despite being the lowest-ranking purist possible, put a horribly bitter taste in his mouth.

"But no matter…Even I was level two at some point, though it pains me to admit it."

Alrin forced a smile.

"You may notice feeling a little different right about now," Halvdan said. "That is what we magic folk refer to as the Void. You will do well to get familiar with it. Explore every part of it until you recognize it better than your own reflection."

"It's…it's incredible," Alrin muttered. It was as if an entire realm of power had been there all along, just waiting to be tapped into. He closed his eyes and explored its boundaries. The newness was exhilarating. It was as if he were staring into his own soul. Each ensigni was no longer just a number, but rather a crystal-clear pool, and he could see straight to the bottom. It all felt strangely familiar to when the Trace had taken over. Though, of course, when the Trace had taken over, the pools had been bottomless.

"You said it stores our memories?" Alrin asked.

"It does," Halvdan said cautiously, "but you need to learn how to protect them first."

But Alrin barely even heard him. He didn't care...He couldn't wait any longer. He wasn't sure if the memory even existed, but he was determined to find out. He thought back to the last memory he'd had before he fell at Batara, and as soon as the memory crossed his mind, he opened his eyes and was suddenly standing at the edge of the cliffs.

Everything felt so real. It was like watching a dream that he already knew the ending to. Every detail was vividly intact—every tree, every cloud, every smell. He could even feel the wind whipping through his hair.

"Better not miss," Thrain suddenly whispered next to him. "That's our last arrow."

"I won't," Alrin felt himself answer. His feet started moving toward the edge, and he felt the bowstring draw back and press against his chin. He peered over the ledge and saw the deer grazing below them. But just as Alrin was about to release the arrow, he felt it.

It was like a prickle on the back of his neck—as if someone was watching him. Cold needles rushed through his body. He didn't know how, but he could tell something was in the memory with him...changing it.

He felt the bow relax back down to his side as the sky grew darker and darker. A thunderstorm materialized above him and the wind began to pick up, moaning as it whipped through the trees.

Thrain never mentioned any of this, Alrin thought to himself. Surely he would've.

He peered back over the ledge to try to find the deer again, but it had vanished. "Uh, Thrain...what's happening?" His voice shook. He spun around to where Thrain had just been, but instead of his brother, it was the deer standing there. Mouth foaming, eyes blood red, it lowered his head at him as if on the verge of charging.

It wasn't a memory anymore—it was a nightmare.

The deer began to creep forward, forcing Alrin closer and closer to the edge.

"Thrain!" he called out again, though his voice felt as if it belonged to someone else. Alrin continued backpedaling away from the demonic creature, and just as his heels found the edge of the cliff, he happened to look up and see Halvdan staring at him from behind one of the trees.

The memory faded to black and he was back in Halvdan's office.

"How...," Alrin sputtered. His mouth was dry and he could hardly speak. A cold sweat ran down the back of his neck. "You...you can change them?"

"I can't change what actually happened, but I can certainly change what you remember," Halvdan said menacingly. "Once in control, I can make you see anything I want you to see, or do anything I want you to do. In the hands of someone strong enough, you're as helpless as a puppet on a string."

Alrin's heart pounded so hard it hurt. There was so much he wanted to go back and relive, but after seeing Halvdan in a memory where he hadn't been, Alrin doubted he would ever try it again.

"Now you see why the Void is so important to protect. If you don't know how to guard your memories, they aren't just yours anymore."

"How far back can I go?" Alrin asked, his heart still sprinting.

"For now, only a day or two," Halvdan replied. "But as you grow stronger, the memories will become more and more clear. And in time you'll even be able to see as far back as..."

"My father?" Alrin blurted out. He wasn't sure why it was the first thing he thought of. He was too young to remember anything about his father, but that was what likely captivated him most. As with the unexplainable gap in his memory, Alrin knew he would always be curious. Until those gaps were filled in, he would always return to the questions of his past.

"Yes, even your father." Halvdan nodded slowly. "But there is only so much to be learned from one's past, Alrin. It is only the steps that lie ahead of us that can be changed, not those that have already been taken."

Alrin nodded.

"Now try again," said Halvdan. "Choose a memory that is strong. And one where you would immediately recognize if anything were changed."

Alrin tried hard to think of something that had happened within the last few days. The first thing that came to mind was his hidden path by the river. He had walked it nearly every day of his life, and no one knew it better. But the idea of seeing Halvdan's face staring at him from around another tree still sent a chill up his spine. *No,* Alrin told himself. *No more trees.*

Then he thought of just the right memory. And it was the strongest one he could think of.

"I think I've got it," Alrin said.

"Good. Once you sense something trying to break in and change it…hold on to it."

Alrin took a deep breath. After several moments of forcing the thought of Batara out of his mind, he very hesitantly closed his eyes and the memory flashed in front of him.

He found himself sitting at the table with Thrain in their tiny, overly cramped family room. The smell of wood burning in the fireplace filled the air as Aurora fumbled with something around the house. Alrin couldn't tell if this was an actual memory or a combination of several, but it felt as real as being there.

Aurora walked over to them with a sort of half grin at the corner of her mouth. Then, as she had so many times before, she moved the hair out of their eyes and kissed them lightly on the forehead. Alrin could feel his face scrunch into a ball and his hand instinctively move to wipe the kiss away. Even in a memory, he seemed to care only because Thrain was around.

The memory was so simple, yet so forceful. If anything was strong enough to keep Halvdan out, it would surely be this. What greater force is there than the strength of family, after all?

And that's when Alrin felt it again. It was as if the memory were a bubble and someone had pressed a knife firmly against it. The sky turned black, and the entire house began to shake. The floorboards beneath them started to creak and splinter, but even as everything around them sounded as if it was being ripped apart, Aurora and Thrain didn't seem to notice. Very calmly they reached out and grabbed Alrin by the hands.

The house continued to shake for a moment or two, but then everything fell silent. The blue of the sky returned, and Alrin opened his eyes.

Even Halvdan seemed shocked that it had worked.

"The memory must be strong," he said. "It's incredibly rare for someone to do it on their first try. Whatever it is, hold to this memory. It will be your anchor through even the fiercest storm."

Alrin finally relaxed, and it wasn't until then that he realized his entire body had been clenched.

Halvdan got up from his seat and moved silently toward the door. "Now comes the fun part," he said heartily, and then grabbed the stone that was propped against the shelf. "Remember our first rule?"

Alrin nodded as he caught the stone Halvdan tossed him.

"Well, that sacrifice doesn't always have to come from you directly. You can store mana in stones such as this one. Just as with spell components, you can stumble across a few of them in the wild if you know where to look. But the best ones come from deep within the runithium mines of Brugden."

Alrin gazed at the stone, remembering the sharp sting he'd felt when his hand was stuck in the wall. *So this is where the magic came from*, he realized. He turned the stone in his hand and it glistened in the sunlight. It was dark gray with specks of eggshell blue sprinkled throughout it.

"What happens when all the energy is gone?" Alrin asked.

"Then whatever spell it was sustaining will end. Not to worry, though; that particular stone is charged with enough energy to take down a few dozen men before it runs out."

The stone fascinated him. It looked so ordinary. He never would've guessed it was anything more than a peculiar rock if he'd come across it in the woods—not even one he would add to the collection in his puzzle box. He suddenly couldn't help but wonder how many he had unwittingly skipped across the surface of a pond in his lifetime.

"Our next stop," Halvdan said, "is to visit Mason's rune shop and get you one of your own."

"Really?" Alrin exclaimed.

"Should be open by now," Halvdan said, judging by the light entering the window. "Be warned, though, with that fresh number two on your hand, he will likely try and sell you everything under the sun. He can smell a new student a mile away."

Alrin jumped to his feet.

"And better let me do the talking," Halvdan added. He then pointed to his head and said, "I think a few lights may have burned out a long time ago, if you catch my drift. He'd likely forget his own name if it weren't written on his sign out front."

Alrin followed him out of the guild, keeping a watchful eye for the one person he greatly desired to see, but desperately didn't want to be seen by…Trishna. Even though they were in the same guild now, he still had a gut feeling that she wouldn't want him there. He knew they were bound to run into each other sooner or later, but until Alrin had the chance to level a few times, he was clinging to the hope of its being later rather than sooner. Luckily for him, she was nowhere to be found.

Once they were outside, Halvdan led him into the shop directly across the street. "Mason Murray's Runestone Emporium" was carved into a wooden sign above the door. A bell chimed as the door opened and closed behind them.

Alrin's eyes immediately caught thousands of small glass vials lining the walls. Long wooden shelves with circular holes cut out of them held rows upon rows of perfectly aligned spell components. Alrin had never seen anything like it. The vials of several rows were full of brightly glowing liquid. Reds, blues, greens…and each had a small paper tag fastened to it by a string. Other shelves were organized by the names of spells. *Mana Elixir, Strength Potion, Serum of the Sages, Bane of Beleag'r, Vial of Veracity.* At the top of the shelf was listed the name of the spell and all the ingredients needed to make it. Alrin knew this because he instantly recognized one of them: "*Healing Tincture*—Bistort and Wormwood: 15S a bundle."

Alrin continued around the room until he came across several glass cases that held the runestones. He leaned down and pressed his forehead against the glass, eager to get a better look at them. The stones were carefully placed in what looked like large egg crates and wrapped in a glossy, velvetlike material. Just as he'd suspected, they looked no different from the one he had seen at Halvdan's—perfectly ordinary.

As he gazed into the glass, an old man suddenly popped up from directly behind it. Alrin nearly toppled over from surprise. The old man must have either been tinkering with something on the floor or sleeping, because he seemed to appear out of thin air.

"Halvdan! Good to see you." His eyes suddenly turned to Alrin's ensignis. "I see you brought me a new student," he said, staring at him as a salivating dog would at a piece of meat.

Mason Murray was quite the odd-looking fellow. He was much older than Halvdan, and much chubbier. What was left of the small ring of hair on his head was slicked over to one side, making his baldness even more noticeable. He had big, round eyes that were far too close together, a pair of thick glasses that he wore down by the tip of his nose, and the remnant of a smile was ever present across his face.

"Good morning, old friend," Halvdan said with a nod. "I'd like you to meet Alrin Turner."

"Mason Murray, at your service," he said, reaching out for Alrin's hand and shaking it vigorously. "Turner," he said. "Well, ain't that something."

"It's nice to meet you, sir," Alrin said timidly.

"So what can I get you today, Master Afrin?" Mason looked at him very vacantly and blinked much faster than anyone should blink behind a thick pair of slanted glasses.

"Um." Alrin looked back to Halvdan, who had a big I-told-you-so expression across his face. "It's AL-rin, sir. And I was hoping to look at some of your mana stones, please."

"Of course, of course." Mason tore over to one of the cases on the far side of the store and returned with one of the egg crates. "These are the finest stones in Everglen," he said proudly. "Straight from the runithium mines of Brugden. Enchanted by none other than their magic-leader, Eldron Warwick himself. You will find none finer."

Alrin picked up the first stone on his left. On either side, small flakes of yellow were sprinkled throughout it. Catching the light at just the right angle, the stone glistened like yellow glass. As he went to place the stone back down, he saw a piece of paper where it had been, with two small inscriptions written on it: "0.1" and "1G, 20S."

"What do these numbers and letters on here mean?" Alrin asked.

"Wow, he must be brand new," Mason said with the glimmer of a sale in his eyes. "The first thing you need to know about mana stones is that you can't retrieve all the mana you put into them. It all depends on how purely refined the runithium ore and how powerful the incantation that is bound to it. This particular stone, shown by the first number, gives back one-tenth of the mana that you put into it. The second number, of course, is the price." A thin, slanted smile appeared at the corner of his face. "This stone is one gold and twenty silver...a bargain if I do say so myself."

Alrin nearly choked. He doubted he'd even seen that much at the same time. During the last harvest season, he'd worked an entire week helping Mrs. Rider with her crops in order to save up for a new bowstring that he needed. It had been backbreaking labor, sunup to sundown, and he'd received only two silver pieces at the end of the week.

Alrin thought for a moment. *That's over a year of work!* There was no way he was going to be able to save that much. Then, purely out of curiosity, he picked up the first stone on his right; it reflected a beautiful flash of green across the ceiling. It reminded him of a color that he'd only ever seen deep in the woods before. He was almost too afraid to look. "0.5" and "8G, 50S."

Alrin grimaced.

"So, Cauldron," Mason said, still struggling to fully grasp his name. "What'll it be?"

"Sorry, sir, do you have anything cheaper?" Alrin said, still holding the stone in his hand. "I'm afraid I can't afford these."

Suddenly a large bag clanked onto the glass beside him.

"We'll take that one," Halvdan said, dumping out a pile of coins onto the case. He counted out nine pieces of gold and put them in Mason's eagerly outstretched hand. "If I can also get some sage and yarrow with whatever is left."

"Absolutely!" Mason rushed to a shelf with remarkable speed and pulled out the spell components that Halvdan had requested from their respective vials. "You'll be needing some flasks, then, too, yes?"

"If you can spare them," Halvdan answered.

"Anything you need," Mason replied as though he was giving Halvdan an excellent deal, but judging by the look on Halvdan's face, this was most certainly not the case.

"What are those for?" Alrin asked curiously.

"Mana elixir," Halvdan answered. "The stone only returns half the mana you put into it. The elixir will restore what you've used so you can train much faster."

"Thank you," Alrin said softly. "I will pay you back as soon as I can."

"Nonsense. Think nothing of it."

Mason brought everything over and set it down in front of them. "Go ahead," he said. "Give it a go."

Alrin hesitated. They still hadn't gotten that far in his training.

When Mason sensed that it was Alrin's first time, he was so giddy that he nearly knocked his own glasses off his face. "Just reach into the Void and pass some of the mana into the stone," said Mason energetically. "I'm no expert like Halvdan here, but it really is that simple."

Alrin closed his eyes and wrapped his fingers around the stone, gripping it tightly. As he reached into the Void and focused on his newfound power, before he knew it, faint beams of green light cracked between his fingers and he suddenly felt waves of energy leaving him. It really was as effortless and involuntary as Mason had suggested. Almost like breathing. When Alrin stopped the flow of energy, the stone dimmed and he felt noticeably more tired.

"Well, ain't that something!" Mason exclaimed, very pleased that he had successfully instructed him. "Now then, try to draw everything back in."

Alrin reached into the Void once more; this time he could sense another source of power. It was like standing in a dark room and seeing a bright light concealed behind a door. With the stone in his hand, it felt like an extension of his own power. As soon as he attempted to draw from it, the energy flowed back into him with another flash of green from the stone.

"Ha!" Mason let out giddily. "Don't grow too fond of that two on your hand, my boy! With this stone here, you'll be leveling in no time."

Alrin felt somewhat restored, but as the tag around the stone suggested, he had a lot less energy than when he'd started.

"I wouldn't expect anything less from a Turner," Mason said. "The son of Meldun, I reckon?"

"Yes, sir," Alrin answered, quite surprised that Mason had remembered his last name, but even more so that he knew of his father. "You knew him?" Alrin asked excitedly.

"There's not a person in Everglen who doesn't know your father," Mason chuckled. "It's been a few weeks since he's been in the shop. How is the old ball of muscle?"

Halvdan suddenly cleared his throat...and Alrin's stomach all but disappeared. "He...died shortly after I was born."

Mason glanced up at Halvdan and his face turned bright pink. "Forgive me," he said, awkwardly adjusting his glasses. "I must have confused him with someone else. You know, my memory isn't what it used to be, after all. Good day, Master Turner." With that, Mason scurried to the back of his shop and tried his best to seem overwhelmingly busy with work that suddenly needed tending to.

Alrin turned and followed Halvdan out of the shop, and that's when he felt the sickening feeling wash over him that he'd felt when Halvdan had changed his memory.

CHAPTER EIGHT

TWO BIRDS WITH ONE STONE

Alrin trudged behind, bound in another deep staring contest with the ground. Hanging at his side was the dazzling new mana stone that he'd already all but forgotten.

It felt as if he'd just been punched in the stomach. In the last few days alone, Alrin's world had been turned upside down. He'd not only mysteriously cheated his own death and had no idea how, learned that the most powerful beings in Dalroth were out there searching for him, and been taken under the wing of the mightiest guild leader that Everglen had ever known, but now the only certainty he'd grown up having had just been stripped away in an instant.

Before he knew it, they were standing in the inner courtyard of the magic guild.

"Halvdan," Alrin said softly.

Stopping and turning, Halvdan folded his arms sternly across his chest and waited for the question that he already knew was coming.

"Is my father really dead?"

"I don't think I'm the person to answer that," he said at once.

Alrin drooped his head. It was more than enough of the answer that he couldn't bear to hear. Maybe Thrain was right. Maybe everything their mother had told them was a lie.

"But I'll make you a deal," said Halvdan. "Now that your Void has been awakened, there is something that belongs to you. Something that your father left for you a long time ago."

Enough of the air that had been knocked out of Alrin returned for him to say, "Really? What is it?"

Halvdan reached into his robe and pulled out the sage and yarrow that he'd just purchased. He clenched them tightly in his fist and held them over a flask. "If you can get your magic to level eight," he said, pausing as a blue liquid funneled from his hand and into the glass bottle, "I will bring you to a place that your father and I used to visit when we were younger. A place hidden in Everglen that no one else has ever seen. It is there that you will find not only what he left you, but perhaps even some of the answers that you seek." Halvdan recorked the flask, which was now brimming with a glowing blue potion.

Alrin pulled Darius Glade's list of magic levels from his pocket. "Hydrokinesis," he said, looking down at level eight. "Isn't that…water manipulation?"

"Indeed it is," Halvdan answered, "and a comfortable mastery of it is necessary for where you're going."

A sudden spark of motivation flashed across Alrin's eyes.

"This is where I leave you," Halvdan said, handing him the potion. "Whenever your mana is running low, just a little swig of this will restore it."

Alrin lifted the potion and stared into the strange effervescent mixture. "And if this runs out?"

"Take a look at the quest board. There's always good ways to boost your levels on there. When I see you next, I expect to see that eight on your hand. Until then, happy leveling."

With that, Halvdan left.

"Thanks again," Alrin called out as he watched Halvdan retreat to his wing of the guild. A puff of white smoke appeared above his chimney and gradually started to grow—as did Alrin's excitement. With his new mana stone in one hand and the potion in the other, he set off to find a quiet corner to begin his training.

The next several hours were filled with endless repetition. He pushed every ounce of energy he had into the stone, then drew it back out again. Over and over and over. He managed to do this about eight or nine times before his fatigue finally forced him to stop and take a sip of the potion. It had a pleasant tinge of sweetness to it, like the taste of honeysuckle, but even better was the incredible rush of energy it gave him. It was like jumping into the Narew River after a long day in the sun. It was instant rejuvenation. With even the smallest sip, he felt fully restored and was able to continue.

Soon into his training, Alrin couldn't help but lose himself in his thoughts. The idea of his father's still being alive continued to creep back into his mind no matter how many times he forced it out. What was it that his father could have left him...and where was this hidden place that no one had ever seen? Most importantly...if he was still alive, where had he been all this time? Alrin became so wrapped up in these questions, in fact, that he lost count of what cycle he was on and quickly found out what happens when your mana runs out.

While he was nearly possessed by the idea of having run into his father without even knowing it, the green light of the stone flickered, and all at once the room started to spin. He reached out for the potion as fast as he could, and what little actually made it to his mouth (and not down the front of his shirt) came not a second too late. Just as the vial made it to his lips, his vision started to blur.

It took several minutes for the room to stop moving, but as it did, the reality dawned on him of just how close he had come to passing out—or worse. It was at that moment that he vowed to stay as far from that boundary as he possibly could.

With what little of the potion that remained now soaking through his clothes, and frightfully concerned that he'd just survived yet another near-death experience, he decided it would be wise to quit while he was ahead. When he finally looked at his hand, his mouth fell open.

2-7-2.

It was so close. He could feel it on his fingertips.

If only he could charge the stone a time or two more, he could go straight to Halvdan and maybe—just maybe—get some of the answers he so desperately wanted.

He looked down at his shirt, and for a moment thought seriously about trying to suck some of the potion out of it. But having to explain why his shirt was in his mouth to anyone who happened to pass by sounded less than desirable. Everyone already hated him, so he really didn't want to add something like that to their list of reasons why. There was no telling how long it would take to live that one down.

It was hard to believe that he'd gotten so far in just a single day. He couldn't wait to see Halvdan's face when he showed him, or better yet, the look on Thrain's. But even after all the excitement, the only thing on his mind was reaching level eight. He hated to admit it, but he was starting to understand the obsession. The triumph that burned with each new level lived only long enough to be immediately smothered by the insatiable craving for the next. It was like an itch that only got worse the more you scratched it.

He took a different route home that afternoon so he could pass by the quest board as Halvdan had suggested. Just as he'd feared, students were everywhere. He even took the most indirect path in an attempt to avoid as many stares as possible, but it only seemed to draw more attention. He'd grown accustomed to stares, but these were entirely different. He clung to the hope that it was because of the large stain on his shirt, but it didn't take long to realize that that wasn't what they were staring at.

"Is that Alrin?" he heard a lanky, dark-haired boy ask someone from his intellect guild. "Was that a seven on his hand?" another girl whispered to a group of her friends as he walked by. "There's no way…It had to be a one," said another.

Alrin wasn't sure which kind of stare was worse. The people who saw him didn't even try to hide that they were talking about him. Everyone acted as though they'd never seen him before, which Alrin may have very well thought was the case if it hadn't been for the fact that he was so universally despised.

As Alrin reached the quest boards, a small grin crept over his face because he noticed that for the first time ever, one word wasn't being mentioned among all the whispers. *Lurker.*

He tried his best to convince himself that he hated the attention, but he knew that was only his mother's words echoing in his mind. In all honesty, he sort of liked it.

But as Alrin turned to the board facing Halvdan's guild, his momentum vanished. As usual, all the good quests had been taken. There was only a single sheet of paper on the board, and it looked as if it had been there for months. Having somehow survived an untold number of thunderstorms, it was nearly plastered to the board, and the ink was almost entirely smudged off. Alrin pulled it down and read it.

Help needed at the farm. Lunch provided.
Thankfully yours,

~ Mrs. Rider ~

Alrin felt his blood start to boil.

Mrs. Rider's husband had passed away many years ago. The several acres of farmland that she owned was all that she had left, and it was getting less and less green every year. He and Thrain always made an effort to help out a few days each harvest season, despite how many times she kindly insisted that they shouldn't beforehand, and then firmly demanded they receive payment for it afterward. She had never once, as far as Alrin knew, openly asked for help…until now.

Alrin clenched the flyer in his fist and started trembling with anger. It made him sick to imagine how many people had seen it and simply left it there. The worst part was that he knew exactly why no one had taken it down yet—because helping her wouldn't increase one's ensignis.

It didn't even cross his mind to take his hidden path home. He made it a point to glare down every person he passed, making sure every one of them saw what he was holding. He wasn't sure whether it was his ensignis or not, but he knew that the person walking the path home that afternoon was far different from the one who'd walked it that morning.

He barely made it home in time for supper, though apparently still just in time to be ambushed with questions as to where he'd been all day. His meal, which he ate entirely with his left hand in order to keep his ensignis hidden under the table, was cold. It wasn't until he mentioned that he planned on helping Mrs. Rider the next morning that Aurora's curiosity finally subsided. This seemed to appease her, at least, but the same could not be said about Thrain.

There was no use trying to get anything past him. He could read Alrin all too well. He sat quietly the whole time that Alrin ate, just listening and squinting ever so slightly at Alrin's hidden arm under the table. As soon as the dishes were clear and Aurora went to bed—that's when the real questioning began.

Thrain could hardly contain his excitement once Alrin told him he'd been invited into the magic guild. Alrin showed him "The Magical List of *Do's, Don'ts and Distant Dreams*," and then pulled his book from between the wall and his bed. The symbol on the front made Thrain's eyes light up like moons. Once Alrin had finished reading him "The Tale of the Dinivus Brothers," Thrain said he remembered it too. Aurora had read it to them almost every night, Thrain mentioned, and she had always finished the story by saying, "It was never their power that made them so powerful."

Thrain shook his head a lot that night. He would get really still, and then, with every thought he stumbled upon, his head would start shaking again. It had never made sense to him when he was little, he said, but he wasn't surprised to learn that her lies had started that early on.

In the best words Alrin could find, he explained what it had been like when his magic was awoken, and everything about the Void and the whirlwind of emotions from being able to watch his memories. But the part Thrain seemed most interested in was that Alrin could tell each time that he was close to leveling. "That would come in handy," Thrain said, but as soon as he realized that the only way Alrin would know about it was by leveling himself, he almost tackled him to find out what his ensignis were. "It's a surprise!" Alrin repeated over and over again, keeping his hand hidden behind his back.

Next he showed Thrain the stone, and told him what had happened in Mason's store that morning. Their voices lowered to near whispers as they talked about the possibility of their father's still being alive. After much discussion, they decided to find out as much as they could before confronting Aurora about it.

"First we need proof," Alrin said connivingly, and, luckily, he knew just where to find it. "Halvdan said I have to get to level eight," Alrin said, "and we just might have the proof we need."

"Level eight!" Thrain exclaimed. "That's going to take years."

And that's when Alrin removed his hand from under his pillow and slowly turned it over.

At the sight of his ensignis, a look of amazement spread across Thrain's face. But very slowly that amazement disappeared and turned into the same look Alrin had seen on everyone else that day. As if his brother didn't even recognize him.

"It's getting pretty late," Thrain said suddenly, then turned over and faced the wall.

"Umm, is everything all right?" Alrin asked.

"Yeah. Just tired," Thrain answered. "Good night."

"...Night," Alrin whispered.

It was quite obvious that everything was not all right. He rested his head against his pillow and stared out the window by his bed. It had never crossed his mind that Thrain might actually be jealous of his ensignis. Maybe it should have. After all, it had taken him only a single day to reach a level it had taken Thrain years to achieve.

And just like that, Alrin hated his ensignis all over again. Before falling asleep, he reached over to the wall.

Thump-thump, thump-thump.

They always came in twos. Like a heartbeat. But this time there was no answer.

The next morning came faster than Alrin would've liked it to. He hoped that Thrain had slept it off and was ready to talk, but when he turned over, Thrain's bed was already empty. As more and more light poured into his window, he made a concerted effort to roll back over and fall asleep, but as he did, he made the mistake of looking at his hand again. Even with a single glance, the obsession returned.

Alrin hated how much power the numbers were starting to have over him. It was like trying to break a bad habit. The more he focused on avoiding them, the more he found himself staring.

He reached up to his window and fumbled for his puzzle box. Alrin always knew if he needed his jacket that day just from how cold the box was. Today was definitely a jacket day. After twisting the lid and aligning the prongs, he took out the mana stone, Glade's list, and Mrs. Rider's flyer and tucked them in his pocket.

Roughly a mile away, Mrs. Rider was the closest thing they had to a neighbor. Rather than taking the Narew path or even the main road, Alrin decided to take the most direct route and cut through several fields of waist-high grass. On a normal day this would undoubtedly be the fastest way, but today…it was a huge mistake. He immediately found himself having to snake his way through the labyrinth of mud that was left over after the snow had melted. With every step he felt his shoes growing heavier, so that by the time he finally made it to her house, he must have been six inches taller.

Mrs. Rider was already hard at work in her cornfields, plucking off the remaining ears from their stalks and tossing them into a large wooden crate. As she looked up and saw Alrin walking toward her with the flyer in his hand, the biggest smile spread across her face.

"Good morning, Mrs. Rider!" Alrin said, walking up to her. Despite her slumped posture and wrinkled hands, the wooden crate next to her was filling up remarkably fast.

She stood up stiffly and wiped the sweat from her forehead. "You know, there must've been hundreds of people that pass by that every day," she said. "I was starting to think there wasn't a decent person left in this town."

Mrs. Rider was an elderly woman (in her seventies or eighties if Alrin had to guess), dark-skinned and alarmingly skinny. But the most recognizable feature about her, by far, was that she was one of the kindest people Alrin had ever known.

"Here, I can do that," Alrin offered, starting at once on some of the stalks next to him. "How many do we need?"

"As many as we can get," she said, still smiling at him. "With the early freeze this year, we're going to lose so many. I just hope there's enough to last us the winter." She dusted off her hands and caught her breath. It was obvious that she'd already been out there for several hours. "Here, let me go get us something to drink," she said.

She returned moments later with a glass of raspberry leaf tea; by then Alrin had already cleared a small circle around him. "Thank you," he said, taking the glass and gulping it down. "You know, I really don't mind doing this," he said, returning the glass with a less-than-subtle hint. He could tell she was exhausted, but knew that she would never own up to it. She would likely work another few hours just to prove him wrong.

"Are you sure?" she asked. "I did need to go into town for a few things."

"Positive," said Alrin. "I'll have this crate overflowing in no time."

Mrs. Rider grinned. "Don't work yourself to death, honey. I won't be long." She started for the main road, but before she got there, she turned. "You know, if there was an ensigni for kindness," she hollered back to him, "you would, without a doubt, be Everglen's guild leader."

As she turned again to leave, Alrin felt his face turn bright red. The irony of what she'd said stuck in his mind, and he thought for quite a while on just how different the world would be if kindness were indeed measured by one of their ensignis. He laughed just imagining everyone trying to "out-nice" one another, and couldn't help but be reminded of Thrain's humble bragging.

It was a cool day, but the stalks stood higher than he by several feet, more than enough to prevent any sort of refreshing breeze from reaching him. The sun poured down on his face and the realization quickly hit that he had once again volunteered himself for another taxing and time-consuming task on Mrs. Rider's farm. The pile of corn grew painfully slowly. There were rows upon endless rows; thousands of perfectly aligned soldiers of sweat just waiting to be plucked.

He took a deep breath and continued working. He tried his best to occupy his mind to pass the time, and before long all he could think about was reaching level eight. He couldn't for the life of him think of a single reason water manipulation would give him answers about his father.

Lost in the idea of how good it would feel for an orb of water to hit him in the face right about then, Alrin reached for another stalk, and two doves roosting nearby sprang up and soared into the air. The idea hit him like a brick. "Of course," he said aloud. "Why didn't I think of it sooner?" He pulled the magic list from his pocket and searched it for a spell he'd seen performed in Halvdan's guild a few days earlier.

"That's it!" he exclaimed once he saw it. "Level four…levitation."

He remembered seeing the two girls passing the stone back and forth through the air. *It can't be too hard*, he thought to himself. From what he'd overheard Halvdan telling Trishna, if you simply focused hard enough and channeled enough mana into whatever object you were trying to manipulate, it should eventually obey.

If he could somehow figure it out on his own, he would not only be able to fill the crate in no time, but it might just be enough to get him to level eight. *Two birds with one stone*, he thought excitedly. Then he couldn't help but roll his eyes at what had given him the idea in the first place. "Two birds with one stone," he said, chuckling. "No doubt Thrain would've punched me for that one."

Alrin's first attempts at levitation proved wildly unsuccessful. If someone had passed by at that particular moment, in fact, they would've surely thought he was a raving lunatic. He held an ear of corn right in front of his face and stared at it so fiercely that it must have looked as if he were in the middle of a heated argument. But just as he was about to give up and throw it to the ground, it wobbled.

Then, a few tries later, it started shaking.

Before he knew it, the corn had risen from his hand and was hovering in front of him.

He just stared at it in disbelief for a very long time, but once the shock finally wore off, it got really exciting. He raised it, lowered it, spun it around in circles, and then, finally, moved it slowly over the crate and let go. It landed with a thud and rolled down the pile to join the rest. Alrin looked up to the endless rows in front of him, and a grin appeared across his face. He knew the rest of the day was going to be spectacular.

Starting out, he focused on just a few stalks at a time. He didn't want to get ahead of himself and risk using all his energy. Remembering what had happened the day before, he reached into his pocket and wrapped his hand around the mana stone.

He reached into the Void and could still sense the faint light under the doorway. *Good, there's a little left—just in case.*

He opened his eyes and lifted. But when nothing budged, he tapped into the Void for more power.

He picked a single stalk this time and focused on each ear of corn so intensely that he was sure they would burst and shoot popcorn all over the place. Holding his breath, he lunged upward with his entire body as if he were about to leap off the ground, and as he did, dozens of ears shot hundreds of feet into the air. He raced back to Mrs. Rider's porch as fast as he could so as not to be pelted as they plummeted back to the ground.

"A little somewhere in between," he laughed as several thuds sounded on the metal roof above him.

Before long Alrin had levitation mastered. He could grab several dozen ears of corn at a time, pluck them from their stalks, and rest them gently in the crate.

It was the most fun Alrin could remember ever having. He probably would've done it all day if he could, but with each and every load, he felt his mana slowly fading. Right when it was almost too low for comfort, it was like a switch in his head was engaged. He didn't even have to look. Halvdan was right—he already knew.

2-8-3.

Somewhere between the loads, he'd leveled in both magic and intellect.

And that's when he heard a sudden gasp from right behind him. "Bless my soul."

He turned to see Mrs. Rider carrying the basket of goods she'd bought from town. Her jaw had nearly hit the ground when she'd seen the mound of green that lay before her.

"Thank you so much, Alrin," she said, her eyes welling up a little. "That's going to last all winter, and then some."

"Don't mention it," Alrin said warmly. "I'm only sorry I didn't come sooner."

"Oh, hush, child. You need never say sorry to me," she said cheerfully. "You have no idea how much this means. Now come inside so I can fix you something to eat."

Alrin glanced down at the 8 on his hand as if it were screaming that he was late for something. "Um, I really should be going. I have to meet someone, if that's OK."

"All right, honey. But wait there just a moment...I have something for you."

She hurried inside before Alrin could object and promptly returned with something in her hand.

"Mrs. Rider, you really don't..."

"I insist," she sharply interrupted. "And I'll hear nothin' more about it."

She raised her hand toward him and tapped her foot against the ground, waiting for Alrin to open his.

Every time Alrin came to her farm, this was the battle he faced. And each and every time, this was the battle he lost.

"Don't think I haven't noticed your ensignis," she said snidely. "With that shiny new intellect level of yours, I was hoping you would be smarter than this."

Alrin smiled and finally gave in. He opened his hand at the same time that she dropped a small silver coin into it.

The most he managed to get out was a shaky "Thank you." He wasn't sure what to say. It was far too generous.

"Now I know it isn't much," she said, "but despite what the rest of the world says around here, a heart like yours shouldn't go unrewarded."

Alrin thanked her again and offered to move the corn inside for her, but once more she refused. He could tell it was another battle that he was destined to lose, so he tucked the coin into his pocket and headed into town.

As he reached the guild, he was met by even more stares, but one in particular stopped him in his tracks. It was finally the person he'd been hoping to bump into.

"There you are!" Trishna yelled at him across the courtyard. Waves of nervousness tingled throughout his body. For the first time in his life, Alrin had ensignis he could be proud of. But after seeing the look on her face, he wanted to hide them more than ever.

CHAPTER NINE

WHEN YOU PASS THROUGH
THE WATER

Trishna headed straight for him like a raging bull, glaring at his ensignis. If looks could kill, Alrin most assuredly would have died. Trailing right at her heels like a midday shadow was her little sister Sirena.

"Er, hi, Trishna," Alrin said, trying to nervously test the waters before she reached him. He wasn't sure why she was so angry. Maybe she blamed him for Halvdan's taking her out of the Trials.

"How are you level eight?" she asked, ignoring any sort of pleasantry.

Oh. Alrin gulped.

Sirena peeked out from around her sister's leg and waved timidly.

Alrin reached slowly into his pocket, then pulled out the mana stone and showed it to her.

"What! Where did you get that?" she hissed.

Alrin couldn't talk. Suddenly his mouth was very dry.

"Wait, what percent is that?" she hollered, and when Alrin didn't answer right away, she folded her arms over her chest and waited. The 10 of her magic level caught Alrin's eye.

"Fifty…," he squeaked.

"I've had my eye on that stone for months!" she yelled. "Halvdan gave it to you, didn't he? Didn't he!"

Before Alrin could even open his mouth again, Trishna spun around and disappeared into the magic guild, leaving him and Sirena standing there in a cloud of dust.

Just another day in Everglen, Alrin thought to himself. Given her reaction, Alrin pretty much gave up on the hope of ever impressing her right then and there. Even now that they actually had something in common, she seemed only to hate him even more. He took a deep breath and tried to calm whatever it was bubbling up in his stomach. "Hi, Sirena," he said, exhaling. At least there would always be Sirena. No matter what numbers were across his hand, she would always be the person he could count on to see past them. "At least my ensignis haven't changed how you…"

"Woooow," she said suddenly. Beneath her mess of curly hair, she was ogling his hand. "Can you show me some magic?" she asked excitedly.

Alrin suddenly felt a few inches shorter. Any hope he'd had left in humanity had just been deflated.

"Umm…" Alrin looked around nervously. "I don't know if I should." He really didn't want to attract more unwanted attention. It already felt as if the entire world were watching him.

"Please, Alrin, PLEEEASE?" She stood on the tips of her toes and tugged at the edge of his shirt.

No, I probably shouldn't...

At least that should've been his answer. And it likely would have been had he not made the mistake of glancing down and seeing those big pleading brown eyes. She was much more clever than Alrin gave her credit for. Even with all level ones, she had found a foothold in the world to get what she wanted—the irresistible power of persuasive cuteness. And having been raised by someone as stoic as Sagittari, she had developed this power to crumble the resolve of far more immovable men than Alrin, so what chance did he have against it? Even though it was obviously an act, she swelled up her bottom lip as if it had been stung by a bee, and all at once Alrin knew he couldn't say no.

"Oh, all right," Alrin said, chuckling. "I surrender. But you have to promise me something."

Her head started bobbing almost instantly.

"You can't tell your father I showed you magic. I don't think he would like that very much."

She nodded excitedly again as a big, victorious smile spread across her face.

"Defeated by a six-year-old," Alrin said, shaking his head and laughing to himself. He started looking around, trying to think of something to show her, and that's when he saw just the thing: the small quiver of arrows across her back.

Target in mind, Alrin pointed over her shoulder with the most convincing look of surprise. "Did you see that?" he gasped suddenly.

"What!" Sirena spun around and looked behind her, mimicking the same look of concern that Alrin wore.

"There it is again!" Alrin said enthusiastically. "I thought I just saw...a GHOST!"

As she turned around, Alrin levitated one of the arrows off her back and floated it into the air. "Look," he shouted, "There it is! It stole one of your arrows!"

Her face glowed with wonder as soon as she saw it. She ran underneath it and started jumping playfully into the air trying to reach it.

Alrin lowered it just enough to barely escape the reach of her fingertips and then lifted it high into the air again.

"Give it back, you mean old ghost," Sirena said, giggling.

Alrin couldn't help but laugh himself. He'd almost forgotten what it was like to have fun with someone.

Every time he lowered it, she scrunched her face into a ball and jumped as high as she could. And every time, Alrin would raise it just barely out of her reach, leaving her hands empty, but delightfully so.

But then, as silent as the wind, Sagittari appeared out of thin air and snatched the arrow out of the sky. As usual, his footsteps were so eerily quiet that Alrin hadn't even heard him coming—and just like that, the fun was over.

"Shouldn't you be practicing, Sirena?" he asked, clenching the arrow tightly in his fist.

Sirena lowered her eyes to the ground. "I thought maybe I could stay with Trishna and Alrin," she said, cowering. "Just for today?"

Sagittari looked down at Alrin's ensignis, then back up at him. It felt as if even his eyes were arrows. "Maybe some other time," he offered with the most frighteningly forced calmness

Alrin had ever seen. He inspected the arrow carefully, as if Alrin's magic might have somehow sullied its perfection, and then pushed it back into the quiver among the rest. "Now run along," he said. "I'll be there shortly."

Surprisingly, she didn't look too disappointed. Despite being relentlessly steered toward archery by her father, she still somehow seemed to enjoy it. This brought Alrin a bit of peace.

As she passed him, Sirena brought her hand up to her mouth and whispered, "That was fun, Alrin. You make a good ghost."

Alrin forced a smile and watched her skip whimsically along the path toward her father's archery range, humming softly and strumming the string of her bow as if she were playing an instrument. Once she was out of sight, however, Alrin had an overwhelming urge to pull Glade's list from his pocket to see what level was needed to disappear.

"I thought I made it abundantly clear you were to keep her AWAY from magic," Sagittari snarled. He spoke so close to him that Alrin felt the heat of his breath. "You can let Halvdan turn you into one of his pixieish fairies if you want, but I will *not* have both of my daughters subjected to it."

"I didn't mean anything by it." Alrin grimaced. "It won't happen again, I promise."

"And I will make sure of that. If there's one thing that I'm sure of, it's that magic can never be trusted. And now, I'm afraid...neither can you." Sagittari turned his back to him and started walking away. "Oh, and don't worry about the bow I made you. I'm sure it will find a more suitable owner."

Alrin writhed with anger. It took everything he had to hold his tongue as Sagittari rounded the corner and was out of sight. He normally found it very easy to avoid confrontation, but something was noticeably different this time. It may have been from the protective siblinglike bond he'd formed with Sirena, or the confidence that grew within him with each passing level. Either way, he was finding it a whole lot harder to control his anger. He decided it was time to get out of sight, before anything else could happen.

He entered the magic guild, and as he neared Halvdan's wing, he could hear Trishna's voice echoing through the halls.

"You took me out of the Trials so that Iarund could win, and now you're power-leveling him? You've never shown a weakling like that any attention before! Why now?"

Even from where Alrin hid, to one side of the doorway, the word *weakling* felt like a knife to his chest.

"Trishna," Halvdan answered calmly. "He has potential beyond anything I've ever seen. If anything, you should be helping him train."

"What potential does he have that I don't?" Trishna hollered.

Alrin inched closer to the doorway and accidentally scuffed his foot against a loose cobblestone, revealing himself.

The talking inside stopped at once. "Alrin, my boy," Halvdan said from within the room. "How's your training going?"

As Alrin's shaggy hair peeked slowly around the corner, Trishna barged through the doorway and rammed her shoulder straight through his.

"Sorry," Alrin whispered instinctively. Sorry for what he wasn't exactly sure. It was more of a knee-jerk reaction from a lifetime of feeling in the way. If only she would understand that he'd never asked for any of this—that he would gladly switch places if he could.

"Come in. Come in," Halvdan said, beckoning him to a chair beside his desk. "I knew you must have leveled a few times to get that kind of reaction from her, but level eight already..." Halvdan sat back in his chair and pulled at his beard. "Very impressive. I suppose you're anxious to see what your father left you, then?"

"Yes, sir. If it's not too much trouble, that is."

Halvdan chuckled. "Like night and day, you two."

Alrin cracked a courteous grin. He wasn't quite sure to whom he was being compared, but he was still much too nervous to ask.

"All right, then, come with me. Let's not burn precious oil with idle words." Halvdan rose from his chair with a stiff groan and then walked over to a wall and fumbled through some things on a shelf. After his hand passed several potted plants that looked as though they were doing everything they could to get out of his reach, he grabbed several vials of potions, and then together they left. As the door closed behind them, Alrin could hear Moltrix rush over and begin to scratch it, whimpering loudly.

Alrin followed Halvdan closely and kept his eyes to himself. He could feel stares burning holes through him as the other students watched their teacher lead the new mystery pupil out of their guild.

They headed south, taking a small road into town until the trodden path gave way to some tall grass that grew along the border of the Narew River. Alrin couldn't decide what he was more excited about—learning something about his father or finding this secret hideout in Everglen. Maybe it was hidden deep in the mountains behind a large roaring waterfall. Or maybe even under a stone statue with a hidden lever to make stairs suddenly appear. He was so enchanted by his ideas of where it could be that he nearly crashed straight into Halvdan.

"This is it," Halvdan said, stopping abruptly.

Alrin looked around.

This couldn't be it. It *was* hidden, of course, but they were still in the middle of town. In fact, it was the exact spot where Alrin had shot the arrow across the river a few days before. He looked over to the small island and could still see the arrow stuck in the oak tree about halfway up its trunk.

"We used to play here all the time," Halvdan said. "Your father and I. Then, shortly after you were born, your father brought me here. I made a promise that day, that if the time ever came, I would do the same with you."

"If what time came?" Alrin asked.

"Your training. Meldun enjoined me that if your Void was ever awoken, I was to bring you here."

Alrin searched the water for anything out of the ordinary. A strong wind blew in from the north and rustled the few remaining leaves that clung to the lifeless branches of the oak tree. Winter was growing nearer with every passing day. Small ripples in the water splashed rhythmically against the bank at his feet, and a cold shiver crawled up Alrin's spine.

"He never mentioned what he left you," Halvdan continued. "I'm quite fascinated to find out myself."

"Where is it?" Alrin asked, looking around, quite dazed.

"There," Halvdan said, pointing across the water. "When we were little, we built a room inside that island. You have to walk underwater to get to it."

Alrin's eyes grew to the size of chicken eggs. "No way," he whispered.

Water manipulation turned out to be quite similar to levitation, but in every way more difficult. With levitation, you had to focus only on moving something in one direction…maybe two. But in order to lift water into the air, you had to apply force from every direction all at once. And if that wasn't hard enough, Halvdan said he wouldn't allow Alrin to set foot into the river until he was able to lift a perfect orb into the air. "Only someone with enough finesse and mastery to form a perfect sphere will have the ability to survive long enough to make it to the island," Halvdan said.

Alrin hated to admit it, but the longer he struggled with his task, the more he respected Iarund for being able to do it. By the end of the day, after reaching the bottom of what had to be at least six or seven mana potions, he was exhausted and soaked to the bone from being splashed over and over again by his failed attempts. Even then, giving up never even crossed his mind. The mysterious prize that awaited him inside the secret underwater chamber wouldn't let him quit.

"Maybe we should take a break," Halvdan finally suggested, when yet another irregular eyesore rose from the river. "We can start fresh in the morning."

Alrin barely heard a word of it. There were too many answers lying at the bottom of that river for him to stop now. And failing time and time again was starting to drive him mad. He couldn't place his finger on it, but something seemed to be in the way. It was as if something was stopping him from accessing his power fully. As he stared at his reflection in the cool, rippling water, Alrin began to realize something very important. When you've spent your entire life pinned into a corner, you have but two options. Stay huddled in the corner— or lash out against whatever is holding you captive. The thing that Alrin was beginning to realize about himself was that it had never been the weight of the world holding him back, it had been himself. As his reflection stared back, one thing became abundantly clear. If he was going to find the answers he desperately wanted...it was time to lash out.

He felt the power of his ensignis burning inside him. But unlike when the Trace had taken over, this power burned with a different flame. Instead of dousing it like a bucket of water, his anger only fueled it. It seemed as if the more frustrated he became, the more power he had at his disposal. It wasn't until Alrin began to walk this line of desperation and anger that he found the tidal wave of determination that he needed.

He crouched down by the water's edge one last time and envisioned himself forming a cup in it with his hands, just as Halvdan had taught him.

As Alrin tried again, he heard Halvdan get to his feet.

To the surprise of both, a perfect orb of water lifted from the river and floated in front of them. It was so flawless, in fact, that they could hardly see it at all. It looked more like a bubble floating through the air.

If only Thrain were here to see this, Alrin thought, smiling.

He released it and it splashed back into the river.

"You're ready," Halvdan whispered. "Now that you're able to contain it, you'll find that keeping it away from you is a piece of cake. Give it a try."

Alrin stepped to the edge of the Narew and glanced up to the tree in front of him. He lifted his hand, and the water quickly obeyed, retreating from the riverbank and revealing a few stepping stones beneath the water. The sun had almost fallen behind the peaks of the Tatras, but enough light remained to glimmer off the stone's surface and show what was etched into each of the steps.

It was the Trace.

"This goes without saying," Halvdan said, watching him, "but whatever happens, don't release the boundary underwater." He pulled another vial from his robe. "Oh, and here, you'll be needing this. It always got pretty dark down there, so when it does, just give that vial a little shake."

As it landed in Alrin's outstretched hand, a burst of white light appeared.

"What, you're not coming?" Alrin asked, staring at the vial in disbelief.

"It's not my place. It was left for you, and for you alone. I think it would be more appropriate for it to be retrieved in the same manner. I'll be here when you get back."

Alrin thanked him again and turned back to the river. As he stepped down and was about to breach the river's surface, the water retreated and left a dry stone for his foot to land on. With each step he took, the barrier he created pushed the water far enough away for him to find the next Trace-engraved step. Then another…and another. Each symbol that came into view brought a new wave of excitement. Once the water was up to his waist, he turned back to Halvdan. Just as Alrin had suspected, he was standing on the bank of the river combing his hand through his beard as if everything that was happening held some deep significance. Once he noticed Alrin looking at him, he simply smiled and gave a reassuring nod.

The wall of water around Alrin grew steadily higher as he followed the steps down. Although the barrier kept him dry, the bottom of the river was ice cold. When the water was up to his chest, the steps began to slope down more steeply. As the water sloshed around in front of his face, he clenched the vial in his hand and instinctively took a deep breath. Then, as his foot found the next stone, the river rushed in over him.

There was nothing but darkness. He could hear the faint, muffled splashes of the river's surface above him, and nothing else. It took everything in him just to stay calm.

He shook the vial in his hand and light filled the tiny bubble he was in. For a moment Alrin had the urge to reach out and touch the churning wall of water in front of him, but quickly decided against it, envisioning it popping and letting the freezing water rush in. The river was beyond murky and there wasn't more than an inch or two of visibility, but Alrin could make out a few shadows of fish as they swam by and curiously inspected his light. He took another deep breath, and the steps continued down.

The river was deeper than Alrin had ever imagined. Not only did each step put more distance between him and the safety of the surface, but he could feel the boundary growing harder and harder to maintain. The added weight of the water above him seemed to be draining his power with each and every step. He guessed the river had to be thirty feet deep at its lowest point, but there was no way of knowing.

Should've asked Halvdan for another potion, Alrin thought to himself, contemplating turning back and doing exactly that, but his curiosity drove him forward. *It can't be far now,* he thought nervously, *just a few more.*

Then, as he took another step, the barrier in front of him suddenly bulged inward. His heart raced. He was certain the barrier had collapsed, but as he reached out to brace himself against the wall of rushing water, his hands met solid ground.

He had made it at last.

The island looked much different from anything formed by a naturally flowing river. Like the stone beneath him, it was remarkably smooth and obviously crafted by a very skilled hand. At the base of the wall was an opening about waist high, and it was bolstered on either side by a column of thick riveted metal. Alrin crouched down and peered into the entrance to the island, but still couldn't see beyond the wall of thick, murky water. Before he ducked down and crawled inside, his hand met a few words etched into the metal just right of the entrance.

Give what you own, yet others use; a gift most cherished you'll never lose.

He flipped the fading vial twice in his hand and the light returned. He knelt down, read the inscription once more, and began crawling.

Once he entered the tunnel, he felt the weight of the river immediately lifted and he could finally breathe easy again. There were only a few inches between him and the walls that surrounded him, so it was hard not to scrape his forearms and knees against them as he crawled. He did his best to work out the meaning of the riddle he had just seen and who might have written it, but he found it hard to focus. It was like one of Jorund's puzzle boxes. He knew its reason for being there was just as much of a riddle. A hidden meaning within its hidden meaning. He couldn't help but wonder if Jorund had had a hand in all of this as well.

The end of the tunnel reached him before any answers did. And to his dismay, it was yet another wall, no different from the ones to his left and right. He fumbled against it with his hands, searching for anything significant that could point him to a way out.

But there was nothing. Dead end.

He flipped over on his back and searched the ceiling above him. He nearly missed it, at first. He began brushing his hand over the solid metal plating, and as he did, a small portion began to ripple like the surface of the water around him.

"It can't be," he whispered.

As he reached out in front of him, just as he'd suspected, his hand went straight through. At first it startled him to see another lock like the one outside Halvdan's, and he remembered the sting of sharp needles throughout his arm. But at least this time he knew what to do.

Very carefully, he drew the symbol of the Trace into the strange, mystical field...but nothing happened. He drew it again and again until finally, after about a dozen tries, panic started to settle in. For just as outside Halvdan's door, each wrong entry made the field shoot a bolt of pain through his body, sapping his energy, as the field gripped his hand even tighter.

He fought to stay calm as his energy cringed every time he moved and the walls of water slowly closed in around him.

Something I own, but others use. Alrin thought furiously for the answer. *Can't be lost...*

"Advice?" he said aloud, and quickly scribbled the letters into the blurry haze.

Another wave of pain, and the murky water grew closer.

He could feel his vision start to dim, but he tried to ignore it, convincing himself that it was simply the vial of light running out again.

His heart pounded. He searched every corner of the Void for even the smallest bit of remaining power. Then, just as the water was about to reach him and he took what he was afraid would be his last breath of stale air, the answer hit him.

My name!

Frantically he wrote the letters A-L-R-I-N into the magical haze. There was a soft click and the metal panel gave way above him. Just as he climbed up into the ceiling, his boundary collapsed and the freezing water rushed back in.

CHAPTER TEN

HE'S COMING

The room was tall enough for him to stand in, but not by much. Alrin flipped the vial in his hand, and the room filled with just enough light for him to make out what was in it. The thick roots of the oak tree draped from the ceiling above, casting snakelike shadows onto the damp, earthy walls around him. For the most part the room was vastly empty. There was only a small bed beside a wobbly table that held a half-burned candle and a small box. He was instantly reminded of a rickety tree house that he and Thrain had once built in the woods when they were younger. To anyone with less of an imagination, it would've seemed shoddy at best. The walls had looked as though he and Thrain had used anything they could get their hands on and pieced it together with far too many nails (which, Alrin reminded himself, was precisely what they had done).

"Something you own but others use," Alrin uttered between heaving breaths. "Clever." His shaky voice echoed off the walls and made the room feel even smaller than it actually was. The air was moist and heavy, and the nervous lump that had formed in his throat made him feel as if he could hurl at any moment.

He turned toward the hole that he had just climbed through as it filled back in with a terrible gurgling noise. He had no idea how he was going to get back out again. He hardly had the energy to stand, let alone swim back out, and raising another barrier was simply out of the question. But for the moment, finding out what secrets the room possessed captured his attention.

After setting the vial of light down on the table, Alrin rested his weight on the edge of the bed. From its wailing cry, it was a wonder that he didn't fall straight through it. He lifted the small box from the center of the table and searched it over until he found what he'd been almost certain would be there. The small hole. Just as he'd suspected, it was one of Jorund's.

It didn't take long to find the right position to allow the lid to open. The puzzle boxes Jorund made had varying levels of difficulty, and this one was definitely a beginner's. After all the trouble of getting into the room itself, a well-guarded puzzle box would've been overkill.

As the lid slowly creaked open, he caught sight of a few vials of bubbly blue potion, which lifted what felt to be a mountainous weight from his chest. Right beside them…was an odd-looking bracelet.

He lifted it from the box and held it in the light. Alrin had never seen anything like it. It was very thin, yet surprisingly heavy for its size, and made of smooth metallic black stones that glistened like the edge of a sharpened blade. At each end of the bracelet was a clasp, which he immediately used to fasten it around his wrist.

He waited a few moments for something to happen, but gradually his excitement disappeared. This was hardly the answer he was looking for. If anything, it just tossed another log onto the pile of burning questions.

He rested his arm at his side and twisted his wrist back and forth, trying to find a position that would make the added weight a little more comfortable. Alrin had never cared much for jewelry. He could never get used to the foreign sensation of something tightened around his hand or neck. He always feared that a necklace might entangle the feathers of arrows as they swayed across his back, or that a bracelet might impede the draw of his bow. He would have to get used to it, though, he thought. Surely the bracelet served some sort of purpose if his father had gone to these lengths in order to hide it. That was, if it was indeed his father who had left it for him.

He grabbed one of the mana potions out of the box and quickly downed it. The cool liquid ran down the back of his throat and made him painfully aware of just how close he'd come to running out of mana again and drowning. He walked over to the hole in the ground, which looked like nothing more than a shallow puddle, and took another glimpse at his bracelet. When he did, his eyes caught his ensignis.

2-10-4.

"Trishna's not going to be happy when she sees this," he said, gritting his teeth. Though he probably would've given anything not to have stumbled upon this little discovery, it was starting to seem that having near-death experiences was the fastest way to level. "I should really stop trying to make a habit of this," he said to himself sarcastically. Then he raised the barrier around him and hopped back down into the hole.

He made his way out of the tunnel, crawling on his knees and elbows over the cruel, unforgiving metal, and as he reached the end of it, he stood up and arched his back in every direction to work out the discomfort.

Already the weight of the river above him felt easier to repel. The noticeable difference of his new magic level brought a small grin to his face. He located the first Trace-engraved stone at his feet and began to follow them up and away from the island. He couldn't wait to tell Thrain about the secret room. Maybe, after a few more levels, he might even be strong enough to bring Thrain down there with him.

He had no idea how close the surface was until the current of the river suddenly broke over him.

The sun had already disappeared behind the Tatras. It was dark and cold and Alrin was more than ready to be back by the warm fireplace in his cabin. His eyes were still used to the blinding light of the vial, so it took several moments for Halvdan to come into focus. As Alrin climbed out of the river, he finally spotted him with his back turned and his cloak blending in perfectly with the darkness around him.

"I made it!" Alrin said, raising his arm, expecting Halvdan to turn around and see the dazzling new bracelet around his wrist.

But he didn't answer.

"Halvdan?" he said a little louder, but again, no answer.

As he walked closer, he noticed that Halvdan was leaning over something, and as he got closer, he realized that it wasn't some*thing*, but rather some*one*. It was a boy. And he was unconscious and lying flat on his stomach in the dirt, his hair matted with dried blood. Only half his face was showing, and it was swollen and bruised beyond belief, but Alrin recognized him immediately.

Iarund Lucas.

Large gashes had been torn into his back, and the clothes barely clinging to his body were savagely shredded. The cuts were so deep that Alrin winced at the mere sight of them. Across the tattered remnants of his cloak was some sort of emblem, but it was difficult to make out because of all the gashes in the fabric. Alrin grabbed a piece of the torn cloth and carefully replaced it. As he did, he revealed the razor-sharp claws and crouching fangs of a black dragon.

Alrin could hardly bear to look. So many times Alrin had been insulted and ridiculed by him—so many times he'd wished Iarund would get what he deserved. But now those feelings were gone. Nobody deserved this. That's when he finally looked up at Halvdan. "What happened?" he asked in the strongest voice he could find.

Halvdan's eyes were shut and one of his hands rested gently on Iarund's back. Beads of sweat covered his forehead, and across his face was the same look Alrin had hoped to never see again.

"Halvdan!" Alrin said louder, and then raised an arm and shook him by the shoulder.

As soon as his hand touched Halvdan's cloak, an image flooded into his mind.

He was suddenly trapped in some sort of cage. His hands were covered in blood and clenched tightly around thick iron bars in front of him. But they weren't his hands. Through the bars he could see several members of the Verindi staring back at him. Each wore a hideous smile, and the tattoo of a black dragon over one forearm.

No sooner had the image flooded his mind than it disappeared again. "Alrin!" Halvdan gasped, but then quickly raised a finger over his lips as if to quiet him.

"Was...was that me?" Alrin stuttered.

"No. It's Iarund's memories," Halvdan said softly.

Alrin stared down in horror as a wave of nausea tore at his stomach.

"He barely made it back before collapsing," Halvdan said. "The only thing he managed to say was...that he's coming."

Alrin's eyes widened even farther. "Who's coming?"

Halvdan shook his head. "That's precisely what I'm searching for." Then he placed his hand gently back on Iarund. "Grab my shoulder," he said. "As horrible as this may be, I fear you may need to see it."

Alrin's hand trembled as he rested it against Halvdan's shoulder. Closing his eyes, he suddenly found himself staring through the iron bars of his prison once more. Iarund's prison.

They were somewhere deep in the middle of the forest. He could see the shadows of several tents flickering across the towering pines that surrounded a roaring campfire.

He could feel everything Iarund felt. Every searing gash across his back pulsed in agonizing waves of pain. He tasted a metallic bitterness that he knew could only be blood. Even Iarund's emotions felt like his own. Yet all he could do was look on, as helpless as the moon, unable to turn away, like a silent witness in the dark.

His attention suddenly turned to the bars in front of him and he felt his hands rise up and plead against the iron captors with all his might. His hands flinched from the pain, and blood dripped from his fingertips. That's when his eyes turned to his ensignis. Seeing Iarund's levels instead of his was like seeing a different face in a mirror. It was as if he were stuck in a nightmare. No matter how hard he tried to move or turn his head, he couldn't. His entire body was paralyzed into the predetermined steps Iarund had already taken.

Then he heard a soft whimper next to him and felt his head finally move. Beside him were two more cages. One was empty, and in the other was another boy in the same dragon-adorned attire, thrashed to pieces like his own. He was scrawny—smaller even than Alrin—and he had dark, spiked hair and blue, daggerlike tattoos that covered most of his arms and neck. *Another unlucky victor*, Alrin thought gruesomely.

The cages were circular, only an arm's length across, and not even tall enough for someone half their size. What was odd was that the doors seemed to be shut only by a simple metal latch that wasn't even locked. To Alrin it looked as if the door could've been simply pushed open, but from the hopelessness and terror that Iarund was feeling, he knew that they had already tried it.

"We have to get out of here," the boy with tattoos next to him pleaded.

"But how?" Alrin felt Iarund say, the words emanating strangely from his own throat.

"I don't know," whispered the boy. "The latch is guarded by some sort of spell. Every time I try and move it, one of the Verindi looks at me." He slowly raised his arm toward the door of his cage and shook the latch furiously, but it didn't budge.

Then, just as he'd said, one of the Verindi darted his eyes at them.

"Pipe down over there!" the man shouted.

It was he. The one who had seen Alrin in Everglen. Alrin would never forget those eyes. Deep, dark, and piercing.

"Calm yourself, Nabal," another said listlessly, as though he was on the verge of falling asleep. "They will have their turn soon enough."

Whoever he was, Alrin could tell he was their leader. He spoke calmly, and as he did, the others listened. As he rose to his feet and turned toward the cages, Alrin caught a glimpse of his ensignis. 83-74-68. They were the same levels that Thrain had mentioned seeing at the tournament. That one had to be Gwydion.

"You know, if you keep trying to escape, Elinar, you're going to end up like your friend Amundi over here," said Nabal, pointing to someone lying on the ground with arms and legs angled unnaturally to the sides. Nabal suddenly laughed and then kicked the lifeless mass in the ribs.

"My name...is...Valkyrie!" the boy with tattoos shouted angrily, which made each of the Verindi start to chuckle.

Amundi and Elinar were the names of the two closest towns to Everglen. The other two captives, like Iarund, must have won their Trials and been given the same promise of training and glory. Alrin felt another wave of nausea, but he couldn't tell if it was Iarund's or his own.

"All right," Gwydion grumbled. "Let's get this over with. You can release him."

A terrible smile swept across Nabal's face as the latch on Valkyrie's cage suddenly clicked open.

He tried making a run for it, but his feet didn't find the ground more than twice before he froze into place and rose high in the air. He couldn't even scream. His arms and legs shot out to the sides, bound in a spell that Alrin had never seen before, and he continued through the air until he finally stopped in front of Gwydion.

Gwydion raised his hand and placed it over the boy's forehead.

"What's he doing?" Alrin tried to ask, but his words felt stuck in his throat.

Gwydion lowered his hand again and looked annoyingly disappointed. "It's not him," he muttered, and then dropped the terrified boy to the ground.

Now was his chance. "*Run!*" Alrin tried to scream, but again nothing came out.

The boy did run, but before he even reached the nearest tree line, a swirling blast of magic struck him square in the back and he fell into a bed of pine needles.

Alrin felt Iarund's fear as a Verindi he had never seen stood up. "This is a waste of time," he said. "The boy that the prophecy spoke of won't be from these towns. They are nothing but weaklings. Can't we just kill this one and go home?"

They turned to Iarund, who immediately cowered into the back of his cage.

"Well, hold on now," Nabal interjected, as though Iarund were his prize animal awaiting his turn to be judged. "Let's give Everglen a chance." Some of the Verindi started to laugh. "If any of these towns have a chance, it will be this one," Nabal continued. "Before the Trials began, I saw a boy who wasn't even competing shake an entire courtyard. There's no telling what this one can do."

But that's when the rest of the Verindi stopped laughing. "That wasn't just the courtyard," another one of them said, blank-faced. "We felt it too...all the way in Elinar."

Suddenly their leader sprinted to Nabal with blinding speed and grabbed him by the throat. "Who was the boy?" he asked, snarling.

"I...I don't know," answered Nabal, and then pointed quickly at Iarund. "He was there," he said, trying desperately to redirect Gwydion's anger. "Ask him!"

Gwydion released his grip and slowly walked over to Iarund's cage. Alrin could feel the bars behind him press deeper into his back and tears run down his face as Iarund tried hopelessly to hide in the tiny cage. Gwydion knelt down and a lifeless expression swept across his face. "Tell me what you saw," he said. His voice was so deep and cruel that Alrin knew he meant to get an answer by any means necessary.

"He...he," Iarund sobbed, too terrified to even speak.

"Silence," said Gwydion. "Bumbling fool. I'll just see for myself." As he closed his eyes, Gwydion broke into Iarund's mind as if he were simply opening a window and took hold of his every thought and memory.

His power was crippling. It made Iarund's strength seem like nothing more than a drop of rain against a blazing wildfire. Alrin could feel him scanning through every memory until he came to one from right before the competition. He stopped for a moment, temporarily intrigued by the sight of a woman lifting huge boulders high into the air. Alrin's heart pounded in his chest.

Luckily, he quickly lost interest and continued searching, but shortly he found what he was looking for.

Alrin watched in horror the memory of Iarund's darting under a table as the ground shook beneath his feet. He felt Iarund's fear when he turned around and saw Alrin staring down at him, the blinding light of the Trace shooting out over his hand where his ensignis should have been. He barely even recognized himself.

Gwydion released Iarund from his control. "That's him. The one we've been looking for," he said softly. "Give me a name."

"T…Turner," Iarund stammered. "His name is Turner." Alrin's heart froze.

Gwydion rose to his feet and closed his eyes. "Yes," he said in nearly a whisper. "We found him." There was no response. It seemed almost as if Gwydion were talking to himself. "His name is Turner, my lord…of Everglen." He paused. "Likely the same Turner. It must be his son." Another pause. "Nabal missed it," Gwydion continued. "The boy was under his nose the whole time."

"No!" Nabal suddenly screamed. "*Please!* I couldn't have known!"

Gwydion ignored his desperate plea and listened to the silent voice in his head. "It will be done," he said, and then finally opened his eyes.

Nabal dropped to his knees, petrified in fear. "What did he say?" he stammered. "What does he want me to do?"

"Nothing more," Gwydion answered vacantly. "He will take it from here." Nabal watched his leader's every move, sweat pouring from his face. "He did, however, wish for me to extend his gratitude for finding the boy," Gwydion said with an eerie grin.

A look of terror spread across Nabal's face as Gwydion raised a hand and sent fiery tendrils of lightning into his chest. He fell to the ground with a thud.

The magic of Iarund's cage was released, and the door swung open. Alrin watched as a whirlwind of blurred trees flooded Iarund's memory as he narrowly escaped into the forest.

Halvdan lifted his hand from Iarund's body, and the memory faded.

"Wh…who's coming?" Alrin asked frantically.

"…King Abaddon."

CHAPTER ELEVEN

TRAIL OF DESTRUCTION

W hat do I do?" Alrin pleaded.

Halvdan shook his head hopelessly. "It's too late...there's no stopping him."

Alrin looked around desperately. "I...I can hide!" His eyes darted toward the sheltering giants that surrounded Everglen. "I know the mountains better than anyone," he urged. "He'll never find me in there."

Halvdan slowly backed away and looked at him as though he were already dead. "There's no use," he said in a frightening whisper. "His gaze stretches to every corner of Dalroth. Now that he has seen you, there is no hiding."

"But I have to try," Alrin said, trembling. "He lives in Dunblane, yes? That is more than three weeks away. If I can just stay ahead of him long enough, I could..."

"You don't understand." Halvdan shuddered. "You have no idea what his ensignis are capable of. To him, Everglen is seconds away."

The panic started to settle in. No matter where he thought of running, Alrin knew that he'd only be choosing which corner to get backed into. The Tatra Mountains had always been his refuge from the outside world, but now they were nothing but dead ends.

"And yet," whispered Halvdan, "a sliver of hope remains."

"What?" Alrin gasped. "What hope is there?"

"You're still alive. If the king could see you, we would both be dead."

Suddenly the bracelet clasped around Alrin's wrist began to glow. Out of each of the black stones came swirling specks of brilliant blue light. It was as though thousands of tiny fireflies had suddenly woken inside the stones and were trying to find their way out.

As Alrin and Halvdan stared down in amazement, the light disappeared and the stones went dark.

"Is this what your father left you?" Halvdan asked.

"Yes. But I don't know what it does."

"I believe I may," Halvdan said, and then closed his eyes. After only a few seconds, the bracelet started to glow again. "I don't believe it...," he said, opening his eyes again to the glowing bracelet.

"What?" Alrin begged. "What is it?"

Halvdan looked down, almost giddy with excitement. "Your Void is completely hidden from me," he said. "It's like you're invisible."

Alrin stared at the swirling lights as they slowly dimmed again. "But how is that even possible?"

"That's not important right now," Halvdan said. "This buys us time—but Abaddon still knows you're in Everglen. We need to get you out of here. Quick…follow me."

But Alrin didn't move. He couldn't leave…not yet.
"I have to warn my family," he whispered.
"Alrin, you can't go back. If he sees you, it's all over."
Alrin glanced down at Iarund, his body bloody and battered at his feet. As horrible as seeing him was, picturing Thrain or Aurora lying there was even worse. "I have to," Alrin said. "If this were to happen to either of them, it already would be over."

Halvdan started to object, but then silently nodded. "Get them and meet me back here. But bring only what you need. I'll attend to Iarund." He lifted his hand and rested it on Alrin's shoulder. "If Abaddon finds you, Alrin…don't hold back."

Alrin turned to leave but was stopped in his tracks by a terrifying shriek. The heavy calm that rested over the valley was instantly torn apart by the most bloodcurdling cry—and worse still, it sounded like Sagittari.

As Alrin and Halvdan darted through the narrow alleyways between the moonlit buildings, there was no preparing them for what they were about to see. They turned the last corner and saw Sagittari on his knees grabbing fistfuls of dirt and pounding the ground as hard as he could.

Once Halvdan realized what had happened, he reached out to keep Alrin from seeing, but it was too late.

Someone was on the ground in front of Sagittari—and right beside him was a tiny bow.

Alrin pushed through Halvdan's arm and moved closer. His legs felt like lead.

When he saw who was lying there, Alrin nearly crumpled to the ground. It was Sirena…and she wasn't moving.

"Is she…?" Alrin couldn't even find the word. That's when he noticed her ensignis and knew exactly what had happened.

0-2-0. Someone had woken her magic knowing full well that she would die from it.

"It's all my f-fault," Sagittari cried. "She wouldn't have even been here if it w-weren't for m-me…" Drool and tears ran down his face.

"Who did this?" Alrin asked, his voice breaking at the sight of her hand clenched hopelessly around one of her arrows. But he didn't need the answer. He already knew.

"…K-King Abaddon," Sagittari whimpered.

Something very painful happened inside Alrin. He knew it was entirely his fault. He knew the king had come there looking for him and that she had likely been the first one he came across. Alrin could almost picture her skipping along the road and running into him. What kind of monster would do this to such innocence?

Alrin suddenly felt his power pleading to come out. He looked down as light began to burst from his hand and the symbol of the Trace flickered over his ensignis.

*Release it…*Alrin screamed inside his head. His entire body clenched violently and he shook with anger. He hardly even noticed the tears pouring from his face.

RELEASE IT!

Every part of him fought to let his power break loose, but no matter how hard he begged for it to take over, the Trace merely flickered over his hand like a dying candle. Again he could feel it slipping.

Halvdan had to scream his name several times before Alrin finally heard him.

"Alrin! You have to get out of here," he said, staring hard at Alrin's ensignis.

That's when Sagittari reached up and grabbed Alrin by the hand. He was trembling so fiercely that for a moment the anger that boiled in Alrin softened and his heart broke all over again.

"It's Thrain…," Sagittari sputtered. "I'm so s-sorry, Alrin— Abaddon took him."

Alrin's legs moved faster than they ever had before, and his lungs burned the frigid night air quicker than he could even take it in. His hair stung against his back like tiny whips as he sprinted toward home. His pounding heart did nothing more than continue the stream of molten metal through his body, but even so he wouldn't slow down. Thrain and Aurora were all he had left.

It wasn't until their cabin came into view that he stopped. The moment he saw it, he knew instantly why the king had woken Sirena's magic. He'd needed to search her memories to find out where Alrin lived.

Everything was dead. Every tree, every blade of grass, even the boards of the house looked robbed of their color and lifeless.

He moved closer, praying it was only the moonlight playing tricks on him. But it wasn't. A perfect ring of gray circled their entire cabin, engulfing everything in it. And as Alrin moved closer, he could see it spreading.

What evil is this? Alrin thought as he stared at the growing magic. It was like an invisible fire consuming everything it touched as it spread across the ground.

As Alrin stepped across the boundary, the grass beneath his feet turned to dust and plumed into the wind. He suddenly felt his energy being drained. It was like the spell guarding Halvdan's door, only a thousand times worse. With each step closer to their cabin, he felt noticeably weaker. But regardless of the darkness sapping his power, Alrin had to get in.

He darted to the front door and pushed it open. It gave way like a rotten log and crumbled to the floor. The house was barely clinging to itself; everything around him creaked and groaned as if it could give out at any moment.

Then he saw her. She was the only thing untouched by the life-draining magic. Against the faded walls of the house, she looked like a rose bursting from the ashes after a wildfire.

It was Aurora…and she was sitting where she always sat—in her rocking chair in the corner—as solid as stone.

Alrin screamed out her name, but she didn't move.

With every step toward her, Alrin felt his energy melting away.

"Mother!" he cried out, tears running off his cheeks only to be absorbed into thin air before even hitting the floorboards.

As he took another step, his knees buckled and he fell face-first to the floor. The light in his eyes started to dim and the last thing he remembered was being gripped by the ankles and dragged out of the house.

Then darkness.

He fell into the deepest sleep he'd ever been in—a sleep that even he knew straddled the line between dreaming and death.

But even there he found no comfort. The nightmare only continued. He dreamed he was back in the Verindi's cage, pleading against the iron bars as they closed in tighter around him with every struggle. Thrain was there, watching him with a snarling grin. Then suddenly a cold breeze floated into the camp carrying a dark whisper. *"This is why you were chosen."* As the icy words echoed around him, a rumbling growl emerged from Thrain's throat, and he transformed into a fiery black dragon and engulfed Alrin's cage in flames.

CHAPTER TWELVE

INTO THE DARKNESS

Alrin woke up sweating and shivering in Halvdan's guild, the cold, damp sheets beneath him pressed firmly against his body. Moltrix had slept next to his bed the entire night, and once Alrin finally stirred, she stamped her feet against the ground and huffed loudly in order to get Halvdan's attention.

"Hey, girl," Alrin mumbled once he was able to crack an eye open, and softly patted her on the head. He pulled off several layers of blankets and tried to get up, but his body simply refused to move.

"Here," said Halvdan, rushing him a mug of some warm concoction he'd made. It must have contained mana elixir, because as soon as Alrin drank it, he felt worlds better. "She's alive," he said before Alrin could even ask, "which was nearly more than I could've said about you."

Alrin took another sip and the room spun a little less than it had before. "What about Thrain?"

Halvdan shook his head grimly. "I fear Sagittari was right. It appears King Abaddon believes that he's found what he's so desperately been searching for." Halvdan peered down at Alrin's ensignis. "But as fate would have it, he's mistaken Thrain for you."

"What does he want?" Alrin asked. The question alone brought back a whirlwind of pain.

"There will be plenty of time for that," Halvdan answered. "We have a long journey ahead of us."

"Where are we going?"

"To get him back, of course." Halvdan reached into the pocket of his robe and handed Alrin the puzzle box that he kept by his window. "Here," he said, "I thought you might want this."

It nearly crumbled in his hand from the draining power of the king's curse. Alrin carefully maneuvered the lid, then opened it. "How did you manage to get it?"

"Ah," said Halvdan, fiddling with the end of his beard. "My mana flows from a deeper stream than yours." He then went scurrying about the room, knocking over bottles and flipping through stacks of papers, tossing what he needed into a large burlap sack. "The spell you saw was likely the darkest and strongest in our world. You were either very foolish or very brave to enter it. Perhaps a touch of both." Alrin took another gulp from the mug and kept his eyes on the ground. "It's known as the Myoclonus curse," Halvdan continued. "It's said to have been created by Beswic himself when he rose against the Dinivus brothers thousands of years ago. I didn't believe it truly existed until I saw it with my own eyes. The magic sustains itself by drawing the energy from anything and everything around it."

"Can we stop it?"

"There are only two ways I know of," said Halvdan as he stuffed a strange map covered in a labyrinth of trails into his bag. "It can only be stopped by the one who cast it. Or…"

"Or what?" Alrin asked, very afraid of the answer.

"Or whoever cast it is killed. Either way, in order to save Aurora and your brother, the king's reign must come to an end."

That was easier said than done when the king was king only because he was the most powerful person in Dalroth. Alrin didn't even want to know how Halvdan intended to stop him. He didn't care. It didn't matter who stood in their way or if he had to train until it killed him. Somehow they were going to get Thrain back and avenge Sirena's death. "When do we leave?"

"As soon as your energy is restored. There is someone who lives deep within Darkwood Forest who can help us, but we must move quickly if we are to arrive before nightfall. You'd better finish that up."

Alrin downed the rest of the beverage and felt his power instantly return…and then some. He couldn't remember the last time he'd looked at his hand, but when he did, he noticed each of his ensignis was a level higher than before. He looked up at Halvdan, who was holding an empty flask in his hand. "Hero's Draft," he said with a wink. "My last one, too. Thought you could use a little boost after what you've been through."

Alrin managed to let out a rather unconvincing, "Thank you," but the last thing on his mind was his ensignis. He couldn't get the image of being locked in a cage or of Thrain's turning into a dragon out of his mind. If his brother was indeed under the king's control, there was no telling what kind of monster he would become. "I'm ready," Alrin said, rising to his feet.

Halvdan nodded. He picked up his bag and strapped it over his shoulder, and then, after his soft, "Come, Moltrix," she sprang to her feet and followed them excitedly out of the guild.

Everything outside was blanketed by a thick layer of snow. Winter had finally come.

On any other morning, it would've been Alrin's favorite day of the year. Ever since the last bit of snow had melted in the spring, Alrin had looked forward to it. That day should have gone so much differently. Thrain would usually wake up first and play their traditional heartbeat tap against the wall to see if Alrin was up yet. Then, after finishing a hurried breakfast, they would've spent that entire morning hiking through the woods just to see how far they could venture into the vastness of the pristine mountains—maybe stopping once or twice to challenge each other to walk out over a frozen pond and see who chickened out first. Then, when either the sun had started to set or the numbness in their hands had beckoned them home, Alrin would use the same footprints he'd already made so that the canvas of white would be as untouched as possible the next morning. This of course would inspire Thrain to drag his feet through the snow even more just to irritate him, and by the time they made it home, they would be bound in the most glorious snowball fight Everglen had ever seen.

It was painful to think about. Even as the snow fell in sheets around him, the day that should have been felt so very far away.

Alrin walked behind Moltrix and watched as the snow dissolved around each of her fiery footprints. He was actually really glad she was coming with them. He could think of nothing better than having a vicious fire elemental walking beside him in the middle of a snowstorm. The heat radiating from her was so great, in fact, that each time a gust of wind blew past her, the snow had already turned into warm beads of water by the time it reached Alrin's face.

As they reached the last fence of Everglen, Halvdan turned to say a final farewell to their tiny, quiet town in the mountains. There was no telling when they would see it again.

But Alrin didn't turn. He couldn't. He wanted to hold on to his memories just as they were before Abaddon reached in and changed them. He knew saying good-bye would only remind him of just how little there was left to say good-bye to. Their only chance of saving Thrain and stopping the curse from destroying everything behind them…was to focus on what lay ahead.

But not even a dozen steps later, something forced Alrin to turn around anyway.

Moltrix heard it first. Her ears perked up suddenly and she stopped dead in her tracks and looked behind them.

At first Alrin thought it was a mirage. As it got closer, Alrin could see Trishna walking toward them wearing a wolfskin jacket with the hood pulled down over her eyes. But even more surprising than seeing her was seeing the long composite bow she held in her hand.

She walked straight up to Alrin and handed it to him. "Here," she said forcefully, wiping her eyes with her sleeve. It was obvious that she'd been crying all morning. "My father said to give you this. It's never missed its target so it better not start now."

Alrin nearly gasped when he saw it. This wasn't just *one* of Sagittari's bows. This was *his*. Alrin had only heard rumors of it, but in every way imaginable, it lived up to the whispers. Every inch was a sharp, shimmering black and it looked every bit as much a piece of armor as it did a fierce and formidable weapon. Each end of the bow doubled as a dagger, and the bowstring was embedded deep into it so that it could never be changed. Without a doubt, the bow was perfection—and Alrin knew immediately which target Trishna had in mind.

Without another word she walked ahead of them and stood next to Moltrix.

"Are you coming?" she asked suddenly.

Halvdan and Alrin exchanged very similar glances of surprise. It seemed not only that Trishna was mindful of the impossible journey on which they were about to embark, but that she was coming with them and there was to be no further discussion about it.

"Looks like you have a training partner," Halvdan whispered.

Alrin's stomach twisted into knots. Even after everything that had happened, seeing her still gave him butterflies.

Together they left, headlong into the blizzard—Halvdan was first, Trishna second, and Alrin lingering slowly behind. Seeing Moltrix, you would've thought this was the happiest day of her life. She darted back and forth between them, blazing wide trails into the snow-covered ground. As they trudged along silently, watching her, it was painfully obvious that she was the only one looking forward to whatever lay in front of them.

Eventually the storm subsided and, far off in the distance, they watched the mountains gradually turn into rolling hills, and then into open plains.

Once the peaks of the Tatras were behind them, a steady uneasiness started making its way in. Alrin had never seen so much uncovered sky before. For the first time in his life, he was going to know what it was like when the sun touched the horizon. He knew it was absurd, but even as he watched tomorrow's storms brewing in the distance, he had never felt so closed in. The openness was too unnatural. The only thing that brought him peace was that when he closed his eyes, he could still see the border of the mountains as if he were sitting on the moss-covered stump outside their cabin. It was like staring into a light and still being able to see its shadow long after it was gone. But as they walked, even that light began to slowly fade.

They walked in silence for hours, except for a muffled sniffle that came from Trishna's direction every so often. Each time Alrin turned to make sure she was OK, she sharply insisted it was only her nose running from the cold.

She was definitely her father's daughter. So strenuously apathetic. She wouldn't be caught dead letting a tear fall from her face.

"I miss her too," Alrin said, after he had finally worked up the courage. But just as he anticipated, she averted her eyes even more and didn't say a word. When Alrin heard the sniffling begin again a few moments later, he nearly walked up to put an arm around her, but decided against it out of fear of being punched in the jaw.

Alrin tried his best to take his mind off Sirena and Thrain by removing Sagittari's bow from his back and admiring it once again. It was the most exquisite thing he'd ever seen. If only he had some arrows, he thought, he could get in a little target practice while they walked to pass the time. He pulled back on the string to test it, but to his dismay, it didn't budge an inch. He tried again, even harder this time.

"You have to be level fifty in strength to pull it back," Trishna muttered, her back turned to him. "Not even sure why my father insisted that you have it—probably just another of his sadistic attempts at motivation."

Alrin lowered the bow back to his side, quite embarrassed. *How did she even…?* It was as if she had eyes in the back of her head. *Who cares,* he thought. *Nothing to shoot at anyway.*

He decided to pass the time by keeping his attention on Moltrix as she sprinted playfully off into the distance any time a bird flew overhead. But keeping his eyes on her for too long across the snow-covered plains, he started feeling woozy. He still wasn't accustomed to being able to see such great distances. Watching her entertained him for only a few minutes, and then the deafening silence crept back in.

"Halvdan," Alrin said, no longer able to bear it. "Do you believe the legend of Visarga? I mean, the story of the three brothers. Do you think they really existed?"

Halvdan pondered this awhile. "Well, answer me this," he finally said. "What did you first learn about magic?"

Alrin could see Trishna roll her eyes, which brought a small grin to his face. He could tell that she'd been prompted to recite the answer a thousand times before. Either that or she too was slightly annoyed by the way Halvdan was answering a question with a question. One of Halvdan's wonderful teaching techniques, Alrin was starting to realize.

"All magic requires sacrifice," Alrin droned monotonously.

Halvdan nodded. "Well, there are things in this world that seem to ignore this rule, things that would make sense only if the legends were true."

"What things?" Alrin asked.

"The seven Talismans of Triem, for example."

"You can't actually believe those are real," Trishna said suddenly. Hearing her speak caught them both by surprise.

"In fact I do," Halvdan answered her, "and there are many others who believe it as well. King Abaddon and his Verindi being many of them. As the story goes, Beswic, who was born an ordinary man, was able to amass a power so great that it rivaled even that of the brothers. It is said that this power actually came from seven talismans that the brothers forged that were meant as gifts for the people. Each of these items held unlimited power and sacrificed nothing from those who wielded them. It was these talismans that made Beswic virtually unstoppable."

A question suddenly popped into Alrin's head that he was almost too scared to ask. "How many does the king have?" he asked nervously.

"Only one that I know of," Halvdan answered. "A helmet that brings sight to all corners of Dalroth and can transport him wherever he chooses."

Alrin gulped. "Where are the others?"

"The others…are out of his reach," Halvdan answered. "But with each of his ensignis at ninety-nine, the king has very little use for them."

Alrin suddenly felt sick to his stomach. He'd never fully grasped what they were up against until that very moment. "What hope is there in defeating ensignis like that?" Alrin whispered hopelessly.

"Our only hope lies in the one thing that has defeated his kind before—the Dorekstone. It was the power in this stone that defeated Beswic, so again it will be used to defeat

Abaddon. It is all that is left of the Dinivus brothers, and it is said to still hold the secret to their unlimited power. The king believes that Thrain is the key to finding it, so for the sake of your brother—and the rest of the world—we must find it before he does."

Far off in the distance, a thin line of green appeared across the horizon that marked the edge of Darkwood Forest. It took nearly another hour to reach it, but once they did, it made sense that they had been able to see it from so far away. The pines rose up higher than any Alrin had ever seen. The base of each tree was several feet across and grew so close to the ones beside it that finding a straight path through was nearly impossible.

Several miles in, Alrin stopped for a breather and looked up the trunk of one so tall that it disappeared into the clouds above them. It had to be thousands of years old.

When Halvdan turned back and saw Alrin admiring it, he walked up and rested his hand against the monstrous trunk.

"Beautiful, isn't it," he said.

Still very much out of breath, Alrin nodded and tilted his head back, searching for the top. "It just doesn't make sense how so much hate can exist in the same world with so much beauty."

Halvdan smiled. "Come on…we're almost there."

They followed Halvdan for another mile or two through the forest. The trees grew even taller and closer together than they had before, and Alrin quickly found that the Darkwood Forest was very aptly named. It was only midafternoon and the sun had all but disappeared behind the dense canopy, and the temperature was plummeting.

Alrin never found the path that they were allegedly following and was starting to feel as if they were moving in circles.

Trishna felt it too. "Are you sure you know where we're going?" she asked, her breath clearly visible.

Alrin moved closer to Moltrix in order to stay warm.

"Not much further," Halvdan reassured them.

"You never mentioned where we're going," Alrin said, "or who it was that's supposed to be helping us."

Before Halvdan could answer, Moltrix crouched low to the ground and growled ferociously. Her whole body started to glow bright red, and her three tails fanned out and burst into flames. Alrin had to stand back and shield his face from the heat that came from her body.

"What is it, girl?" he asked nervously as she stared fiercely into the woods.

At the top of a hill and moving slowly toward them were two shadowy figures. One was a woman, and the other was the biggest man Alrin had ever seen. At his waist was a giant two-handed sword with a glistening red hilt. He stepped into Moltrix's light and removed the hood of his cloak. He had a short, scruffy beard and long blond hair that was held back behind his ears.

He couldn't pinpoint it, but Alrin felt as if he'd met the man before. But then his eyes gave it away. They were a deep emerald green as piercing as the blade strapped to his waist. Alrin could almost swear he was staring at a stronger version of his brother.

"I always knew it would be you," the man said to him in a warm voice. "I don't know how, but I always knew." He moved closer into the light that was still shooting in waves from Moltrix's body. "I am Meldun...your father."

Alrin looked at Halvdan, hoping it was just a cruel joke. "My father is dead," Alrin muttered.

"So the world had to believe," Meldun answered. "For the protection of my family." He then looked very disheartened. "Not that it did much good. Despite everything I've done, I still couldn't move you out of Abaddon's reach. No matter. That can still all be undone now that you're here."

Alrin waited to feel something…anything, really. Anger that he'd been lied to his entire life, or joy that his father was still alive. But nothing came. He couldn't explain it, but he felt oddly disconnected from the man claiming to be his father. There was only a gaping hole where he knew there should've been some sort of emotion.

Halvdan walked up to him and they grasped each other's arm and embraced. That's when Alrin noticed a glove very similar to Halvdan's concealing Meldun's ensignis.

"It's been too long, old friend," said Meldun. "Thank you for watching over him and bringing him here safely." He then turned to Moltrix, who still seemed moments away from attacking. "Come now, you overgrown candle. You remember me." Meldun hunched over and held his hand out in front of her.

She inched forward still baring her razor-sharp teeth. Once she was close enough, she sniffed his outstretched hand and instantly doused her fiery tails. She rose up on her hind legs and wrapped her huge paws around him as if they were two long-lost friends finally reunited.

Meldun laughed. "It's good to see you too," he said, but then quickly jumped back. The front of his cloak was singed black where Moltrix had pressed against it.

"Sorry about that," Halvdan apologized. "Capricious beast. She's been unusually temperamental lately."

"Think nothing of it," Meldun said, continuing to pat his jacket as if he were putting out an invisible fire, and that's when he noticed Trishna gawking at him.

"Forgive me, my dear, you must be Trishna." Meldun walked up and shook her by the hand. "My heart is truly broken for your loss."

A wave of shock spread over her and her eyes turned watery again. "How did you know about Sirena?"

Meldun glanced over. "Halvdan has told me everything."

At this the woman who had come with Meldun stepped forward. She was dark-skinned and her face was covered in blue tattoos. "We each have lost someone dear to us," she said, shaking Alrin's hand and then Trishna's. "Abaddon will pay for what he has done. I assure you."

Alrin stared at the blue, daggerlike tattoos covering her body. He knew at once where he'd seen them before.

"The boy from Elinar," Alrin exclaimed. "The one in the Verindi camp..." Alrin thought for a moment. "Valkyrie! Valkyrie was his name...Did you know him?"

At this the woman drooped her head toward the ground.

"This is Veda," Meldun said. "Veda Valkyrie. The boy you saw was her son."

"I'm...so sorry," Alrin muttered. "I didn't..."

He wanted to hide in a hole. He didn't know what to say. His first instinct was to tell her that her son had fought courageously or that he'd been brave until the very end, but he couldn't even say that. The Verindi had robbed him of everything before finally killing him. And the worst part was that it had seemed to faze them about as much as taking out the garbage.

"Veda will be a vital piece to the puzzle," said Meldun. "Of course, the final piece being you, Son."

For the moment Alrin was forcing himself to look past the fact that his father was still alive. A man who he'd been told his entire life had died shortly after he was born.

"What puzzle is that exactly?"

Meldun shot Halvdan a look. "Have you told him nothing?"

"I thought it would be best to keep him in the dark," said Halvdan. "His curiosity dwarfs even yours, if you can imagine it. Any question I entertained would've been followed by only another that I wasn't prepared to answer. He shares your blood, after all."

Meldun smiled. "I suppose you're right. Well, I think it's about time that we bring you out of the darkness," he said, looking at Alrin. "Come. We have much to discuss." Then he turned and started to lead them deeper into the forest. "Speaking of darkness—Halvdan, how about a little light?"

Halvdan glanced at Alrin and Trishna almost instinctively. "I suppose you're right. There's no use holding back anymore." He raised his arm into the air and shot an orb of light high into the trees. Everything around them lit up brighter than day. Halvdan took a deep breath, as if a huge weight had suddenly been lifted from him. "Ahh," he sighed. "It feels good to use my power again."

Alrin and Trishna stared at each other in disbelief. Neither of them had ever seen his ensignis, of course (they'd always been covered by his glove), but neither of them would've guessed he could do something like that. Alrin pulled Glade's list from his pocket and searched it for anything that looked like what Halvdan had just conjured.

37—Lunar Flare
42—Camouflage Other IV
56—Augury

Suddenly Trishna walked up behind him and pointed to a spell much farther down the list than where he was searching.

76—Illuminate

For the first time ever, Alrin thought he and Trishna had something in common. Halvdan was more powerful than either of them had ever imagined. But the most alarming part wasn't that Halvdan had kept his power from them, it was how Alrin felt once he finally saw it. He was envious of it. He was starting to understand why Thrain had acted the way he did when he saw Aurora reveal her power. She always said the only reason she and Halvdan kept their ensignis hidden was that it was their way of showing the world that power didn't matter.

It would be like telling a beggar that wealth wasn't everything when you were the richest person in town. It was all just convenient deceit.

Alrin looked down at his ensignis in disgust. The numbers staring back only reminded him of just how useless he would be at helping save Thrain and Aurora.

"What good am I?" Alrin said aloud as he and Trishna followed Meldun deeper into the forest.

"Do what I do," Trishna said to him. "Turn your anger into motivation."

CHAPTER THIRTEEN

JORUND'S PUZZLE BOX

They arrived at Meldun's just shy of a mile later. To Alrin, the smoke rising from the chimney and the scent of smoldering pine sparked an overwhelming nostalgia for home. For a moment he even thought he saw his mother's face peering at them through a window, but he quickly realized that no matter how hard he wished it, this dream wasn't going to end.

Once they were inside, Moltrix made herself comfortable by the fire and swished her tails back and forth through the flames while the others unburdened themselves from the tiresome journey. All except for Halvdan, who stood at the doorway and waved his arm over the threshold. Almost at once a shimmering barrier spread across it and encircled the entire house.

"There," he said, "now we're hidden from any eyes that may be searching."

Despite his best attempt to keep his eyes to himself, Alrin couldn't help but watch everything Meldun and Veda were doing. He'd never seen anyone like either of them before. Meldun was so brawny that when he sat in his twice-normal-size chair, it creaked so loud that Alrin just knew it would give out under his weight. The way his muscles bulged at even the slightest movement made even the simplest tasks look extraordinary. Lifting a glass of water to his mouth, he looked as if he were pulling the weight of the world off its hinges.

Then there was Veda, who was the exact opposite. She moved so gracefully that even the act of removing her jacket seemed meticulously practiced to perfection. She glided soundlessly across the room and sat in the chair closest to Alrin. The blue tattoos across her face continued down her arms and back, covering every inch of her exposed skin. Around her waist Alrin noticed a belt made of stones remarkably similar to the ones clasped around his wrist. Somehow, even while facing in the opposite direction, she still knew that she was being watched.

"Is there something you wish to ask me?" she asked quietly.

Luckily, the chatter that filled the small room was loud enough to prevent anyone other than Alrin from hearing her. He was so caught off guard by how observant she was that the best thing could think of was, "I was just curious what all the blue tattoos meant."

Veda smiled. "They are called Aerean lines," she said very precisely. "The people of Elinar hold wisdom above all else. With each new level achieved, another mark is given."

There were so many that Alrin couldn't even begin to count them. He knew it would be much simpler to just look at her ensignis, but when he tried, it didn't surprise him to see yet another glove just like the ones Meldun and Halvdan wore. "I was almost sure you would ask a question about your father," she continued.

Alrin stood from his chair and began perusing the room, knowing all the while that he was being carefully watched. Even though he had no feelings toward his father, it would be a lie to say that he didn't have questions.

"There were nothing but questions when I believed he was dead," Alrin said. "Now that I know he's not...I can't even think of one." He grabbed a small wooden box on a shelf and searched it over until he found the tiny hole in the bottom. Another of Jorund's. He fiddled several moving latches until it popped open and he read the inscription underneath the lid.

Knowing time as night and day,
Far from you he will never stray.
Though its loyalty is strongest at its peak,
When in darkness, you will never seek.

Veda seemed entertained by his answer, but Alrin had the gut feeling that she could see right through it.

Without a word she rose from her seat at the same time the groaning of Meldun's chair announced he was getting out of his. Even though her mouth never moved, Alrin knew she had somehow tipped Meldun off that Alrin had many questions. It was painfully obvious that Meldun was trying to nonchalantly make his way over, but Alrin could tell that finesse was definitely not his strong suit. He moved about as gracefully as a tree falling in a forest.

"I see you found the bracelet I left you," Meldun said as he walked up next to him.

Alrin continued fiddling with the box, trying his best to seem distracted. "It's a good thing I have a knack for riddles," Alrin said awkwardly. "Nearly died down there."

"Yeah, you can blame Halvdan for that one," Meldun said, chuckling. "I never much cared for them. Do you know the answer to that one?"

Alrin looked at the box in his hand and thought for a moment. "Your shadow."

"Very impressive," said Meldun. "Halvdan was right. You're much brighter than your ensigni gives you credit for. But have you figured out the real riddle? The riddle as to why Jorund carves holes into everything he makes?"

Alrin's eyes lit up. For as long as he could remember, he had longed to know the meaning of this. "I always thought it was so that Jorund knew they were his."

"That was my first thought too," said Meldun. "But your mother and I asked him the same question when we bought yours. At first he thought we were simply asking why he placed riddles there to begin with, but when I told him that I knew the box and the hole itself were the true riddle, he could never give me a straight answer. He only smiled and said that it would mean something different to everybody."

Meldun leaned his weight against a bookshelf and unknowingly bulged every muscle in his arm.

"Why does he do it, then?" Alrin asked, trying his best not to get caught staring.

"Well, one day a child came into his guild and asked him the same thing and Jorund gave him a much different answer. Would you like to hear what he told him?"

Alrin nodded eagerly.

"Well, after solving his puzzle box and finding the hole at the bottom, the boy came in thinking it was broken. 'Not at all,' Jorund told him. 'This box tells an amazing tale. Haven't you ever heard the tale of the oracle and the magic sand?'"

Alrin didn't realize how intently he was listening until he noticed his own head shaking from side to side.

"There was once a quiet village," began Meldun. "A village of farmers, merchants, and blacksmiths. It was a peaceful town—surrounded by golden meadows, sparkling rivers, and the richest earth you've ever seen. Having more than they could ever want, the villagers lived in a time of peace and plenty. But then, one day, a terrible wizard passed through, and the instant he laid eyes upon it, he wanted everything for himself. Being naught but lowly tradesmen, the villagers were helpless against him, for the wizard's power came from a mystic and magical sand. Knowing that he alone could remove it, he cast a powerful spell over the land, turning their golden meadows to ash and their sparkling rivers to dust, and enchanting the earth to never again see even a single blade of grass.

"It wasn't long before the villagers knew that the only way to survive was to leave the land they loved behind. One by one they moved away until there was but one person left. An old and humble toy maker. He was clearly no match for the wizard in strength and magic, but he was very cunning and very wise. One day he disguised himself in a cloak and told the wizard that he was an oracle, gifted with the power to see the future. He then gave the wizard a prophecy that by the same time the very next day, someone would have stolen the sand and banished the wizard forever. 'There is but one way to prevent this,' said the disguised toy maker, handing him a small wooden puzzle box. 'Hide your sand in this very box and I shall cast a powerful spell so that it will open to no one but you.'

"The wizard was also very cunning, so, in order not to be deceived, he took the box and cast his own spell over it instead. Indeed, from that day on, no one could open it but he, but little did he know of the tiny hole carved into the bottom. That very night the toy maker followed the wizard home and collected every grain of sand that fell to the ground. When the wizard woke the next morning, he knew that he'd been deceived, for when he opened it, the box was empty.

"Just as he'd foretold, the lowly toy maker wielded the power of the sand, banishing the wizard forever and restoring their land to all its glory. From that day on, the old toy maker was known far and wide as a gifted and powerful oracle. For even without the gifts of magic, strength, or even foresight, he was wise enough to know that even the strongest of men can meet their downfall on the path they take to avoid it."

Alrin smiled. It now made sense that some of the boxes Jorund made were so hard to open. "So that's the reason he gives children," Alrin said, "but there has to be more to it if he says it means something different to everybody."

Meldun looked at him proudly. "You definitely have a knack for riddles, don't you? Well, one day during my training I found out what it meant to me. I came to the realization that no matter how hard I trained, or how powerful my ensignis became, it would never be enough. I could feel a hole engrained within me that could never be satisfied. It was like trying to fill this box with sand. No matter how much power I filled it with, it would be empty again the next morning. It was this emptiness that kept me going. Even though it never stayed full, it needed to be filled nonetheless."

Alrin thought this over for a while. Who knew, maybe his father wasn't just a big ball of muscle as Mason had suggested. "Is that why you left Everglen?" Alrin asked. "In a search to fill this void?"

Meldun hesitated. "I have to admit…at first, yes. But not in the way you think. At about your age, I left Everglen in the search for more power. As I went from town to town growing stronger, I eventually found myself in a position to see people for what they really are. Eventually you come to realize that when you find yourself between someone and the thing they want most, there's nothing a person won't do. It wasn't until Dunblane that I decided to take my family away from this obsession with power."

Alrin's eyes widened. "You lived in Dunblane?"

"I did," Meldun said, chuckling. "Where do you think I met your mother?"

"What?" Alrin exclaimed. "But I thought you needed one of your ensignis to be over eighty to live there."

"You do," Meldun said, quite puzzled. "Wait—you're telling me that you never looked at her hand…not even once?"

"No," Alrin almost yelled. "She always wore one of those blasted gloves!"

Meldun let out a deep and thunderous laugh. "That does sound just like her." By now everyone in the room was listening to their conversation. "Sorry, Alrin. I thought surely you knew."

Alrin folded his arms over his chest. "And next I bet you're going to tell me that Thrain was born there too," he huffed sarcastically. But when he looked up, Meldun's face was scrunched up as if he'd just swallowed a bug.

"You *can't* be serious! Wait, was I born there?"

"No," Meldun said, smiling reassuringly. "You were born in Everglen."

Alrin couldn't believe it. He almost wished they'd just left him in the dark. After all of that, being clueless again sounded pretty great. He couldn't help but wonder how much Thrain knew of all of this. "Well, at least that explains why Thrain has such a big head," Alrin said, chuckling. "Any other surprises I need to know about?"

"Actually…yes," Meldun answered in an alarmingly serious voice. "There's one more thing. Shortly after we moved back to Everglen, the king received a prophecy that a boy had been born. A boy who would one day be able to wield the power of the Dinivus brothers. He sent word to his followers to return to Dunblane to help in his search. If they refused, they and their entire families would be killed." The room grew very still. "So as you can see," said Meldun, raising up his sleeve, "I had no other choice but to leave."

As he looked down, Alrin turned ghostly pale.

Across Meldun's forearm was the crouching dragon of the Verindi.

Alrin nearly choked on the words as they came out. "You're…you're one of them!"

CHAPTER FOURTEEN

MOLTRIX'S BIRTHDAY

I t felt as if he were back in Iarund's nightmarish memory.

Meldun's hands went up as if he was trying to prove he wasn't a threat. "I *was* one of them," he said urgently. "But that was a long time ago. I left the moment I saw Abaddon for the monster he truly was."

Alrin couldn't breathe. It was as if his heart had already conditioned itself to burst from his chest at the very first sign of a dragon. "But he wouldn't just allow someone to stop being a Verindi," Alrin stammered. "I mean—he can see everything. Be anywhere. How do we know he's not standing outside this very moment, watching us through the window?" Alrin hadn't really thought what he said all the way through, and as soon as it left his mouth, he had an overwhelming desire to be the farthest away from the window.

Veda's voice suddenly came from the next room. "Because you never search for something that you already believe you possess," she said calmly. She rose from her chair so fluidly that it almost looked as if she were floating.

"Thrain…," Alrin whispered.

Veda nodded. "You're safe here," she said, placing an arm around him and inviting him to sit back down at the table. Alrin wasn't sure if it was because he knew each of her tattoos stood for a level of wisdom, but he sensed truth behind everything she said. Something strangely pacifying took place when she spoke, and he couldn't help but be reminded of Aurora.

"So this prophecy," Alrin said, "you think it's about me?"

Alrin waited for an answer and was relieved when he heard Veda's voice again. "As the legend goes," she said gently, "the Dorekstone was hidden until someone worthy presented themselves. Several days ago, when you fell from the cliffs at Batara…something happened."

Alrin searched the faces of everyone around the room. Apparently it was no secret. "H…how did you know about Batara?"

"Scrying, of course." She sounded slightly confused by the question. "Halvdan scried us the instant you told him."

As usual, Alrin was a mouse in a maze. Around every exciting new corner he only found himself deeper and deeper in his labyrinth of questions, and he was beginning to wonder if there would ever be a way out. "Err…what's scrying?" he asked timidly.

At this, Trishna could no longer hold her tongue. "You must be joking!" she yelled. "How is he supposed to be the one to defeat the most powerful being in all of Dalroth when he doesn't even know what scrying is?"

Alrin sank into his chair. He was used to insults, but whenever they came from her, he wanted to shrivel into a corner.

Veda looked rather concerned as well. "*Scrying*," she said in a strenuously patient manner, "is unlocked at level forty. You have the ability to speak with anyone you wish, no matter the distance between you." She paused and gave him an expectant stare, knowing there would surely be another question, but Alrin refrained despite several that immediately bounced into his head. "Several days ago, when the Trace appeared on your hand," Veda continued, "something else happened. A door opened that has never before been opened. Until that day it had never been more than a stone wall in the Longshire ruins with a symbol over it. And I think we all know which symbol it was."

"What do you think it means?" Trishna asked. And it was a good thing she did, because Alrin certainly wasn't about to.

Veda met the glances of Meldun and Halvdan. "It is there," she said ominously, "that our power will be tested. The first test of three, to be exact. Tests that, if passed, will lead us to the Dorekstone."

"Does the king know about them?" asked Trishna.

A horrible silence filled the room.

"Yes," said Meldun. "But he doesn't know their locations…not yet. But that isn't for a lack of trying, I can assure you. Of the many atrocities I witnessed as part of the Verindi, there is one that will haunt me until the end of my days. We were commanded to scour the land for a certain man, and were to stop at nothing until we found him. This man was rumored to be the highest sage in Dalroth, known for his vast knowledge on the Dinivus brothers and the location of the tests." Meldun's eyes didn't move from the center of the table. "We found him in Elinar—Avery was his name. Avery Valkyrie."

Veda cleared her throat. "Many have died trying to protect what little is known about the Dinivus brothers," she said solemnly. "My grandfather was one of them. But I can assure you that his death wasn't in vain. As a part of my training ever since I was a little girl, he would bring me to the strangest and most hidden places and speak of something he possessed that was very dear to him. Something very old and very powerful. Before the Verindi stormed our city searching for him, my grandfather gave me this and entrusted me to guard it as no one else ever would." Veda reached into her pocket and pulled out a brittle piece of old parchment and carefully unfolded it. "I vowed to never let this fall into the hands of a Dragonmark," she said, glancing at Meldun. "But your father has more than expiated his past."

As the paper unfolded, they all craned their necks in over the table.

The page was completely blank except for a few lines of strange symbols written across the top.

"This writing is my grandfather's," said Veda. "It is written in a language that was spoken in the time of the Dinivus brothers. My grandfather spent countless hours teaching me as a child."

"You can read it?" Trishna asked.

Veda smiled conceitedly. "Every star in the sky and grain of sand in the sea has a name to those who were there during their placement." They all stared at one another awkwardly. Veda rolled her eyes. "Yes, I can read it," she snapped. "But it's a riddle—and a very hard one at that. One that even I have yet to solve."

"Let Alrin have a go," Meldun chimed in. "He's the riddle master, after all."

Alrin shied from the compliment. He couldn't tell if his father's confidence in him was genuine or simply a feeble attempt to make amends for a lifetime of absence. But either way, it felt good for someone to seem as if he believed in him.

"Very well…," Veda said rather skeptically. She looked down at the page and translated the riddle from the ancient text:

Never born, it only dies.
Even fed, its hunger cries.
Heartless flutters, wingless soars,
Fingers crack, voiceless roars.

Everyone turned to Alrin expectantly.

But Halvdan answered first. "Wind, I'll bet," he said confidently, then, with a simple nod from him, the front door swung open and a gush of wind rushed into the room and over the table. But as it passed over the page, his spell rebounded. With a loud fizzle and a burning smell of fireworks, Halvdan went sprawling backward, chair and all, onto the floor. Alrin tried his best to smother his laughter but did a rather lousy job of it.

Even Trishna laughed.

Her smile was an eclipse. Without even realizing it, Alrin was watching her. He simply couldn't turn away from something so rare, but knew he was risking injury if he got caught staring too long.

"You really believe I haven't tried that yet?" Veda said, chuckling. "Besides, my grandfather despised magic. Whatever means by which he intended this message to be revealed, magic won't be involved, I assure you."

"Aye, I can see that," Halvdan grumbled from the floor. "Thanks for the warning." He teetered back and forth over his chair with his feet and beard sticking straight into the air. Meldun let out a deep, hearty laugh, and then with a single finger reached over and flipped him effortlessly back up to the table.

That's when Trishna caught Alrin still looking at her and immediately wiped the smile from her face. "So what sort of tests will we be facing?" she asked, shooting Alrin a what-are-you-looking-at glare.

"No one knows," Veda answered. "Not even my grandfather knew. But we can be sure that they will only recognize feats of power deemed worthy in the eyes of the Dinivus brothers."

"So basically all ninety-nines?" Trishna grumbled. "And King Abaddon is the only person in the entire world with that kind of power. Perfect."

"That's not exactly true," Veda said with a grin. She raised her right hand above the table at the same time as Meldun and Halvdan. Then, all together, they removed the gloves concealing their ensignis.

This was one of the few moments that Alrin had waited his entire life for. The moment of seeing Halvdan's ensignis. Every level they revealed was impressively high, of course, some even well into the eighties, but each person had a single number that Alrin had never dreamed he would see in person. Each proudly displayed a 99—Veda in wisdom, Meldun in strength, and Halvdan in magic.

Alrin's and Trishna's eyes couldn't have grown any larger if three piles of gold had been lying there on the table.

"Now you can see," said Halvdan, "why it was so important that I keep these hidden in Everglen. If word ever got out, then it would've been only a matter of time until the king came looking for them. And there's no telling what might've happened—to me or to all of Everglen, for that matter."

"Fifteen years have passed," spoke Meldun, "since Veda's grandfather was murdered and the king's true intentions came to light. From that day forward, we have kept our ensignis hidden from the world and trained in secret for one single purpose. Together we will find the Dorekstone and rid the world of Abaddon once and for all."

Halvdan, Veda, and Meldun spent the next several hours reminiscing about the years they'd spent training to achieve their 99s. Of course, this quickly sparked a competition over who could tell the best story.

There was Donfeldur—the Highsage of Yerivan—who'd told Veda to select any book in his entire library, and then boasted that he would know how many pages the book contained. The hardest thing Veda had ever had to do, she explained, was stand there and try to seem impressed, when she knew not only how many pages there were, but how many times each and every word was used, having only read the book once.

Meldun told of the time he visited Eld-lor, his old strength-master in the city of Brugden. Eld-lor needed help felling trees to construct a new wing for his guild, and (to the surprise of no one at the table) this was a competition in itself. The two men agreed that after just two hours' time, they would return and compare how many trees they had cut down. It took Meldun a total of five minutes, he bragged, to cleave an entire grove of the forest with his red-hilted sword. He became so bored while he waited that he fell asleep, waking up in time to ensure his victory, of course, but only by a margin that would seem inconspicuous.

But Halvdan's tale was the unanimous victor. He told a story of something that had happened shortly after he achieved level ninety in magic and unlocked the ability to slow down time. He was teaching levitation to a student in Everglen by throwing various things into the sky so the student could practice stopping them right before they reached his hands. The student quickly became cocky and boasted that he would one day be even stronger than Halvdan. So Halvdan picked up a watermelon and hurled it into the air. Then, just before it reached the student, Halvdan slowed down time, walked straight up to him, and lowered his hands so that it smacked him right in the face.

The entire room exploded with laughter, but Trishna was particularly delighted, for she knew exactly whom Halvdan was talking about.

"I remember that!" she laughed. "Iarund. That was Iarund, wasn't it?"

Halvdan nodded gleefully. "If he learned anything from me that day," Halvdan said, "it was a little bit about humility...and maybe how hard it can be to get watermelon out of your hair."

Everyone but Alrin roared with laughter. If it had been anyone else, Alrin would've likely been rolling on the ground with the rest of them. But just the mentioning of Iarund's name made him feel sick to his stomach.

"Humility?" Meldun said, still chuckling. "What do you know of humility? Even your story sounds an awful lot like humble bragging to me."

"Maybe so," Halvdan said, stroking his beard and grinning proudly. "Maybe so."

Alrin had been lost in another powerful bout of the stares, still fixated on the image of Iarund lying on the ground, when he heard his father mention the words *humble bragging*. It almost felt as if someone had prodded him in the side. Everything hurt all at the same time. That was something Thrain used to say.

Alrin stood up quietly, politely excused himself from the table, and walked over to where Moltrix was curled up unnaturally close to the fire. Even with his back turned, he could feel the mood of the entire room change, and he knew without a doubt that everyone's eyes were following him.

"So if the prophecy speaks of him," Trishna whispered, "what part does he play in all of this?"

Veda hesitated. "That...remains to be seen."

Alrin stared into the flames, and before he knew it, he was asleep.

Sometime in the middle of the night, a bright light flashed into his eyes and stirred him. Prying open a tired eye, he saw Moltrix beside him snoring rhythmically through a dream and Trishna fast asleep on the couch. He looked around the room for a minute or two, trying to find what light could've roused him, but eventually rested his head back down and pulled up the thick wool blanket that someone had draped over him.

Then it happened again.

Alrin sat up and waited. Now he was certain it wasn't a dream. When he looked down and saw light fading away into his bracelet, his heart froze. Someone was looking for him again.

Flash-flash. Flash-flash.

The pattern…the one like a heartbeat. *It has to be him*, Alrin thought excitedly. He unclasped the bracelet and began to remove it, but that's when someone's voice stopped him.

"What are you doing?" Alrin looked over and saw Trishna glaring at him. "What are you doing?" she wailed again. "Don't take that off!"

"It's Thrain," Alrin said. "It's him! I know it is."

There was a look of pure terror in her eyes. "Thrain would have to be level forty already to use scrying. There's no way he leveled that much in one day. DON'T…TAKE…IT…OFF."

Alrin looked down at his bracelet again. Maybe she was right. "You don't think…it could be Abaddon, do you?"

"Of course I do," she said menacingly. "I know you're only level four in intellect, but seriously, Alrin, I thought you would be smarter than that." She shook her head in disgust and flipped back over so she didn't have to face him. "I don't care what Veda said. If you're supposed to be the *one* thing that can stop him, then of course he's looking for you, you idiot."

There was a long spell of silence. Alrin rolled over and stared at the coals that were still faintly glowing in the fireplace.

For a moment no one spoke. But then Trishna exhaled loudly and flipped back over. "I'm sorry," she finally muttered. She got off the couch and walked over to the front door and opened it. Before stepping out into the cold, she turned. "I'm not sure why I said that."

Alrin grabbed the blanket from the floor and followed her outside, where she was standing, arms folded, staring up through the pine needles as small wisps of snow swirled around her in the moonlight.

"I miss her too," Alrin said softly as he walked up behind her and wrapped the blanket over her shoulders.

The moon disappeared behind a thick layer of clouds and the flakes started growing larger.

"I woke up just now and for a moment everything was OK," Trishna said, wiping her eyes. "Then I remembered all over again." She sniffed and wiped her nose. "You meant the world to her, you know."

Alrin tried his best to fight against the knot forming in his own throat. "She probably meant even more to me than I did to her. Sirena was the only friend I had."

"Oh, that's not true," Trishna said almost patronizingly, then sniffed again.

Alrin was sure that she was about to blame her sniffling on the cold again. But she didn't. She even allowed a few tears to run halfway down her cheeks before wiping them away. As much as it killed him to see her hurting, each tear was like a ray of sunshine breaking through the storm. She wasn't scared to look weak in front of him anymore. Maybe she was finally starting to let him in.

"Actually she was," Alrin said, grinning. "One day when I was walking home, I pretended to reach down and tie my shoes seven times just to avoid people that were walking by. Sirena was the only person that saw anything other than my ensignis."

Trishna smiled and pulled the blanket tighter around her.

"What's left of us without our ensignis?" she asked. "It's who we are."

"I dunno," Alrin answered. "I guess I've always held on to the hope of there being something more than that. I can't believe they're all this life has to offer."

"What if they are, though?" Trishna asked. "What if that's all there is?"

"Then I will have spent my life holding on to the hope that there is something greater than just myself. And I will be OK with that."

Trishna twisted her mouth and gave him a playful squinty stare. "You really are a strange one, aren't you?"

Alrin smiled. "I know it's hard to believe, but you're not the first person to say that."

Trishna smiled back. And it must have been a bigger one than she intended because she wiped it away almost immediately, then tried to play it off as if it had never happened.

But Alrin wasn't about to let this one get away. "You know, you should really smile more. It suits you."

Trishna clenched her jaw and pursed her lips. It was obvious that she was doing everything in her power not to let another one slip out so easily. She turned her head upward to the sky and inhaled deeply. "It's nice out here," she said, ignoring him. "It's so quiet."

Alrin was about to agree, but was interrupted by a sudden fireball exploding out the front door of Meldun's cabin.

"Uh...what was that?"

They turned, looked at each other only briefly, and then sprinted inside.

Halvdan, Veda, and Meldun came rushing out of a side hallway as if prepared for battle.

"*What happened?*" Meldun hollered, drawing his sword and holding it, white-knuckled, out into the darkness.

Halvdan opened the palm of his hand and every candle in the room lit at precisely the same time. "Relax, everyone," he said calmly. "It's only Moltrix."

Beside the fireplace where she'd been sleeping, there was now nothing but a small pile of ashes.

Meldun lowered his sword. "I'm sorry, old friend," he said, putting his hand on Halvdan's shoulder. "She must have gotten too close to the fire."

"It's quite all right," said Halvdan, surprisingly unaffected.

"She was the most loyal of beasts," Meldun offered consolingly. "She will never be forgotten."

"It's really OK. She's much easier to feed this way."

Meldun looked disgusted. "Loss is difficult to bear, but there are far better ways of dealing with grief."

Halvdan chuckled. "No, you don't understand. Here, let me show you." He walked over to the fireplace and took a knee next to the pile of ash. "Come on out, girl," he said, rubbing his fingers together close to the ground. Out of the ash wriggled the tiny head of what looked to be a baby orange tiger, her face all covered in soot.

"Oh my goodness, she's the cutest thing ever!" Trishna exclaimed, running up to her and picking Moltrix up in her arms.

Moltrix began to purr loudly as she flipped through the air her three tiny tails, which were now no larger than Trishna's fingers.

"Fire elementals: Part tiger. Part phoenix," Halvdan said. "The most majestic of creatures." Halvdan looked around the room, inspecting the damage. "Apologies, Meldun. I didn't realize her birthday would be this soon. Hope she didn't burn nothin' important."

Alrin's stomach jumped into his throat. He had forgotten all about Sagittari's bow. He looked over to the corner where he'd left it, and with a huge sigh of relief saw that it was perfectly intact.

But that's when Veda let out a terrible shriek. "My grandfather's page!" she exclaimed. "I left it here on the table!" She scrambled around the room, tossing over chairs and looking under bookcases.

"Oh no. I'm afraid it must've burned up in the fire," Meldun said grimly.

"Then we are lost!" Veda cried. "That page was the only thing that would show us the locations of the other tests."

As Alrin watched her search frantically through the charred remains of everything that had been lapped up by the tongue of Moltrix's flames, an idea suddenly came to him. "What was it that your grandfather used to tell you?" he asked. "You had to protect it like no one else would? Maybe that's it, then. Maybe the only way to protect something that important is by doing something no one else would—destroying it."

"'Wingless soars, voiceless roars,'" Halvdan said, looking to Veda. "Fire would make sense." He walked up the table and examined it closer, shining a light onto it from his outstretched hand. "Would you look at that," he said. "It seems Alrin has solved your grandfather's riddle after all!"

Where the paper once had been, a perfect map of Dalroth was now burned into the table. It was very similar to those Alrin had seen pinned up in Halvdan's guild, except for the three symbols of the Trace burned into different locations on the map. The closest one was just outside Elinar, and below the symbol were the words *"Longshire Ruins."*

Trishna rushed to the table and rested her hand against Alrin's back as she leaned in to get a closer look. That's amazing!" she exclaimed. Moltrix, who was still curled up comfortably in her arms, blinked down curiously at the table, trying to see what all the fuss was about.

Alrin felt his face turn red. Even after she removed her hand, he could still feel where it had been.

"It seems he has," Veda whispered as she studied the image burned into the wood, but there was no excitement in her voice. "Though ideas are oftentimes like our friend Moltrix here. They are rarely born...only reborn. I must have somehow given you the answer." Her face made it painfully obvious that not having been the one to decipher her grandfather's riddle came as a huge blow to her ego. "Destroy it," she said coldly. "I know exactly where the other two locations are...I should've known all along."

Meldun nodded and unsheathed his sword. He looked eager to finally be able to display his awesome strength.

"Wait," Halvdan interrupted. "Allow me. I haven't been able to use this spell in years." In an instant the table rose into the air, and at the same moment that Halvdan opened his fist, it splintered into tiny fragments and fell to the floor in a pile of dust.

Meldun sighed and disappointedly returned his weapon to his hip. "Show-off," he grumbled under his breath.

Moltrix let out a small squeak of a yawn and then jumped out of Trishna's arms and started scratching at Halvdan's leg.

"Ah, looks like someone's hungry," Halvdan said, reaching down and scratching under her chin.

Alrin realized he was too, for at that same moment, his stomach grumbled loud enough for everyone to hear.

"Then let's eat and be on our way," Veda said, staring ominously out the window as the first light of day cracked through the trees. "The tests of the Dinivus brothers await us."

CHAPTER FIFTEEN

THE WARRIOR WITHIN

The farther north they traveled, the deeper winter had already sunk its claws into Dalroth's frostbitten flesh.

In order to stay warm, they took turns carrying Moltrix inside their jackets. Of course Moltrix didn't mind much. Each time, she would curl up into a tiny warm ball and fall fast asleep. Everyone took a turn except Meldun, who, exactly like Thrain, seemed to be the sort of person who needed a constant reminder it was winter. Alrin could've sworn he even saw him sweating at one point, despite the torrents of snow plummeting down around him.

The more Alrin watched him, the more he began to realize that his father was everything that he wasn't. Strong, fearless, and unshakably confident. But at that particular moment, the only quality Alrin wished he'd inherited was his ability to be blissfully unaffected by the cold.

Veda hardly wasted a second. She made Alrin tell her about each time the Trace had appeared on his hand, because, in her words, "Halvdan's account wasn't detailed enough for my liking." He told her what little he could remember about Batara and about the time in the courtyard when he'd stood up to Iarund. "Everything felt so real," he told her, "and yet so imaginary. It's kind of hard to explain. It felt unstoppable…and yet so fragile. I guess I could describe it like a really high waterfall. If you could somehow stand on either end at the same time, it would seem like a roaring river, but also a gentle mist."

Once he had said this, a small wrinkle appeared over Veda's brow and she grew very quiet. Alrin usually kept his thoughts to himself out of fear of being mocked for them. Even if you said something clever, you could easily get ridiculed if you didn't have the ensigni levels to back it up. He could tell that she was searching for a deeper meaning, when he really hadn't intended for there to be one. He'd spent his whole life outside, so finding such comparisons came naturally. The woods just always made sense to him. Everything had a place. Everything had a purpose.

It was Meldun who finally broke the silence. "Better look out, Veda," he said, smirking. "Seems like you may have some competition on your hands. That sounded an awful lot like wisdom to me—and, unlike most of the things you say, that *actually* made sense." From the look on his face as he said it, Meldun was particularly delighted with himself.

But Veda most certainly was not. Most of the time, the jagged tattoos around her eyes made it difficult for anyone to tell exactly which way she was looking, but this was definitely not one of those times. She was staring holes not through

Meldun, but straight through Alrin, almost as though he was the one who had said it. He was immediately reminded how even opening one's mouth could seem like a threat to someone's ensignis. He quickly retreated back into himself. He didn't know why he'd thought being outside Everglen would be any different.

That night, when they made camp, everyone ventured out in different directions for firewood. Alrin was careful to take as long as he possibly could so that he could return last and make sure he brought back less than everyone else. He didn't want to give anyone the opportunity to resent him for carrying more than they had. Luckily, it wasn't much of a competition, because, by the time he'd made it back, Meldun had returned with what appeared to be a good chunk of the forest under his arm. Alrin walked over and placed his embarrassingly small pile of sticks and twigs next to the giant pile. "Tinder," he said, feeling the blood rush to his cheeks. "I thought some smaller stuff would help to get it started."

They all stared awkwardly at one another, and then, without a word, Halvdan slowly lifted his hand toward the pile and everything burst into flames.

"Oh." Alrin gulped, moving back from the heat. He'd forgotten how useless a lot of things were around magic. "How about I find something for us to sit on, then?"

"No need," Meldun said suddenly, and he walked over to where his sword rested against a large pine tree. After a few swings up the trunk with his invisibly fast blade, the tree fell with a thunderous snapping of branches, and several perfectly smooth logs rolled to the ground at Alrin's feet.

"Er…never mind," Alrin said stiffly. "Just sit over here and stay out of the way, then? Yes? Fantastic."

Besides the small grin that Meldun gave purely out of courtesy, the look on everyone's face told him that was an excellent idea. He didn't think he would ever get used to being around this kind of power. He'd always felt two steps behind everyone else growing up, but two steps around ensignis like these felt like miles.

Aside from the occasional word or two that night, no one really spoke. Especially to him. Veda because she never talked much to begin with; Trishna because her occasional glare indicated she still slightly despised him; and Meldun and Halvdan because their minds seemed too burdened for them to even lift their eyes from the fire.

It wasn't until everyone had fallen asleep that it happened.
Flash-flash, flash-flash.

It was the bracelet again. Alrin sat up and quickly shielded the light. He didn't care what anyone said, it had to be Thrain. That pattern was like a secret handshake. It felt as if they were back in their room and Thrain was knocking against the wall to see if he was still awake.

It flashed again.

Alrin looked around to make sure everyone was still sleeping—Trishna especially. She wouldn't like what he was about to do. Then, before she or anyone else had the chance to talk him out of it, he removed the bracelet from his wrist.

A cold chill crawled up his spine.

"*Are you there?*" came a voice.

Alrin whirled around. It felt as if it were coming from every direction all at once.

"Alrin, can you hear me?"

Alrin's heart pounded. He hadn't been sure if he would ever hear that voice again.

"Thrain!" Alrin almost yelled. "You're alive!"

"Yes," Thrain answered. It was definitely he, but there was something very strange about his voice. Alrin could sense that something was terribly wrong.

"It's true, then," Alrin whispered. "Level forty in magic already. How is that even possible?"

"There's not much time. I have to warn you."

Alrin froze. "Warn me about what?"

It sounded as if Thrain was struggling to catch his breath between every word. *"Hide...you have to hide. Whatever you do, don't come after me."*

"Why? What does he want with you?"

Thrain paused to catch his breath. Each word he spoke winced like knives to his throat and sounded as if it could be his last. *"He's training me for some kind of tests. I...I told him I was you."*

"What!" gasped Alrin, much louder than he'd intended. He heard Meldun stir, but thankfully his snoring resumed almost immediately. "Why?" Alrin asked, much softer this time. "Why would you do that?"

"It was the only way I could protect you..."

"But we know how to stop him," whispered Alrin. "I'm training for the tests too. Even now we're on our way to Longsh..."

"Don't!" Thrain sharply cut him off. *"Don't tell me. If I know what you're planning, he'll find out...if he hasn't already."*

Alrin bit down. He feared that anything that came out of his mouth could ruin everything. Or even worse, it might cause his brother even more pain. But there was one thing he just couldn't hold in. It was the burning coal that would only do more damage the longer he held on to it. "There's something you need to know," Alrin whispered, not sure how to say it. "Our father is alive."

It took a while for Thrain to finally answer him. *"Don't trust anyone, Alrin—not even me after this. I'll erase as much of this memory as I can, but I'm afraid even that won't be enough. You have no idea what he's capable of…"*

Thrain's voice started to trail off.

"Wait!" Alrin cried. "When will I be able to talk to you again?"

Then, in a whisper that sent chills throughout his body, Thrain said, *"You won't."* And just like that, he was gone.

Alrin waited an eternity for another flicker of the bracelet, or for his brother's voice to appear from the darkness again, but he was answered only by the eerie howl of the wind as it whistled through the treetops above. His eyes ticked back and forth between his bracelet and his ensignis like a broken clock. Ignorant of itself and unbound by an hourglass, each minute felt like hours. He tried to convince himself that Thrain hadn't heard what he'd said about their father, but he couldn't silence the thought that Thrain had already known.

3-11-5. No matter how hard he tried, he couldn't take his eyes off his ensignis. They only reminded him how helpless he was. Helpless to save Thrain and Aurora. Helpless to avenge Sirena's death. Helpless to pass the tests awaiting him, which could be the only way to stop the monster responsible for it all. Helpless to even calm his racing mind and get some much-needed rest. Just being the only one awake infuriated him. It only further pointed out how unlike the others he actually was.

3-11-5. He glared at the numbers as if they were deformities he'd been born with. Deformities he'd always been blind to and only now learned existed. His entire life he'd been called a lurker, and he'd played the part perfectly. Always peeking over the fence of power like a timid spectator, admiring what he saw but never thinking it could be he. Only now, everything he saw was suddenly turning into everything he needed. Somehow Thrain had made it to level forty in a single day, and Alrin was determined to find out how. It was starting to become abundantly clear that there were shortcuts, and he had a strong suspicion that Halvdan, Meldun, and Veda had used them. If it was true that Alrin couldn't trust anyone, then he knew it was time to start trusting himself. He decided that, the following morning, there would be no more secrets…

Alrin didn't have to wait long before the right moment presented itself. He thought it might prove difficult (especially around the all-perceiving eyes of Veda) to bring up faster ways of training without revealing he already knew they existed—or that he'd spoken with Thrain the night before. But as luck would have it, Trishna brought up the topic of their ensignis and they became so enamored of their own achievements that Alrin could ask practically anything behind the flattery of her questioning.

"It must have taken decades," said Trishna, gawking at their hands.

"Actually, it only took about three months for me to get from eighty to ninety-nine," Halvdan said proudly.

"Just two weeks for me," Meldun bragged.

"Pssh," spit Halvdan defensively. "That's only because someone called you a weakling and it sent you into one of your blinding fits for nearly two weeks."

Meldun roared with laughter. "So what?" he said. "Only took two weeks."

Halvdan shook his head and then leaned down to Alrin and Trishna, hiding the corner of his mouth with his hand. "Seriously, though, don't ever call him a weakling," he whispered. "Even as a joke. He's likely to tear down a mountain if you do."

Trishna and Alrin smiled nervously, but each sensed the seriousness behind Halvdan's warning.

"I'm sure whoever called him that had level ninety-nine in stupidity," Trishna quipped. Meldun agreed, and the color began to return to his face.

And that's when Alrin saw his opportunity. "But isn't each level harder to reach than the last?" he asked.

"Exponentially," Veda answered loftily. "Especially after seventy or so."

"Then what's your secret?" asked Alrin. "Leveling that fast doesn't even seem possible."

Meldun opened his mouth to answer, but before doing so, he glanced to Veda almost as though he were seeking her approval.

"That kind of training," said Meldun after receiving a slight nod, "is only possible the same way *that* keeps you hidden." He pointed suddenly to Alrin's bracelet. "As I'm sure you've gathered, that isn't just an ordinary hunk of metal around your wrist. It's one of the seven Talismans of Triem. Forged by the Dinivus brothers themselves." Meldun gave him a sideways squint. "Surely you didn't think I went to all that trouble hiding a worthless trinket, did you?"

Trishna rushed over and grabbed Alrin's arm. "You can't be serious!" she exclaimed. "They really exist?"

"Very much so," Meldun answered her. "And there was a time when Abaddon believed they were the keys to finding the Dorekstone. I don't care to know who all he killed gathering them, but once he finally did, and no closer to the stone than when he'd started, he hid them away deep inside one of his treasure rooms."

"How do you know all this?" Alrin asked.

"Your father wasn't just *one* of the Verindi," Halvdan chimed in. "Before he left, he was Abaddon's right hand and leader of the king's army."

Meldun looked intensely proud yet equally ashamed upon hearing this. "The night that Veda's grandfather died," he said, "I may have gone in and taken a few things."

"This bracelet?" whispered Alrin.

"Yes. And possibly a few others…" Meldun removed the sword clasped to his hip and flipped it brilliantly through the air, only for the ruby-red handle to land perfectly in his outstretched hand. "The sword of strength!" he said, handing it to Alrin. "Impervious to magic, frost, and flame—and as sharp as the day it was forged."

As Alrin reached out and curled his fingers nervously around the hilt, Meldun let go and the sword fell immediately to the ground. It was astonishingly heavy.

Trishna giggled. "You may want to try using two hands until you've leveled a few times," she said, covering her smile with her hand.

Alrin gave her a look, then heaved the sword into the air with all his might. Immediately he felt the intense power of the blade flowing down into his arms.

"I've grown so attached to it," said Meldun, "that I almost forgot what it felt like to be without it."

"Y…you're letting me use it?" Alrin asked, already astonished by how exhausted he was simply from holding it.

Meldun nodded proudly. "I've longed to see the day when one of my sons began his training. Now that day has come."

That's when Veda walked up to him. "You're going to need more than just that pointy stick if you want to train properly." She unfastened her belt and held it out in front of her. "The belt of wisdom," she said triumphantly, strapping it around his waist. "Before long, the world you once knew will all seem strangely dim."

Almost at once Alrin understood what she meant. Everything seemed clearer, as if a haze had been lifted from his mind. Everything felt new, as if he were looking at the world for the very first time. He turned to Halvdan, and a memory of being in the magic guild flashed into his mind. He couldn't believe he hadn't realized it sooner. "The stone," he said. "The one guarding your door. It was one of the talismans, wasn't it?"

Halvdan combed his fingers through his beard. "The belt is already working, I see." He smiled and then reached into his pocket. "Behold the Dinivus stone," he said, tossing it to Alrin. "Plucked from the stream that never runs dry."

As soon as it landed in the palm of his hand, Alrin sensed its blinding power. It was the same power he'd felt when the Trace appeared—pure and unwavering.

"It's going to take a hero to stop Abaddon," said Veda. "It's about time you start looking like one."

He glanced up and noticed Trishna looking at him as she never had before. It was something about her eyes. There was something very different about her eyes. Alrin could see a flicker of hope in them.

"Very few have possessed so many at one time," said Meldun. "Use them well, Son, but be careful not to lose yourself in them. If you can't control them, they won't hesitate in controlling you."

A nervous pit began to grow in Alrin's stomach. Everyone looked at him as though he were a mighty warrior, poised at the edge of a glorious battle. And with Sagittari's bow over his back and three Talismans of Triem strapped to him, he was actually starting to feel like one.

As he peered down at the monstrous blade hanging down by his side, the numbers he would never see again caught his eye. 3-11-5. When he looked back up, he instantly knew. Though he wasn't sure which path he had just taken, he knew that in one way or another, it was going to end with Abaddon.

CHAPTER SIXTEEN

RORRIM'S LENS

Every day Alrin would spend a few hours with each of them, learning and perfecting all he could. Even before the first light cracked through the trees, Meldun would toss him the Dinivus sword and teach him a new stance or sword routine (once he could comfortably lift it, that is). Day one of strength training was basically dragging it behind him until his arms felt as if they were going to fall off. But that didn't last long. The sword's power was incredible. After only a few days, Alrin could not only lift it with a single hand, but had turned it into a graceful extension of his own arm. He grew larger and stronger every day, almost as fast as Moltrix.

Yet no matter how battered and sore he was by the time Meldun was finished with him, his day had only just begun. Veda was next, and her lessons were by far the most exhausting. She crammed as much as would fit in his head, and that was just a warm-up.

The first thing Veda taught him was the ancient language spoken in the time of the Dinivus brothers. At first Alrin thought this was a colossal waste of time, regardless of how many times she told him that "anything worth mentioning will be spoken or written in this language." It shouldn't have surprised him to find out that she was right. Alrin had a pretty fair grasp of it after only a few hours of wearing the belt, and he began to realize that some of the words and phrases didn't have an accurate translation at all. They were like brand-new colors that he'd never known were there. There just weren't any words in his language to describe them.

Veda rattled on about histories of great battles and kingdoms from eras that Alrin hadn't even known existed. He learned not only everything there was to know about "The *Magical List of Do's, Don'ts, and Distant Dreams,*" which he still carried in his pocket, but who had discovered each and every spell (and which wizards had died trying to do so). Books weren't necessary, because Veda was basically a walking library. She hardly even paused for a breath before continuing to the next impossible chapter of her training. Alrin was almost certain that everything she was saying was simply going in one ear and out the other, but he soon found that this wasn't the case. Wearing the Dinivus belt, his mind was a steel trap. Anything that went in was in there for good.

She didn't even seem human. She knew everything about everything. At one point Alrin even suggested (within earshot of Halvdan) that she probably knew more about magic than he did. Halvdan strongly objected, of course, until she folded her arms and asked him when the best time of day was to add purified nightshade and henbane to make the strongest batch of a Sleeping Kiss potion. Needless to say, "Err...nighttime?"

was not the correct answer, and from that point on, Halvdan seemed suddenly preoccupied whenever Alrin was training with her.

Then, when either Alrin's head was filled to the brim or Veda was simply too frustrated with him to continue, it was Halvdan's turn. This was Alrin's favorite part of his training—but not because of the exciting new spells he could quickly master, or even because the power of the Dinivus stone would instantly restore him. It was his favorite part of the day because Halvdan allowed Trishna to join them.

Of course, she did everything in her power to continue ignoring him at first, but as time went on and the numbers on his hand continued to grow, so did the number of times Alrin caught her glancing at him.

As the days ticked by, Alrin was starting to wonder if they would ever find the other end of the forest. He longed to feel the sun on his face again and feel the rush of the wind, regardless of how freezing cold it was. But very gradually, the trees began to thin and he knew they must be getting close to Longshire. Veda grew quieter and quieter every day, sometimes not speaking the entire time Alrin was supposed to be training with her. She stayed in a strange, dreamlike trance, only waking from it long enough to give him a complex riddle or something to memorize, but even then he could tell her heart wasn't in it. For a while Alrin thought that maybe she was scrying someone, but when he tested this theory, speaking to everyone else one at a time, nothing would faze her. All he could guess was that she must be thinking about her grandfather. He had taken her to Longshire as a part of her training, after all, so there was no telling what was going through her mind.

Naturally Alrin couldn't just sit back and wonder if she was OK, but when he opened his mouth to ask, she somehow already knew it was coming. "You will do well to reflect on what you've learned," she interrupted him. "Wisdom delights in silence, as a fool delights in words."

Alrin closed his mouth as fast as he had opened it. Nothing ever escaped her. She often bragged about being able to notice everything that was going on around her, and how she had the ability to remember her entire life just as it had happened. As Alrin stared in silence at the ninety-nine tattoos covering her body, he wasn't sure whether that was a gift or a curse. What a burden it must be to remember everything that had ever happened to you like it was yesterday, he thought. Especially when much of your life wasn't worth reliving, as was the case for her. Abaddon had changed only a few weeks of Alrin's life, and it was more than enough to torment him day and night, but Veda's entire life had been taken from her. She would gaze with sadness at every bend in a stream or noticeable boulder jutting out along the ground. What memories they possessed, Alrin would never dare to ask.

Once the trees finally broke, the ruins of the once-great city of Longshire came into view on the horizon. As he stepped out into the sun, he felt as if he could finally breathe again. He immediately understood why horses break into a sprint when they're given an open field. That much power was never meant to be stifled. By then his levels had grown to 26-28-22—Halvdan taking this as a personal victory because apparently there had been a silent wager on who would level him the fastest (even though Meldun insisted he was cheated because of Halvdan's head start). Alrin had never felt so much power before. Every morning it felt as if his clothes were a little tighter than they had been the day before. He noticed that his arms would bend slightly differently and that everything physical he did was getting easier and easier. But the biggest surprise was that even his coordination was improving. He wasn't turning into a big ball of awkward muscle as he'd thought he was going to. His reflexes grew sharper every day, and it felt as if his mind was making new connections with his body every time he moved. He was starting to see why everyone was so obsessed with their ensignis. He could see its being very easy to get lost in them if he wasn't careful, and start caring for nothing else.

Longshire had once been a mighty city carved from stone. On the coast of the Elegian Sea, it had once served as a great trading post that connected Dalroth to the other lands across the waves. During his lessons with Veda, Alrin had learned that the city had been built in honor of Draegan Dinivus, and destroyed shortly after his disappearance in search of the Dorekstone. Enormous statues of warriors, paladins, and knights had once stood higher than even the trees of Darkwood, but were now nothing more than piles of rubble slowly returning to the earth.

Once they finally made it to the collapsed outer wall of the ancient city, it was obvious that Veda had been there before—and it was a very good thing she had been. The ruins were an impossible maze. She led them under fallen temples so massive that they must have once been visible even from Everglen, through narrow stone corridors, and down long, winding stairwells as if they were the halls of some great palace she'd been raised in. Every time they came upon what Alrin assumed was a dead end, it led to yet another passageway that only Veda could see. Finally they reached a large stone wall with a open doorway leading underground.

"This is it," whispered Veda, resting her hand against the stone entrance. "My grandfather would bring me here and stare at this wall for hours. Not even he knew how to open it. I'm afraid his teachings end here." She lowered her hand to a brick that was covered in a large snowdrift and began to slowly brush it away. "Whatever power saved you that day at Batara," she said, looking to Alrin, "it also opened this door."

Alrin nearly stopped breathing when he saw what she uncovered. The symbol of the Trace was chiseled into the stone, and directly below it were the following words:

Vestus q'albras intrentin cantu.

Alrin forced himself closer. He could feel the power of the belt around his waist helping him to remember everything that Veda had taught him. The words were so clear in his mind, it felt as if he'd never learned them at all. It was as if they had always just been there. "'Strength alone shatters weakness within,'" he read.

"Very good," said Veda. "I'm glad to see I didn't waste all that time for nothing." She turned to Meldun, and her mood instantly changed. "Unless Alrin gets to ninety-nine in the next five minutes, Meldun, it looks like this test is going to be yours."

It felt as if a weight had suddenly been lifted. The entire way, Alrin had secretly hoped that passing the tests wouldn't come down to him. After all, any feat of strength he could do was still effortless to Meldun, so if anyone possessed a power that would be worthy in eyes of the Dinivus brothers, it most assuredly wouldn't be coming from him.

That's a relief, Alrin told himself. *Now I just hope Abaddon isn't down there.* The thought alone nearly paralyzed him. It hadn't even occurred to him until now that the king might actually be down there waiting for them. Nausea tore at his stomach, and before he knew it, he was doubled over gasping for air.

An enormous hand suddenly landed across his back. "Looking a little green there, Alrin." Meldun snickered. "No turning back now." And with that, he made a gallant disappearance down the stairs.

Everyone followed him down except for Alrin and Halvdan, who paused for a moment and peered down at Moltrix, who was now almost as high as his knee. "Stay," Halvdan said sternly, which caused her to twist her head to the side and whimper loudly. "No, girl," he scolded. "You have to stay here. It's for your own good, and you know it."

With a very disgruntled huff, Moltrix plopped to the ground, melting every bit of snow around her. "You wouldn't think it," Halvdan said, kneeling down and scratching the top of her head, "but fire elementals are actually very afraid of the dark." He snickered. "Though I do suppose cold, dark tunnels are about as far from fire as you can get."

Moltrix dropped her chin into the growing puddle beneath her, flicking her fiery tails to either side and staring up at them with big, somber eyes. Alrin couldn't help but feel sorry for her. He wouldn't want to stay out there either. But she didn't stay disappointed for long, because it wasn't a second later that a bird flew overhead and she bounded happily to her feet and chased it behind a nearby statue.

"Not too far!" Halvdan yelled after her, but he knew it was hopeless. Playing with the tiny floating creatures was her favorite thing in the world to do, and anytime she saw one, there was no point in trying to stop her. "Wouldn't be surprised if she chased one off the face of the earth one day," Halvdan said, shaking his head, and then turned and took the first step into the cavelike entrance. As his footsteps grew farther and farther away, Alrin quickly decided that finding out whatever was at the bottom of the stairs sounded a whole lot better than standing here by himself. He clutched the Dinivus stone in his pocket and took the first step down into the darkness. It felt like stepping into the Narew River all over again. Only instead of freezing water, it was the fear of what was at the bottom that washed over him with every step.

The end of the stairs opened up into the largest room Alrin had ever seen. Apart from a narrow stone bridge extending straight ahead of them into the darkness, there was nothing but endless pits around them and monstrous columns rising out of the depths and continuing far above where the light of Halvdan's outstretched hand would reach.

Alrin crept toward the ledge and kicked a loose rock over and listened for it to find the bottom. After waiting for what seemed to be a lifetime, Halvdan dropped a ball of fire from his hand, and they watched it shrink until it was dimmer than a star in the night sky. Everyone exchanged nervous glances, and then they continued forward.

Alrin stared in awe at the columns as they passed. There was something strangely magical about their uniformity. There must have been hundreds, thousands even, each one perfectly identical. Rows upon endless rows stretching from their unknown beginnings upward to their unknown ends. There was no way of guessing what heights they had to climb just to hold up the impossibility of the room. They alone knew their own greatness.

As they continued forward, something began to slowly emerge from the darkness in front of them. Trishna saw it first.

"Look," she exclaimed, straining to make out whatever it was. "What is that?"

The light from Halvdan's hand barely broke its surface, but the closer they came to it, the more it began to take form.

"It's a statue," Veda whispered. "Likely that of Draegan Dinivus, the one whose strength ran as deep and as wide as this room."

"Seems a little skinnier than I imagined," Trishna said. "Looks like he could've used a little meat on those bones."

"Quiet!" Meldun hushed her. "Mind what you say in here. If Draegan's pride was as great as his strength, there's no telling what could be summoned from the deep."

"No, she's right," Veda whispered. "That's not Draegan…"

As usual, Alrin was trailing a good ways behind, so the only thing he saw was everyone stopping dead and gaping up at the statue. "What?" he asked nervously. "What is it?"

No one answered him. They all simply moved out of the way for him to see. And Veda was right, it most definitely wasn't a statue of Draegan. It was *Alrin*.

"Wh?…I?…Who?" Alrin stammered.

And he wasn't the only one who seemed to suddenly lose the use of their mouth. Even Veda looked as if anything that was about to come from hers didn't even make sense to her.

No matter how many times Alrin pinched his eyes shut, he opened them again to be somehow staring at himself immortalized in stone. Down to every detail. Every shaggy strand of hair covering his eyes, every tattered and much-too-small piece of clothing he was wearing, even the Dinivus sword and the gash over his shin from when he had accidentally swung it too low. It all was there. But as he looked closer, he noticed something that made it look nothing like him. In all his life, not once had Alrin ever stood like that. Pompously and arrogantly, staring off into the distance as if he were above everyone else. He sort of hated seeing himself that way. Even though the statue captured his appearance perfectly, it was far from capturing him.

"Is this the test?" Trishna asked.

"I…I don't know," Veda answered, looking even more rigid than the statue.

Meldun let out a loud gasp. From the look on his face, you would've thought she'd said something utterly repulsive. "What did you just say?" He chuckled. "I never thought I'd hear those words come out of your mouth."

Veda's eyes turned sharper than daggers. "You seem to forget that I've never been here before," she fumed, and then turned heatedly back to the statue and stared at it even harder. She seemed to trigger an unspoken contest over who could stay quiet the longest, because everyone stood perfectly still as she tried to figure it out.

It didn't take long for the silence to make Alrin feel awkward. He'd never liked attention to begin with, and though they weren't staring at him directly, it still felt quite uncomfortable. In fact, if he'd been equally immersed in staring at himself, he wouldn't have noticed the next statue ahead of them on the bridge.

"Look," Alrin exclaimed, eager to be out of the spotlight. "There's another one."

Every head turned in unison, and Meldun was skittish with excitement. "Now that's more like it!" he yelled, dashing to the statue. "Here you go, Trishna. You said you wanted one with a little more meat on it? Take a look at this one!"

Alrin didn't even need a better look, given the way Meldun was carrying on. It was obvious who it was.

"Never cared much for statues," said Meldun, puffing up like a peacock. "Always thought it would make me look a little stiff. But this one I like."

Just like Alrin's, the one of Meldun looked exactly like him. The only difference being that the I'm-the-greatest-thing-that-ever-lived expression on its face matched Meldun's perfectly. He stood with his arms angled to his waist, mimicking the statue perfectly. But his overwhelming excitement dissolved almost immediately.

"No," he whispered. "No, it can't be…"

"What's wrong?" Alrin trembled, nearly on the verge of turning and sprinting back up the stairs. From the way he was acting, Alrin thought surely he had spotted the king behind the statue, about to jump out and kill them all.

"It's just…" Meldun huffed, "It's just…I don't think they made my arms big enough."

Alrin's eyes nearly fell out of his head, and he felt like turning and jumping straight off the side of the bridge. Despite how endlessly large the room was, it didn't seem big enough for Meldun's ego.

"Oh well," Meldun sighed. "I guess it'll have to do. It's not every day that you get to see such a work of art in person, after all, even if it isn't perfectly accurate." That's when Meldun raised his hand and rested it on the foot of his statue. And when he did, a horrible noise of splitting stone came from directly beneath them.

Alrin wasn't sure who screamed it first, but "*Run*" echoed over and over again in his ear. Before he could even move, a monstrous arm wrapped around him and hoisted him into the air, just as a hole in the bridge appeared and spread toward them like a crack in a frozen pond. The bridge fell away into the darkness below them, and Alrin could hardly grasp what was happening until he saw the black dragon on the arm of the person carrying him. It was Meldun, and even with Alrin bouncing over his shoulder, he was running faster than any human should be able to run.

"Hold on," Meldun said in an alarmingly calm voice. "We're not going to make it."

No sooner had the words left his mouth than Meldun lunged high into the air.

His strength was unthinkable. The force alone was more than enough to knock the air completely out of Alrin's chest. He lifted his head just in time to see the others dive safely onto a platform up ahead—but that was the same moment that Alrin knew he was right. They weren't going to make it.

For a split second, Alrin's eyes met Halvdan's, and he knew he was going to cast something incredible to save them. But as they continued to fall, Halvdan didn't budge. He just stood there looking back, focusing on him, as though he was waiting to see what Alrin would do. Even as Alrin stretched out to reach the platform he had no chance of reaching, Halvdan still did nothing.

The darkness engulfed them.

It wasn't long until the only thing that reached them was the piercing screams from somewhere up above. Alrin closed his eyes and waited. Just as with the rock he'd kicked over the ledge at the beginning, he waited to find the bottom. And the longer he fell, the more he knew that his power wasn't coming.

But suddenly they stopped. Alrin opened his eyes and followed the strange beam of light all the way back to Halvdan's outstretched hands. By the time his feet touched solid ground, there was only one thing running through his mind. Where was the Trace when he needed it?

As Halvdan's magic released him, his legs buckled and he fell to the floor. Trishna rushed over and threw her arms around him, and it wasn't until he felt how badly she was trembling that it dawned on him that the screams he'd heard had been coming from her.

"I thought you were…"

Alrin raised his arms and rested them across her back. "So did I," he whispered.

"So did I!" Veda yelled, glaring at Halvdan. "Exactly what was all that about?"

Even Meldun was ghostly pale. "Have to admit, Halvdan, had me worried there for a second…"

"F-f…forgive me," Halvdan sputtered, never taking his eyes off Alrin's ensignis. "I thought maybe…" but he fell silent and it was obvious that he regretted every second of putting them in danger.

"Never mind," Meldun heaved, trying his best to disguise how frightened he'd just been. "Was that it, then? Did we pass the test?"

"No," whispered Veda. She'd already turned and was looking at what was on the platform with them. "*This* is the test."

On the platform was one thing and one thing only—a statue of Draegan Dinivus. In one hand was a razor-sharp battle-ax, and in the other a monstrous oval shield. The shield stood roughly ten feet high and it shimmered like white glass. With nothing but the darkness of the endless chamber behind it, it looked like a window into another realm.

"I can't believe it exists," Veda gasped. "It's Rorrim's Lens."

In almost a knee-jerk reaction, Meldun began to creep toward it, but he quickly stopped himself. He must have learned his lesson from the first time he'd touched something.

"What is it?" asked Alrin.

"It's another one of the seven," she answered. "It's a mirror—and like all mirrors, it reflects the opposite of what it sees. Instead of your appearance, however, Rorrim's Lens reflects the opposite of your power."

Meldun looked intrigued. "What do you mean?" he asked.

"Go ahead," said Veda, stepping out of the way so he could move closer in front of it. "See for yourself. Just don't touch anything."

As he did, another Meldun appeared in the mirror. But something was strange about him. It was he and it wasn't he. The reflection looked exactly like him but moved independently. It was like seeing another Meldun staring back at them through a window.

"What do you see?" Veda asked him.

"Still see the strongest warrior in Dalroth," boasted Meldun, admiring the impressively muscle-bound warrior looking back at him. "Afraid it must be broken," he said with a chuckle. But as he continued gazing into the mirror, his reflection changed. Instead of the warrior worthy of 99 strength looking back at him, his reflection turned scrawny and frail. The bones of his shoulders and face jutted out from a malnourished frame, like a skeleton wrapped in a thin layer of skin.

"See what I mean?" Veda said. "It reflects the opposite of your power."

Trishna started laughing hysterically. "Look, Alrin!" she said. "I bet that's what you'll look like when you grow up."

Alrin shot her a squinty glare, but was far too entranced by the power of the mirror to come up with anything clever to throw back at her.

"So what test must he pass?" Halvdan suddenly asked.

Veda opened her mouth to answer, but Meldun beat her to it. A clever grin appeared across his face. "Strength alone shatters weakness within." He began popping his knuckles, which sounded like a crackling campfire, and walked toward the mirror utterly certain of what he needed to do. He raised an arm and lunged with blinding ferocity. But his fist stopped about a foot short of the mirror. Everyone looked just as shocked as he did that something had actually been able to survive his attack. He struggled for quite a while, trying with all his might to force his way closer, but when he finally relaxed, his hand shot backward.

The reflection started laughing at him, a deep and terrible laugh.

"Oh, one more thing." Veda smiled. "The shield of Triem creates an impenetrable barrier."

"Of course it does." He laughed. But learning this only seemed to motivate him further. It was as if he'd finally found a challenge worthy of his incredible strength. He looked down at the 99 on his hand, then back up at his reflection as if they were sworn enemies. That's when the Meldun in the mirror opened his mouth and uttered a single word from his corpselike grin:

"WEAKLING."

As soon as Halvdan heard it, he pulled Alrin and Trishna violently out of the way. And it didn't take long for them to see why.

Meldun looked possessed. "Give me my sword," he demanded.

Alrin wasn't about to argue. He pulled it out of its sheath and handed to him as fast as he could, then slowly backed away.

Without hesitating a second, Meldun charged the mirror and stabbed. As the sword hit the barrier, every muscle in his body strained miraculously, but inch by inch the blade moved closer. Meldun's roar was deep and deafening. With a final blast of strength, the tip of his blade scratched against the glass as a crack spread down the mirror from top to bottom. Meldun relaxed his grip and rested the sword at his side.

For a moment the Melduns just stared at one another. The real Meldun, of course, flaunted a grin of victory, but the look coming back from the mirror Alrin would never forget. It wasn't one of defeat, or even anger. It was a look of sorrow. It was the look someone would give after waiting centuries for something, only to have their savior fail at the very end. Just before the mirror shattered into thousands of pieces, the reflection dropped his head and disappeared.

The glass fell in waves and shattered across the floor. Directly behind it, embedded in the shield, was a small hole with something inside. It looked like an oddly shaped hunk of metal, almost like a piece of a machine or a strange gear. Meldun walked up and grabbed it, and everyone crowded around to get a closer look. "Impenetrable barrier...," he muttered, grinning from ear to ear as he grabbed it. Then he turned around and opened his hand for everyone to see.

"What is it?" Trishna asked.

"It's known as a *Triclave*," said Veda, staring down at it. "It's a piece of a key."

Alrin looked closer. Now that she mentioned it, one side did look as if it could be the tooth part of a key. It was E-shaped and contained a hole in the side that looked as if it might fit together with another piece.

"There are three," Veda explained. "One from each test."

"A key to what?" Alrin asked.

Trishna made a very annoyed sound with the back of her throat. "A door, of course, you dummy."

Alrin scrunched his brow at her. "Thanks," he said sarcastically. "But what door?"

"I don't know," Veda said, suddenly eyeing Meldun to make sure he didn't jump at the opportunity again. "But I have a good idea of what we'll find behind it."

Meldun shut his fist tightly around the Triclave. "We have to keep it safe," he said. "Since I was the one who passed the test, I think I should carry it." He looked around for any objections, but after the incredible display of strength everyone had just witnessed, there obviously weren't going to be any.

Suddenly an orange glow appeared behind them, and when they turned, a blazing torch lit each of the columns and the bridge had reappeared, leading straight back to the stairs and out of the chamber. Meldun started walking, and the others immediately followed, carefully stepping over the shards of glass as they went.

Alrin would've followed right away had he not been hit with another powerful bout of the stares. He just couldn't seem to wrap his head around anything that had just happened. Nothing made sense. Why would the Trace save him when he'd fallen from Batara but not now? And if he was the one the legend of Visarga spoke of, why hadn't he been the one to pass the test?

A chill crawled up his back. Nothing about this place made a lick of sense. He turned to leave, and that's when the glass by his feet started to move. All the pieces slowly rose into the air, then, all at once, reformed the mirror.

Alrin couldn't believe his eyes. He turned around to see if anyone else had seen, but the others were already near the stairs, still applauding Meldun for his victory.

Alrin walked toward it, his curiosity pounding. He couldn't help but wonder what the opposite version of himself would look like. He turned briefly, to make sure no one was watching, then very slowly moved in front of the mirror.

At first there was nothing, but then, just as Meldun's had, his reflection suddenly appeared. It was the first time he'd seen himself in weeks. He hardly even recognized himself. He was much stronger now. And much bigger. He was becoming a fine-tuned machine under the weight of his father's training and the power of the Dinivus sword. He looked...a lot like Thrain.

For a moment both Alrins stared at each other, as if each one was waiting for the other to move. Seeing himself move differently from how he was actually moving was like being in another one of his dreams.

"So," Alrin whispered. "This is what the world sees..."

Without a word his reflection looked down at Alrin's ensignis. Despite their being much higher than they had ever been, as soon as he saw them, the same look appeared on his face that Alrin had seen his entire life. As if he was pathetic. As if he didn't even deserve to be breathing the same air.

Alrin tightened his fist and had an overwhelming desire to reach out and punch the glass just as Meldun had tried at first. Maybe he'd never had the desire to train like everyone else because part of him had listened. Maybe this was how he could destroy the weakness within—by lashing out against the only thing holding him back—himself.

As he looked at himself staring back in the mirror, he slowly raised his fist. Then, just as he was about to strike the glass as hard as his strength would let him, he stopped.

"You know," he said, lowering his arm back to his side. "I wonder how much more we could see if we just lifted our eyes from ourselves."

As he was about to turn, something in the mirror changed. At first glance he thought it was showing him Meldun; that was, until he saw his face. It was Alrin, only much older, and much more powerful. Long hair fell across his piercing green eyes. His arms dwarfed even his father's, and they shot out of glistening armor, wielding a jagged, lightning-edged sword. It was the fiercest warrior Alrin had ever seen—and it was he.

Their eyes aligned and his reflection only smiled.

It was a proud smile, one that wouldn't dare be seen across the face of such a mighty warrior gazing at such a weakling. The reflection opened his mouth to speak, but instead of saying the word *weakling* as he had done before, he repeated the words Alrin had seen outside.

"Vestus q'albras intrentin cantu."

A piercing light shot from Alrin's hand. It was blinding, almost too powerful to look at, but just as fast as it appeared, the light of the Trace slowly faded. He looked back up and the mirror was gone.

CHAPTER SEVENTEEN

TRUTH IN THE IMPOSSIBLE

Once Alrin stepped back out in the sun, everyone was there waiting for him. They all looked very relieved when he emerged—to his pleasant surprise, even Trishna.

"About time," she said, trying her best to hide her concern.

Alrin chuckled. "You know that's twice now that you've been worried about me," he teased. "I'm starting to think you don't actually hate me."

"Please," she huffed, rolling her eyes as if that were the most outlandish thing Alrin could have said. "Let's not get ahead of ourselves. We were just starting to wonder if you fell to your death again. Would've been terribly inconvenient to go back in looking for you." She turned her back to him and began to follow Veda out of the ruins, but not before a small grin appeared at the corner of her face.

Her smile was contagious. Without even realizing it, the same one had spread to him.

"You know," said Halvdan, walking up and nudging him with an elbow. "If your ensignis keep leveling like this, you may just have yourself an admirer."

Alrin shifted awkwardly. He hadn't had much practice at receiving compliments yet. They made him feel very uncomfortable. "I'm not so sure that's a good thing," he said finally. "A few weeks ago she didn't even know I existed."

Halvdan nodded. "Unfortunately, dear boy, that's the world we live in. I'll tell you the same thing that I told you when you were younger. Our ensignis decide everything. Even who we end up with," he said with a wink. "You should embrace them! Start using them to your advantage for once."

Alrin felt his face turn very red. "I don't know. I've hated my ensignis my entire life. I don't see that changing anytime soon."

Halvdan nodded. "I too have felt that," he said. "But at times, even hate has its uses. It can be a powerful motivator if channeled properly. Think of it as a potion of sorts. Sometimes it's best to keep it bottled up until the most opportune time."

"I do." Alrin smiled. "Sometimes there's just not a big-enough bottle."

Halvdan laughed. "I still admire that cleverness in you, Alrin. I really do." Then he glanced down at Alrin's hand again and his face turned somber again. "So you really don't know how to make the Trace appear, do you?"

Alrin paused before answering. Thrain's warning still echoed in his mind, so he just shook his head.

"Well, perhaps the way to control it is remembering all those who have hurt you in the past. If memory serves correctly, when the Trace last appeared, you were about to tear Iarund limb from limb."

"Not my proudest moment," Alrin admitted. "But anger only seemed to make it worse."

Halvdan began combing his fingers through his beard. "I don't know what you have to do to make the Trace appear again," he said. "All I know is that we may need it before this journey is at its end. I fear that your father's strength, Veda's wisdom, and all my magic and potions won't be enough. When that time comes, we will look to you."

Then he turned and walked ahead.

Alrin wanted nothing more than to tell him what had just happened in front of the mirror. But even though he trusted Halvdan with his life, he trusted Thrain even more. "Thanks for saving me back there," Alrin called after him.

"Don't mention it," Halvdan yelled back. "Let's just hope you don't have to return the favor someday."

The next test was apparently in the town of Brugden, which gave Alrin a few more weeks to train. And with four of the seven talismans of Triem, his levels grew faster than he'd ever thought possible.

Every day his training intensified. Veda, Meldun, and Halvdan brought his mind and body to the breaking point, and when the power of the talismans revived him, he returned even stronger. Just as Halvdan had suggested, to Alrin's delight (but also frustration), the more powerful he became, the closer Trishna got to him.

After a while Alrin started to notice that she was looking at his ensignis even more than her own, so one day he decided to wear a glove like the rest of them. He convinced the others it was a good idea, saying it would allow him to devote more time to his training, rather than wasting hours of precious daylight staring at his ensignis. In truth he hoped that Trishna would start to see Alrin for who he really was rather than just a bunch of numbers on his hand, but the glove might as well have been a mask. It only seemed to intrigue her more.

Even though Alrin never had a second to himself, it was the loneliest he remembered ever being. There wasn't a soul around whom he could talk to—except Moltrix, of course. But she seemed more interested in the birds flying by than in listening to him worry and complain, and Alrin didn't really blame her. The only chance he had to relax came while he was sleeping, but eventually even sleep lost its luster. No matter how hard he tried, his mind wouldn't stop. It was on repeat, replaying never-ending cycles of fighting strategies, Dalroth's bestiary, and hypothetical battles with powerful creatures.

He could hear Halvdan's voice even in his dreams: "What spell would you use if you came across an onyxium golem and it attacked with *Beleag'r*?…No, no, no. *Illusion* wouldn't be enough! You have to counter with *Phalanx* to exhaust its mana, then cast *Dissipating Aura!*…No, it wouldn't be able to block your counterspell, onyxium golems are level fifty-three and *Augury* isn't until level fifty-six!"

Nearly every dream would end up with him back in the Verindi camp. The king's voice would flow over the wind whispering, *"This is why you were chosen."* Then, no matter how hard he tried to move or wake up, he would be stuck looking on helplessly as Thrain turned into a black dragon and engulfed his cage in flames.

The path to Brugden was treacherous. Meldun recommended they stay as far from the roads as they could, since the Verindi were likely scouring every town and road in between. But the countryside wasn't much safer. The farther from Everglen they ventured, the stronger the creatures they encountered. Veda said that the safest way to Brugden was through Eduwin Valley, which meant they had to find their way across the scorching Black Sands of Deregon.

Alrin had a very hard time believing that it was the safest route, because the path across the desert was home to some of the strongest magical creatures, some of which even Halvdan was too afraid to face. Even from miles away, they could see hordes of halcyon maulers and doryphor giants scouring the land for anyone or anything foolish enough to enter the desert. But at least this way it finally stopped snowing (which was a huge relief to everyone except Moltrix), and they didn't have to worry about bumping into the Verindi because even they weren't dumb enough to step into the barren wasteland.

They ate and drank what they could find, which was scarce at best.

Even if there had been plenty to eat, Alrin would've still had a difficult time staying full. The extra muscle he put on burned anything he ate about ten times faster than what it used to. He was always hungry. And he wasn't the only one. By then Moltrix had returned to her full size, so the occasional rabbit they came across was hardly worth the effort to catch. It took nearly twenty just to get her whimpering to subside.

Finally, one night, when she could no longer bear the growling in her stomach, she disappeared from their camp, returning several hours later with a deer that was even larger than she was. "Must've gone into the Ashvale Mountains," Halvdan said, as she dragged it to his feet and immediately fell asleep. "There's no telling how many she ate." They all started laughing because she began snoring almost immediately thereafter. For the first time in many nights, they remembered what it felt like to fall asleep with full bellies.

The day before they would've reached the city, Veda explained that they weren't going to Brugden right away.

"We have to make a quick stop first," she said.

"There's no time," objected Meldun. "For all we know, the king is already there."

"Need I remind you that he has the Dinivus helmet?" asked Veda. "He can be anywhere he chooses. Besides, Darius Glade lives near here and he scried me a few nights ago saying we would need his help for the second test."

"*Wait*," Alrin exclaimed. "Darius Glade! *The* Darius Glade?"

He couldn't believe it. Darius Glade had been the first one to successfully cast each and every spell on the entire list he kept in his pocket. The one who had single-handedly discovered over thirty spells and incantations. Not to mention he'd literally written the book on herb amalgamation. The man was a living legend, and Alrin was actually going to meet him.

"The Trace that marked the second test appeared right at the center of Brugden," said Veda. "Apparently it has caused quite a stir in the city. Not to mention we have to get past the wraiths that guard the city's borders."

"Get past the wraiths..." Meldun chuckled. "I've been into that city countless times. If those shadow demons think they can stop us, they have another thing coming."

"We will heed his advice," said Veda. "There is none wiser—he was the one who trained my grandfather, after all."

"Wow, he must be ancient," Trishna blurted out, then instantly raised her hands to her mouth wishing she hadn't.

Veda shot her a terrible look. "However, I must warn you," said Veda, "He's lived with nothing but his potions and experiments for who knows how long. Don't be surprised if he's a little…off."

Darius Glade lived on a hill surrounded by beautiful countryside in every direction. His house was perched in a spacious clearing surrounded by tall shade trees, and there was a large wraparound porch with a rocking chair next to the front door. Faded green shutters bordered the windows, and a small reed wind chime played a peaceful tune in the breeze. A lush vegetable garden with bright-red tomatoes and the largest cabbages Alrin had ever seen was at the bottom of the hill alongside a gently flowing stream full of fish. Besides being extraordinarily appetizing to Alrin's bottomless pit of a stomach, it all looked remarkably…ordinary. He didn't see anything that would indicate that whoever lived inside was anything like the person Veda had described.

But then Alrin noticed it. Blue smoke was coming out of the chimney, and the closer they got to his house, the more they could hear a high whistle like that of a boiling kettle. Once they reached the front door, Veda paused to give everyone a look as if to say, "Prepare yourself," then raised her hand to the door.

Knock-knock. Knock-knock.

"Come in or don't, what's the difference!" came a shrill, scratchy voice from within the house.

Veda shot them a quick I-told-you-so glance, then cautiously opened the door.

The pattern of Veda's knock had made Alrin sick to his stomach, but the feeling quickly faded once the door began to creak open and he got a look inside. He couldn't believe the chaos. Bubbling kettles were scattered across the floor and blue clouds of smoke pummeled the ceiling from every direction. Countless flasks and makeshift glassware, fastened together with shoestrings, rose high into the air—some even going through holes in the ceiling that looked as though they'd been cut out to make more room.

As they cautiously made their way into the room, a long, gray-haired cat jumped down from a shelf and scurried across the floor and into the next room.

"Don't worry, Mr. Frills," the old man whispered to his cat, "she isn't here to steal your food." He paused and looked over at Moltrix. "That's not why you're here, is it, girl?"

Moltrix looked just about as confused as the rest of them.

"There. You see?" he said, very relieved, as if she'd answered him. "Oh, Veda, would you mind adding a few tarralyme to that brew of wormbane there?" It didn't seem to dawn on him that anyone else was even in the room. "Don't forget to whistle to them first! But we don't need to remind a Valkyrie of that, now do we…?"

Veda quickly obliged, walking over to some odd-looking plants growing in a window. She plucked a few bright-purple flowers from a vine and then whistled to them just as he'd requested. The flowers immediately began flapping their petals like tiny butterflies and then fluttered into a nearby kettle. A puff of blue smoke rose high into the air and out some of the holes in the ceiling.

Well, that explains the blue smoke, Alrin thought to himself as he watched Darius hustle about the room.

He was nothing like what Alrin had imagined. As Trishna had suggested, there was no better word to describe the man than *ancient*. He was by far the oldest man Alrin had ever seen, though he most certainly didn't act like it. Despite there being hardly a place for his feet to land, he bounced around the room with a childlike nimbleness, dipping his finger into kettles, sniffing puffs of smoke coming out of flasks, and then running up to a window to reposition a curved hunk of metal (which looked as if it may have been part of a breastplate) so it reflected sunlight into a tiny vial at the end of his colossal contraption.

Once everything had his official stamp of approval, he looked up with gleeful anticipation. "Excellent, are we ready?" he asked no one in particular. "It can only work at the final ray of sunlight before the night of a full moon."

He raised his hand toward the kettle that Veda's flowers had fluttered into, and it levitated and poured its contents into a funnel nearby. Alrin followed the strange flow of the mixture as it traveled through the intricate maze of glassware and cauldrons. It sputtered and bubbled, changed colors, and flowed into other kettles, which sent sparking fumes high into the air. Then, after every cauldron and strange ingredient had played its mysterious role, a single drop passed through the sunlight and landed in the vial just as the last sliver of sun fell below the horizon.

Darius rushed in and picked up the vial. "This was two months in the making," he whispered in an old, shaky voice. "I hope this works."

Just when Alrin was certain he couldn't be any more confused than he already was, Darius raised the vial to his lips and downed the liquid in a single gulp. Everyone waited anxiously for whatever marvelous spectacle of magic was about to occur.

What timing! Alrin thought. He couldn't believe that he was actually present for the newest groundbreaking discovery. He couldn't wait to tell Thrain.

"Hmm…" Darius whispered. "Very interesting."

"What?" Veda almost yelled from excitement. "What does it mean?"

Darius smacked his tongue against the roof of his mouth, tasting the fruits of his two-month endeavor.

"Just as I suspected," he said. "Womblebees and fairy trees have nothing to do with magic."

Alrin and Trishna looked at each other and choked back what would've been very inopportune bursts of laughter. Veda had been right. The man was completely mental.

Meldun seemed beside himself. "Complete waste of time," he muttered under his breath. "We could be at Brugden by now." Darius heard him and slowly walked up. Even though he tried his best to hide it, Meldun looked quite intimidated.

"Hmm," Darius grumbled, looking Meldun over. "Powerful ensignis, this one. But if I were to guess, I would bet wisdom falls on you like fodder to a flockless field, doesn't it, boy?" Then he turned to Veda. "You failed to mention there was a Dragonmark in your company."

"Forgive me," she answered. "Master Glade, I would like for you to meet Meldun Turner. He's the one I told you about. The one who secured the Talismans, making all this possible."

"Ahh yes…Turner," he said, looking him over again. "A name that will surely survive the ages."

Meldun swelled with pride. Apparently he'd missed the whole part where his intelligence had just been insulted.

"And I'm Trishna," she said, politely extending her arm. She was very eager to meet him. "It's such an honor to meet you, Master Glade. I've studied so much of your work."

"Please, call me Enoch," he said, shaking her outstretched hand.

"Oh," said Trishna. "Is that, uh…a middle name?"

"No," he answered, looking very puzzled by the question. "Just one that I've come to like."

Trishna slowly backed away, nodding as if it made perfect sense, but it was obvious that she just didn't want to be the closest one to him.

Then he turned to Alrin.

Before Alrin even had a chance to speak, Darius's voice entered his mind.

"Stay true to the path that lays ahead, Trace-bearer, for it is far too narrow to stray."

Alrin panicked and looked down at his bracelet. The stones were completely dim, but somehow Darius was getting past it.

"Come," Darius said aloud, turning toward the others, "We have much to discuss, and our time grows near."

As they followed him into the next room, Mr. Frills leaped off a shelf right by Meldun's head, startling everyone, then sprinted under a table next to his food and guarded it very closely.

It was starting to become abundantly clear that they weren't used to visitors. Neither of them had the slightest inkling how to act around other people.

Everyone followed Darius to a large wooden table and took a seat around it. Everyone but Alrin, that is; he was still far too spooked to sit down. He still couldn't figure out how Darius had gotten past his bracelet. They all waited for Darius to speak, which took quite some time. A light rain began to fall outside, and he sat quietly by the window and seemed delightedly distracted by it.

"The sun rises and the sun falls, then hurries back to where it rises," Darius said finally, as if he suddenly remembered he wasn't alone. "But not everything is meaningless…"

Veda looked around uncomfortably. "I suppose," she answered amicably, all the while growing increasingly more impatient. "You…invited us here to help with the second test?"

"Indeed I have. But first…" he said, turning toward Meldun. "May I see it?"

Everyone at the table knew exactly what he was referring to, but Meldun instinctively acted clueless.

"The Triclave," Darius insisted. "May I see it?"

Meldun situated himself uneasily in his chair. "Forgive me, ancient one," he said, clearing his throat, "I think it would be wise to keep it hidden."

Alrin and Trishna attempted to exchange inconspicuous smiles, but they failed miserably and received prompt kicks under the table from Veda.

Darius reverted his gaze back out the window. "Wise," he repeated softly. "Yes, I'm sure you're right. Whether worthless or priceless, I'm certain it's a prize worthy of its owner."

Meldun glowed as he always did when being given a compliment, even though Alrin had the sneaking suspicion that it was not meant to be one.

"There is but one way to pass the second test," Darius said abruptly. "One that will save hours for a few, and years for many. But not one at this table will be able to solve it…"

Silence filled the room as they waited for him to continue. "Wait. Is that all?" Meldun glowered. "Wonderful, another riddle." Darius kept silent and continued staring out the rain-streaked window. Meldun rose from the table with a jolt and his chair screeched across the floor. But before he could open his mouth, Veda silenced him.

"Calm yourself," she blurted out. "He gave us far more than you realize. Alrin," she said, turning to him, "do you still have the list of magic levels with you?"

"Yes, I have it right here." Alrin fumbled into his pocket and began emptying it out. The list was wrapped around the Dinivus stone, so when he removed it, the stone landed with a thud on the table.

Veda reached out and unfolded the list. As she did, the small silver coin that Mrs. Rider had given Alrin rolled to the center of the table and tumbled to rest. Alrin couldn't believe he still had it. It was beyond worthless at this point, and he would've undoubtedly thrown it away by now or skipped it across a pond had he but remembered it was there.

Yet it wasn't until Darius heard the sound of the coin that he finally turned his attention from the window.

"It's amazing how much power can fit into one tiny pocket," he said softly.

Meldun, Veda, and Halvdan looked very nervous. There, resting on the table like nothing more than a paperweight, was the all-powerful Dinivus stone. An object of unlimited magic. In the hands of Darius Glade, it would bring forth a power the likes of which Dalroth had never seen. In his hands it would be a path to unstoppable greatness.

Very shakily Darius reached out and picked up the stone and coin, then slowly returned them to Alrin. Once they were safely back in Alrin's hands, everyone could breathe again. As his gaze turned back to the window, Darius's voice suddenly entered his mind again.

"Keep it close," Darius said to only him, somehow still mysteriously bypassing his bracelet. *"Only with it will you be able to unlock your true power."*

Veda handed the list of magic levels to Meldun. "Here," she said. "Read the first spell next to '99.' Not one at this table can solve it, because it will take all of us."

Meldun looked down at the bottom of the list. "'Time Shield,'" he read aloud. "What is that supposed to mean?"

"Worry not, Turner," said Darius. "Though a great many have seen and even more have heard, there are few who know its meaning."

"What meaning?" Meldun growled. "I've about had it with your riddles."

"It is the test of Oswyn Dinivus," Darius said calmly, "the granter of all wisdom to this realm. If there is any hope in passing the second test, dear friends, the truth lies in the impossibility of it."

Veda removed her glove to reveal her level ninety-nine in wisdom. "This burden falls on me, Master Glade. Please, tell us what you know."

"There are ten wheels," Darius said, barely reacting at the sight of her ensignis, "spinning at random. On each wheel there is a symbol. Your task is simple. Stop the wheels when each symbol is perfectly aligned."

"Wait, that's it?" Meldun chuckled. "I had to get past an unbreakable shield, forged by the Dinivus brothers themselves, and she has to stop a bunch of spinning wheels?"

"As I said," continued Darius, "the wheels move at random. Some are fast, some are slow. One second they are moving one direction, and the next they are spinning the opposite without your ever realizing it. The combinations are endless."

"How do I align them?" Veda asked.

"As I said, it's impossible." He looked at her as if the answer were clear. "And when the likelihood of something is that infinitesimally small, once it actually happens, there is but one logical conclusion. That it was never random to begin with."

"Again with the riddles!" Meldun yelled, and slammed his fist against the table, making sure his dragon and ensignis were in clear view.

"What he's saying is that even though the wheels move at random," said Veda, "the one who solves it was never meant to be. If it was truly random, then everyone would have the same chance of solving it."

"Yes," said Darius, staring out the window. "The one who solves it was always meant to do so. The truth…lies in the impossibility."

Meldun rose from the table. Having more of an answer than he'd ever expected from the old man, he'd decided it was time for them to leave. Even though they were all very much unsure whether Darius had helped them at all, they respectfully thanked him nonetheless.

He led them through his tangle of an experiment to the front door and wished them well. As Alrin walked past the vegetable garden at the bottom of the hill, Darius's voice entered his mind one last time. *The sun rises and the sun falls, then hurries back to where it rises.*

Alrin froze. That's what Thrain had heard him say after he woke up at Batara. When Alrin turned around, Darius was sitting on the porch in his rocking chair, and over his hand was the glowing symbol of the Trace.

CHAPTER EIGHTEEN

WHISPERS IN THE DARK

Halvdan jostled him awake the next morning to a black cloud covering the sky. Alrin climbed a nearby hill next to where they camped, where the others were huddled together looking out on the horizon. That's when Alrin realized the blackness in the sky wasn't a cloud at all. Thick pillars of smoke were rising out of Brugden.

"What happened?" Alrin whispered as he gazed out over the burning city. He searched everyone's face for even the smallest ray of good news. But he didn't find it.

The city was built into the side of Mount Dorgundul, the highest mountain in all of Dalroth. Its solitary peak rose from the plains like an unwavering beacon, declaring the city's majesty to all who looked upon her. Even with half the city ablaze, it was still magnificent to behold.

"So how do you suppose we get past the shadow wraiths?" Halvdan suddenly asked.

Alrin had learned of them only briefly during his training, but the name was more than enough to send a shiver down his spine. They were by far the most terrifying creatures he'd learned about. They were transparent, vaporlike beings that would all but disappear if a strong-enough breeze passed through them. They walked in the realms of both the dead and the living, holding on to life just enough to escape death, but clinging to death just enough to avoid ever truly living.

Killing a wraith was no easy task. They weren't natural beings, so killing one required something far greater than natural weapons. Seeking them out to level your ensignis was suicide because if you somehow managed to kill one of them, there were always dozens more lurking nearby. They did, however, leave behind Soul Gems—the most sought-after treasure in the entire book *Legendary Loot: Dalroth's Deepest and Darkest Places*.

It was said that the power within these gems had the ability to extend one's life, and that many of the wraiths that could be found roaming the shadows of dungeons were still alive from the days of the Dinivus brothers. Even though killing a wraith like that would be nearly impossible, getting ahold of one of those gems would change your life forever.

Only someone with a death wish or completely blinded by greed would dare to seek one out. The crux of it was that the only way into the city—the infamous Bone Gate of Brugden—was guarded by an entire horde of them.

"Leave the wraiths to me," said Meldun. "I've been into the city countless times. Just don't look at their ensignis, and they will give us passage."

Alrin cleared his throat. "Umm, I noticed you didn't say *safe* passage." He said it only to try to ease the tension, but as he watched Meldun turn disturbingly quiet, he got the feeling that Meldun might have left the word out on purpose.

"Just stay close," he said, and then began to lead them down the hillside.

As they grew steadily nearer, the outer walls rose higher out of the ground like mountains themselves. There was no way of knowing how many generations had dedicated their entire lives to carving out the city. Every inch of stone was covered in intricate textures, and instead of columns, renowned sculptures held up the entire city.

"I never knew people were capable of this," Alrin gulped.

"And to think," said Veda, "Mount Dorgundul once had an elder sister right beside her."

"What?" Trishna gasped. "Elder as in taller?"

Veda nodded. "Where do you think they got the stone?"

Trishna looked dazed. "You're telling me that they tore down the tallest mountain in the world only to build a city on the second tallest right beside it? Why not the other way around?"

"To show the world they were the tallest," said Veda. "So that the mightiest rock in Dalroth would be nothing more than cobblestones beneath their feet."

It grew darker the closer they got to Brugden, and the smoke thickened above them, which took quite a toll on everyone's nerves. Once the gate was within sight, Meldun, Halvdan, and Veda slowed to nearly a stop. Moments earlier they had been barreling fearlessly down the hillside, but at the mere sight of the gate they were obviously rethinking their strategy.

"Don't worry," Alrin said, seeing Trishna in nearly a panic. "We have three ninety-nines with us, and a fire elemental." At this point Moltrix was staring into the darkness beyond the gate and visibly shaking. And the others weren't doing much better. "See, they're not worried," Alrin said comically. "There's no reason for us to be."

A nervous smile spread across Trishna's face. "They're not scared for themselves," she answered. "They're scared for us. The wraiths attack anyone under level fifty who tries to enter."

"Oh." Alrin gulped. His mouth suddenly went very dry. He hadn't looked at his ensignis in weeks. As he began to remove the glove from his hand, he saw Trishna look down with him. 51-58-52.

"That's not possible…," she whispered. Then their eyes turned to hers.

12-16-13. She had leveled incredibly fast the last several weeks herself, but without the items of Triem, her training had been frivolous next to his.

"You don't have to go in, you know," Alrin offered. He watched her consider staying outside for a moment, but when she refused, he wasn't surprised in the least.

"It's OK," she said softly. "Meldun said I'll be fine. I trust him. Don't you?"

But Alrin didn't. He wished he did—he wished for nothing more than to be able to say the comforting words she was begging to hear, that they were safe in Meldun's hands. But he couldn't. Even though he didn't have a reason not to at this point, he still couldn't lie, even if it would make her feel better. "You're the only person I trust," Alrin whispered.

Her reaction was instinctive. She did what she would always do: looked the other way and pretended he didn't exist.

Alrin immediately wished he could take it back. He couldn't believe he'd been dumb enough to think she could ever see him any other way. Even after weeks of spending every waking second together, after all the hours he'd spent training and studying alongside her, he was still just two-thirteen.

But then, just when he was certain he'd blown his only chance, he felt her hand slide inside his…and her other hand wrap around his arm.

He felt his face fill up with color.

At that moment he could have defeated a whole army of wraiths.

"I'm not sure what to trust anymore," she whispered.

"You know I wouldn't let anything happen to you. You can trust that." Her hand tightened around his.

"It was during the Games," she said quietly, "when you were at the archery range with Sirena."

"What was?" Alrin asked.

"The first time I saw you. I mean, I'd seen you countless times before that. But that was the first time I saw *you*." Trishna smiled, then lowered her head. But that's when Alrin caught her glancing toward his ensignis again.

His heart sank. There it was again—his worst fear finding its way to the surface. He'd always had the terrible feeling she was falling only for the numbers on his hand. Nothing more. "Or do you mean that was just the first time you saw the Trace?" he asked, pulling his hand away.

"I didn't mean it like that," she said. "I've never known anything else my entire life." She took Alrin's glove and pulled it back over his ensignis. "I just want you to know I'm trying."

Halvdan's voice immediately silenced them. "Quiet, you two…we're here."

The Bone Gate stood before them, a marvelous blockade of shattered men and mountain, and beyond it was a dark tunnel that led under the wall and into the city.

Moltrix let out a deep and threatening growl as fire ignited across her body.

"You sure about this, Meldun?" Halvdan asked as he reached down and tried to prevent Moltrix from sprinting away. "She senses the wraiths."

Meldun turned toward the gate and peered into the darkness. "I need my sword," he said, and promptly retrieved it from Alrin's side. "If anything should happen in there, it will still do the most damage in my hands."

"You're probably right," said Halvdan, his voice nearly trembling. "Forgive me, Alrin, but I must ask for my stone back. Just for the time being."

As Alrin reached into his pocket and slowly handed it to him, he tried his best to hide how painful it was to part with. It was the one thing that Darius had actually been perfectly clear about. To keep it close because he wouldn't be able to unlock his power without it.

Then Alrin turned to Veda, and before she even asked, he unstrapped the belt from around his waist and handed it over to her. Not that it would do her any good, Alrin realized. She was already at level ninety-nine, but he could tell that she still wanted it.

"Stay close," commanded Meldun as he began creeping toward the gate. With the Dinivus sword clenched firmly at his side, he slowly stepped into the shadow.

"Well, here goes nothing," said Trishna as she fell in line right after them.

"Wait!" Alrin cried, but it was too late.

The smoke in the tunnel was nearly suffocating, and there was only enough light from Moltrix's flames to know which way was forward. Covering the walls were large holes almost like open, vertical graves, and up ahead of them was a glowing line, stretched wall to wall, across the floor.

"We have to be quick," Veda whispered. "Once we cross that line, we are at the mercy of the wraiths."

Alrin and Trishna stayed back and watched everyone else cross the line uneventfully.

But then it was their turn. As they stepped up to it, they noticed the line was actually glowing words from the ancient language.

"Do I even want to know?" Trishna asked.

Alrin looked down and read the incantation to himself. "*Sworn to the mountain, earth and stone. Add the weak to our gate of bone.*"

"Probably not," he said, looking back up. He felt her hand grab his again; then together they stepped across the boundary.

They listened and waited, each expecting the worst. There was no telling what kind of magic the wraiths were capable of. For all he knew, they could collapse the tunnel on them, freeze them with the Myoclonus curse as his mother had been frozen, or even rip them away into the darkness.

But nothing happened.

"Hmm," Trishna whispered. "Maybe they left once they realized there wasn't a city left to protect." Her voice echoed unnaturally through the tunnel. It seemed as if every hole in the wall was echoing what she'd just whispered.

And that's when the eyes appeared, two bright pearl-like eyes from deep within the shadows next to them. With the eyes came a whisper.

"*Fool…*" Its voice rumbled through the tunnel, and a shadowy creature emerged from the wall. All they could see was its eyes, because its body was even more transparent than the smoke around it.

Meldun stepped forward and turned the dragon on his arm toward the shadow. "I am Verindi, sworn to the same master as you, shadow walker. Let us pass."

The eyes stared down at his arm. "*We serve no Verindi,*" the shadow rumbled. "*You stake no claim here, Dragonmark.*" The shadow continued forward, its glowing eyes floating steadily toward Trishna.

Like a flash of lightning, Meldun's sword pierced through the middle of the shadow's body. "You may not heed my words," Meldun roared, "but you will heed my blade!"

The shadow flickered slightly, then let out a deep and terrible laugh. "*You cast your strength like a stone into the dark. What hope does stone have against the will of shadow?*"

Meldun froze. Even with the insult to his strength, there was no blackout rage, no amazing display of power…His face filled with terror as he realized, probably for the first time in his life, that his strength was useless. The wraith floated straight through him and again set its eyes on Trishna.

Suddenly Halvdan jumped in front of it. "That all depends on the stone," he said with a snarl. With the Dinivus stone clenched in his hand, he raised his arm toward the wraith. "ADHUC MORTEM!" A blinding light shot from his hand and struck the monster dead on.

The wraith dimmed slightly, but its terrible laugh only grew louder. "*You think your magic runs deeper than mine?*" it bellowed. "*I have blotted out more men then you have seen days!*"

Alrin looked on helplessly. Even with Halvdan's powerful spell continuing to flow through it, the wraith continued moving toward Trishna. Its eyes were locked on her as if reaching her was the only thing it cared about.

As it got closer, its ensignis began to appear. Somehow the ninety-nine barrier didn't apply to it, for they were all well into the hundreds. Alrin stepped in front of her, his hands trembling. He was the last thing standing in its way.

"Alrin!" Halvdan yelled, still giving the wraith everything he had. "It's time! *RELEASE IT!*"

"I...I don't know how!"

"Think of all the men they've killed!" Halvdan yelled. "Think of Sirena!"

Alrin tried as hard as he could. He closed his eyes and found the memory of Sirena. He could still see her brown curly hair lying in the dirt as vividly as when it had been there. And it was all his fault. If he'd never gone to the games in the first place, the Verindi wouldn't have seen him, the king wouldn't have gone to Everglen looking for him, and she would still be alive...It was all his fault.

He felt the Trace flicker over his hand.

He tried to focus on the pain. He tried to remember every time someone had cursed him for being weak, every insidious stare that had made him cower into himself even more. Rage burned inside him, but the more it grew, the further away his power felt. Alrin opened his eyes and began to panic.

"My father's bow!" Trishna suddenly yelled from behind him. "You're level fifty now, you can use it!"

"What good is a bow without any arrows?" Alrin yelled back at her.

"You don't need any! Just pull it back!"

As fast as he could, Alrin tore Sagittari's bow off his back and curled two fingers around the string as if he'd nocked an arrow. Though it felt unnatural to do so, he raised the bow toward the wraith and pulled back on the empty string. And as he did, a bright line appeared exactly where an arrow would've been.

He pulled back as hard as he could, and the string hummed as it flexed. As he released the string, the magical arrow launched forward faster than anything he'd ever seen and pierced the wraith's body.

It let out a terrible cry and its eyes immediately began to dim. It flickered and thinned, like the waning smoke of an extinguished candle. Just before it vanished, a terrible laugh rang through the corridor. *"Your fate has been sealed."*

As Halvdan's magic disappeared, a purple crystal dropped to the ground, and the wraith was gone.

"Hurry, we have to go," said Veda, rushing in to grab the Soul Gem. But as soon as she lifted it from the ground, a new set of eyes appeared within the tomblike holes beside her.

Within seconds they were surrounded. Waves of darkness poured from the walls, and hundreds of tiny, beady eyes closed in around them.

Alrin pulled back on the string and another arrow appeared. But he knew it was hopeless. Wraiths were everywhere. It would've been easier to stop a swarm of bees with a slingshot.

"Alrin!" Halvdan screamed. "You have to release it! *Now!"*

That's when a pair of glowing eyes moved right in front of his face. Bright horrible pearls, glowing with the light of the thousands of men whose eyes they'd dimmed.

But as the shadow stared into him, it whispered something that made everything stop, even the other wraiths.

"Lord Thrain!"

Every wraith turned toward Alrin, and at the sight of him fled back into the darkness.

"Forgive us," the wraith begged as it slowly backed away. *"We weren't aware of your return."*

As Alrin watched it disappear back into the wall, he could've sworn he saw it trembling. *"Thrain?"* he whispered, frozen in fear. He knew it could mean only one thing. His brother had already been there, and he was more powerful than Alrin had ever imagined. His name alone sent even the darkest of creatures scattering like roaches.

"What happened to you, Thrain?" Alrin uttered painfully.

Then, before the wraiths could change their minds, they hurried out of the tunnel and into the city.

CHAPTER NINETEEN

DISTRACTED POWER

Is this what I think it is?" Alrin hunched over to catch his breath while staring down at the mystical bow still clenched in his hand.

Veda had evidently arrived at the same conclusion, because she was inspecting it very closely. "Have you ever seen it before?" she asked, turning to Meldun.

Meldun only shook his head. He seemed to still be recovering from his encounter with the wraiths.

"I suppose there's only one way to know for sure," Veda said. She turned her head upward and began to scan the skies. "Alrin, do you see that flag at the top of the city?"

Alrin stared straight up, and at the peak of the mountain he saw a small bell tower with a single flag flapping in the wind. "You mean that one?" he asked, shaking his head at the impossibility of what she was about to ask. "The one I can barely see?"

"Yes," Veda answered sternly. "I want you to try and shoot it."

Alrin chuckled. He was the best archer there, of course (though he would never dare to admit it out loud), but he knew that even with 99 strength, he couldn't shoot an arrow a fraction of the way up the colossal city, let alone hit a tiny pole at the top of it. It just wasn't possible.

As he looked back down at Veda, his smile disappeared. She was deadly serious. "All right," he said, "but when the wind catches it and it comes straight back at our heads, I don't want to hear any complaints when we all have to dive under something."

He raised the bow straight into the air, and as he began to pull back against the string, Veda stopped him.

"With your eyes closed," she ordered.

Alrin didn't say a word. He smiled a dubious smile, closed his eyes just as she'd requested, and slowly pulled back. As the bow stretched back to his chin, he heard faint gasps as the glowing magical arrow appeared once more.

He didn't even bother aiming, because he knew it would be pointless even with his eyes open. He simply pulled the string back as far as the 51 of his strength would take it, and released. When he opened his eyes, he saw exactly what he'd expected—the arrow rose high into the air and then very slowly began to arch its way back toward them. But just as he was about to dive inside a nearby building, the bow in his hand started to glow. It was the same orange glow of the arrow, bright and unexplainable.

Alrin searched the sky until he found the arrow between the waves of smoke rising from the burning rooftops. His body turned rigid. Instead of falling back to the earth as it should have, it was gaining speed. It climbed higher and higher until it finally disappeared into the burning sky. As Alrin squinted upward, he heard a tiny snap like the breaking of a twig and watched as the top half of the flag disappeared behind the roof.

He almost couldn't bear to see the smug little grin across Veda's face.

"You see," she gloated. "The bow has never missed its target because it *can't* miss." But her expression instantly changed. "Though I would love to know how someone in Everglen came to possess a Dinivus weapon," she said, turning to Trishna.

"Don't look at me," Trishna exclaimed. "I was about to ask you the same thing!"

"Never mind," Veda said sharply. "We're running out of time. If the king has already been here, the second test may already be gone. We must hurry."

Brugden was utterly destroyed. The city had once been connected by intricate bridges and stairwells carved completely out of granite, but these were now lying in piles of aweless wonder. They passed a monument that had once held extravagant stained-glass murals spanning each of its hundred-foot walls, but the only picture the shards of glass painted now was of a graveyard of color as the sun beamed through the shattered fragments across the ground.

There were, however, a few shops that had miraculously avoided the destruction. One was a small bakery, and according to a small sign in the window, it was the last one standing in the entire city. The short, chubby man who owned it looked as if he was making a fortune, bringing out tray after tray of the most intoxicating foods, taking full advantage of the suffering townspeople.

"Fresh pastries!" the baker yelled to them as they passed. "Get them while they last. Only five gold a dozen!"

"Five a dozen," laughed Halvdan. "Hit our head on something, have we?"

"Supply and demand, my friend," the baker said nastily. "Supply and demand." Then with a wink he disappeared quickly around a corner to find a desperate customer.

Veda led them down the few remaining alleyways that weren't blocked by giant slabs of stone while they stayed out of sight as best they could, and Alrin finally had the chance to ask about something that had just happened.

"What spell was that back there?" he asked Halvdan. "The one on the wraiths? I've never heard you mention it before, and it's certainly not anywhere on Glade's list."

"And there's a reason for that," Halvdan answered. "You won't find it in a book either—at least not in any library you'd wish to be in. The spell saps the power of whomever you cast it on, as well as your own. Like all magic this powerful, it comes with a terrible price. It can't be stopped until either you or your opponent dies. It's dangerous because you can never know who is the strongest when it comes to magic. Even if your level is higher, you never know what they could have hidden. By the time you learn they have a few mana potions, for example, it's already too late. If I didn't have the Dinivus stone, I can guarantee that I wouldn't be standing here right now."

Hmm..."Adhuc mortem," Alrin thought. That could come in handy if he happened to come across Abaddon. If he ever got the stone back from Halvdan, that was.

As they continued deeper into the city, Alrin was amazed at how strong the people of Brugden were. The weakest ensigni he came across was just as strong as any of his. At one point he saw a girl no older than he walking next to a building as it suddenly collapsed. As Alrin screamed for her to move out of the way, the girl simply lifted her hands, suspending the entire building in the air, then easily shoved it aside. It was the most awesome display of power Alrin had ever seen, and from the look on her face, it was about as hard as catching a leaf falling from a tree.

It was Everglen all over again. The power around every turn was baffling.

After the girl hurled the wall effortlessly into a pile next to her, she turned to see who had dared to question her power. Then, just like the wraiths, as soon as the girl got one look at Alrin's face, she turned and fled around a corner.

"Do you think it's Moltrix they're afraid of?" Trishna asked.

"It's me," Alrin said rigidly. "They think I'm Thrain too." His stomach turned inside out. "You don't think the king made him do all this, do you? Thrain wouldn't hurt anyone."

"He would," said Veda, "if he didn't have a choice."

They continued toward the center of Brugden, and, from the look of a few intact street signs, in the direction of Brugden's guilds.

"So if you have to be above fifty to live here," Trishna began, "what happens to the people that are born here?"

It was a good question, come to think of it. Alrin had only seen maybe one or two children, but they'd each had ensignis well above his own.

"They have until the age of fifteen," Veda answered. "If they can't make it to fifty by then, they either leave the city until they do…or their families disown them and they are forced to beg on the streets."

"That's barbaric," Trishna gasped.

"Yes, well, they see it differently here." Veda smiled. "Some see it…as motivation."

As they rounded a corner, Brugden's guilds came into view. Although they were much larger than Everglen's, Alrin had the strangest feeling that he was home. He'd always heard that the guilds were arranged the same triangular pattern in every town, but he'd never imagined the layout would be this similar. There was even a fence outside the magic guild like the one where he'd watched Halvdan instruct Trishna on how to perform the wind wave. Everything felt the same.

It made him miss his little sanctuary in the mountains even more. He missed the mossy tree stump that overlooked the small pond next to their cabin. He missed exploring the woods and going to Batara—despite that it was there that everything had started. As odd as it seemed, he even missed chopping wood outside their cabin. The most Alrin had had to worry about back then was missing the center of the log and making a chunk ricochet off and hit him in the shin. The shadow of the Tatras that he had always been able to shut his eyes and see was gone.

But most of all, he missed his brother.

The courtyard was deserted. Word had likely spread that the one responsible for its destruction had returned. As they reached the center of the guilds, Alrin expected to see a quest board like the one he'd torn Mrs. Rider's flyer from, but instead there were stairs leading underground with the strangest humming noise rising from them. It sounded like the flutter of far-off wings, except it was constant and almost sounded mechanical. Alrin reached into his pocket and rubbed the silver coin nervously between his fingers.

"Good," Veda muttered. "It's still here." She started down the stairs, but right before she did she noticed something. "Look, Alrin," she said, pointing across the courtyard toward someone watching them. "At least there's one person left who's not afraid of you."

The boy was young. He couldn't have been a day older than fifteen. His face was filthy and his hair was unkempt—as were his worn-out clothes, draped over him like rags. He was likely one of the unfortunates who hadn't made it to fifty in time, Alrin realized painfully.

He didn't understand why, but seeing the boy was comforting. Maybe it was because he was reminded of himself. Discarded. Overlooked. Born into a town where no one wanted him. Not to mention Alrin had already grown accustomed to people running in the other direction at the mere sight of him, so making actual eye contact with someone was refreshing.

Alrin raised his hand and politely waved, but as soon as he did, the boy darted back behind the corner.

"Never mind." Veda chuckled. "Maybe there's not."

Alrin let out a heavy sigh and followed Veda down the stairs, but about halfway down, something on the wall made him forget all about the boy and the burning city above him. The symbol of the Trace was written into the wall just as it had been atop the stairs at Longshire.

The whirring noise grew louder with each step down. When he reached the bottom of the stairs, he half expected to enter another room of bottomless pits, but this room was the exact opposite. It was small and confined, with hardly enough room to stand in.

"Cozy," said Meldun sarcastically. It was the first thing he'd said since his encounter with the wraith. He obviously wasn't taking the blow to his pride very lightly.

At the center of the room, atop an intricate stone platform, was exactly what Darius Glade had described; ten identical wheels spinning around a column like rings would spin around a broomstick. "He was right," Veda whispered, as she lightly rested a finger against one of them. "They're changing directions…and you can't even tell."

"How do we stop them?" Trishna asked.

"There has to be…" Veda said, looking around for a moment. "Ahh, here we are." She walked over to the side of the platform to where a small lever was attached to the wall and pressed it.

The wheels jolted to a stop, and just as they'd expected, a small symbol of the Trace was etched into each of them.

Veda released the lever and the wheels instantly regained their incredible speed. "It doesn't make sense," she whispered as she pressed the lever again. The wheels stopped instantly once more. "Oswyn Dinivus had the power of wisdom. I thought surely his test would be some sort of elaborate riddle or intricate puzzle. It doesn't seem like there's anything to figure out." She scanned the room. "Everyone look around," she said suddenly. "There has to be something. A hidden lever or maybe a stone you can push against to reveal some sort of clue."

They all did as she said, and began searching every corner of the small, stony cave. Even Moltrix acted as if she wanted to help, though she didn't have the foggiest idea what they were doing. She stayed at Halvdan's heels, sniffing every wall he was pushing against, and then looking up at him with big curious eyes.

"Look," Meldun suddenly announced. "Here's something."

On one of the stone tiles across the floor were words just like the ones they'd seen outside Longshire. "Faculis estraviré steria mortus."

"'Distracted power will be your ruin,'" Veda and Alrin read simultaneously.

Veda turned deathly quiet and stared at the words as if trying to unlock their secret meaning. "Well, that hardly helps at all," she said finally.

"There's only one way I know of to slow them down," said Halvdan, pulling the Dinivus stone from his pocket.

Veda nodded. "Let's try something Darius mentioned first, then we will give that a try."

Meldun let out a snarky laugh that echoed throughout the room. "Nothing useful ever came out of that old kook's mouth. I don't see why we should start listening to him now."

"My grandfather once told me that everything Darius said turned out to be some cryptic riddle designed for him to figure out. Maybe a little cryptic is what we need right now." She turned to Alrin. "Care to give it a try?"

"We tried this already," Meldun said. "If Alrin were the one meant to solve it, than he would've been the one to break the mirror at Longshire." He looked down as though he'd suddenly remembered Alrin was standing there. "No offense, Alrin."

"None taken." Alrin chuckled. "I couldn't agree more. I don't have more of a chance of solving it than anyone else standing here. If I had to put my money on it, I bet Moltrix has the best chance by simply wandering around and bumping into the lever by accident."

As soon as she heard her name, Moltrix's ears perked up and she got very excited. She lifted her front paw and began to scratch against the wall, doing everything in her power to help. Everyone laughed as they watched her. It had been the only way Alrin could think of to get the attention off him again, but now that he thought about it, it didn't seem like such a bad idea.

"Still, it's worth a shot," Veda said, motioning toward the lever. "Come on, Alrin. Come claim your destiny."

Alrin gulped and then hesitantly obliged. He walked over to the lever, his fingertips numb and tingling. As he pressed it, he heard the wheels grind to a stop, and everyone rushed over to look at them. "What happened?" he asked nervously. "Did it work?"

For a moment everyone just stared like they couldn't believe what they were looking at.

*There's no way…*Alrin thought. Surely he hadn't just solved it on his first try. *That's not even possible…*

His heart pounded in his chest.

But that's when Trishna began laughing hysterically. "You…" she stammered between bursts of giggling. "You can't even see a single symbol. Not even one! That's probably the furthest from solving it you can get!"

Alrin felt his face turn red. "See," he said, embarrassed, "same chance as everyone else." He released the lever and the humming of the wheels returned. He actually felt somewhat relieved that it hadn't worked. The only thing worse would've been if it had actually worked on the first try. He hated being in the spotlight.

"Hmm," Halvdan mumbled. "I thought surely that would work. I guess that only leaves us with one option. Veda, Meldun, are you ready?"

Before they answered, the sound of footsteps came from the top of the stairs.

In a flash Meldun drew his sword and was leaning against the wall next to the entrance of the room, and Halvdan did the same against the wall on the opposite side, clenching the Dinivus stone tightly in his fist.

The footsteps grew closer.

They looked to Veda as she watched the feet appear at the top of the steps. Alrin saw them at the same time she did. The feet were bare, and with each step the tattered clothes they had seen moments earlier slowly came into view. Veda raised her arm in the air, commanding the men to hold, just as the boy took the final step into the room.

Meldun lowered his sword and breathed a huge sigh of relief. "It isn't safe for you in here," he said nastily.

Of course the first thing Alrin noticed was the boy's ensignis. 34-23-42. Then he noticed the rest. The boy had short black hair and a narrow face, and looked frightfully skinny (although just about anyone looked scrawny next to Meldun).

Only a few weeks ago, Alrin would have marveled at this boy's power. He would've been the star pupil of every guild in Everglen and would've won the Verindi Trials barely lifting a finger. But in Brugden—the boy was worthless.

If only he'd been born in Everglen, Alrin thought. *His life would have been so different.* Who knows, perhaps in another life they could've even been friends. He would've given anything to have cheered this boy on as he went head-to-head against Iarund in the Trials. How amazing it would've been to have seen Iarund get humiliated by a fifteen-year-old in front of the entire town. But just as fast as the thought entered Alrin's mind, the image of Iarund's gashed body replaced it, and he immediately regretted having thought it at all.

That's when Alrin noticed that he was in another deep bout of the stares and was still looking straight at the boy. He shook his head and politely looked away. But he couldn't get over how familiar the boy looked—the way he moved, the way he averted his eyes when someone was watching him.

It was he, Alrin realized. The boy was Brugden's version of himself.

"Did you hear me?" Meldun bellowed. "You don't belong here."

The boy finally looked up at Meldun, but he didn't even flinch at his incredible size. It was obvious that he had grown accustomed to being the weakest one in the room.

"Please," he said in a very timid voice. "Would you mind helping me?"

The boy's request seemed to upset Meldun even more. "Not now," he said, staring down angrily. "Can't you see we're busy?"

The boy stared down at his feet. "I don't mind waiting," he said softly.

Meldun looked at the others as if searching for a reason not to go off. "Perhaps later," he said with his very last bit of patience, "but for now, how about you just stay out of the way."

Without saying another word, the boy walked over to the farthest corner and sat down on the floor.

They all quickly returned to what they had been doing. Veda, Meldun, and Halvdan were used to being watched, so it wasn't long before they forgot that the boy was even there.

"This is going to take each of us," Veda said. "Halvdan, you raise the Time Shield. Meldun, do what you can to slow the wheels, and I will look for any patterns to emerge."

Suddenly a tiny voice came from the corner, catching everyone by surprise. "What's a Time Shield?" the boy asked.

All heads turned at the exact same time.

Alrin winced as he prepared for another onslaught of insults from Meldun. *Oh, please be quiet*, Alrin thought, barely peeking at him.

"It's a barrier," Halvdan answered before Meldun had the chance to, the guild instructor in him thankfully coming out. "Inside the barrier time moves much differently."

"Differently how?" the boy asked.

Halvdan started laughing and began pulling at his beard. "Well, that depends on how strong the person is that casts it."

"Oh," the child answered. "Well, how strong are *you*?" he asked, not even missing a beat.

"Now that's far enough!" Meldun yelled. "Insolent lurker! Do you even realize who you're speaking to?"

Halvdan raised an arm toward Meldun. "Quite all right, quite all right," he offered, trying to placate Meldun's temper. "There was once a time when our curiosity got the best of us as well." He turned his attention back to the boy. "What's your name, son?"

"Oswyn," he answered quietly. "The ones who gave it to me thought it would ensure a bright future." He pointed toward his ensignis with his eyes. "Didn't seem to work." Alrin wondered why he didn't use the word *parents*, but realized that it was likely because he no longer had any.

Halvdan smiled. "Well, Oswyn, you are in for quite a treat." He took off his glove and revealed his 99, as did Veda, and then Meldun. "Inside the time barrier, a second turns into hours, a day into an eternity."

The boy didn't even seem to notice their ensignis. "How do you plan on slowing the wheels?"

This time it was Veda who calmed Meldun before he exploded.

"Distracted power will be your ruin," she reminded him.

Luckily it seemed to work. Meldun wrapped his glove around the blade of his sword and climbed on top of the platform next to the spinning wheels. "Enough of this," he said, glaring at the boy still huddled in the corner. "We need to do this now." He lowered the sword next to the wheels as if he were going to grind the edge of the blade against them.

Veda nodded. "Halvdan, raise the barrier."

A wave of focus spread over him as Halvdan pressed his palms together, focusing his energy with everything he had. The entire room began to shake, raining down dust from the ceiling. When Halvdan pulled his hands apart, an electrified orb appeared around him, sparking and shooting bolts of light in every direction. It looked as if a thunderstorm was forming right in his hands, or he were tearing a rift between worlds. The barrier continued to grow until it had completely engulfed Meldun and Veda.

Everything inside the barrier turned into a blur. When Alrin looked closer, he could sometimes see Veda or Meldun freeze in place long enough to be seen for a fraction of a second before instantly vanishing again.

"Are you seeing this?" Alrin hollered to Trishna.

"I don't get it," she said, squinting through the hair that was whipping against her face. "I thought it would slow time down."

"He said it turns a second into hours," Alrin yelled over the rushing wind. "For every second spent out here, hours must pass inside the barrier." That's when Alrin remembered the boy sitting in the corner, but when he looked over to where he'd been not moments earlier, the corner was empty.

When Alrin found him again, he was only a few steps away from the Time Shield.

"*Nooo!*" Alrin screamed, but the boy didn't stop. Alrin lunged after him, pleading for him to stop, but by the time he reached him, Oswyn had already stepped into the Time Shield.

It couldn't have been more than half a second before Alrin entered, but it was more than enough time inside the barrier for Meldun to have completely lost it. "Get out of here!" Meldun screamed. The veins in his neck looked as if they would burst at any moment. "I can see why your parents abandoned you. I would've done the same thing!"

That's when he finally looked up and noticed Alrin standing there.

"You mean like you abandoned me and Thrain?" Alrin said suddenly. He knew Meldun's words hadn't been meant for him, but they stung just as badly as if they had been. He waited for the look of regret to spread across Meldun's face, then put his arm around the boy. "Come on," he said, leading Oswyn back across the barrier. "Let's leave them to their power."

"Alrin, wait…," Meldun shouted after him. "I didn't mean it like that…Alr—!" But his voice disappeared as they stepped back across the barrier.

"What happened?" Trishna asked, seeing the both of them utterly demoralized. "You weren't in there more than a second."

The boy hung his head and sprinted up the stairs.

"Oswyn, wait!" Alrin shouted after him. "Hold on!"

The boy had already made it to the top of the stairs. He stopped but kept his back turned.

"I'm sorry. He's not normally like that," Alrin said, catching up to him. "It's just these Dinivus tests...and the Trace..." Alrin leaned over, trying to catch his breath. "You know what...I don't know why I'm trying to defend him. It's sickening how everyone treats you. Your numbers don't make you less of a person than anyone else...I wish our ensignis would just disappear."

That's when Oswyn finally turned around. His eyes went straight to Alrin's. He never even tried to sneak a glimpse at his ensignis. It was as if they didn't even exist to him. "Please," whispered the boy, just as he had the first time. "Would you mind helping me?"

Alrin stood up straight. It was strange how he asked it, as if he did it a thousand times a day and yet everyone gave him the same answer.

"Of course," Alrin answered. "I'd be happy to. What can I do?"

"Well...," the boy whispered up at him, his eyes glistening. "Anything."

"Hmm." Alrin patted his pockets, and looked around awkwardly. "I don't..." But then he remembered the silver coin. It wasn't much, but it was more than nothing. Yet he didn't feel right just handing it to him. It had been nearly worthless to begin with, and was even more so now that Oswyn's town was virtually destroyed. No, it wasn't enough.

"Hold on," said Alrin, "I'll be right back."

Alrin sprinted toward the only shop he remembered having seen intact on the way in. He darted through alleyways until the sweet aroma of fresh bread reached through the smoke and lured him in.

He caught the baker just as he was leaving his store with another tray of food.

"Excuse me," Alrin said just as the baker was raising a boundary spell over his front door. It still surprised Alrin to see that even a baker's ensignis were over fifty. "How many can I buy with one piece of silver?"

"Bah!" The man laughed greedily. "Six a dozen," he said. "They're going faster than I can make them." But when he turned around, his grin vanished completely. Just one look at Alrin's face and he nearly dropped his entire tray of food. "It's *y…you*!" he gasped. "Here. Take them all, please!" He backed up against his front door, paralyzed with fear.

"I don't want them all," Alrin said calmly. "I just want a fair price. Now how many could I normally buy for one piece of silver?"

The baker hesitated. "How…how many do you want?"

Alrin glared.

"One!" he blurted out. "A piece of silver would normally buy one."

"Fine, then, I'll take one."

The baker wrapped up the biggest pastry he could find as fast as his chubby hands would let him, then handed it over to Alrin. As soon as Alrin had paid him, he disappeared back into his bakery, slammed the front door, and locked it promptly behind him.

Alrin rushed back and found Oswyn exactly where he'd left him.

"Sorry," Alrin said, handing the pastry over to him. "I know it's not much…but it's everything I had."

Oswyn looked down at it, then back up at Alrin. Tears began to stream down his face, wiping away a thin trail of dirt from his cheeks. Then, as a bright smile spread across his face, he muttered something Alrin would've never expected.

"Faculis estraviré steria mortus."

Alrin's eyes widened. "What…what did you just say?"

The boy continued smiling. "You were never distracted from your true power."

Alrin was suddenly forced to turn away as the blinding light of the Trace appeared over his ensignis. When he looked back up, the boy was gone.

CHAPTER TWENTY

UNSPOKEN TRUTH

Alrin stared at the mystical symbol on his hand until finally he heard footsteps emerge from the stairwell behind him.

He threw his hand inside his pocket, and when he turned around he saw Veda walking toward him, the second Triclave in her hand. "There was a pattern after all," she said in nearly a whisper. She looked utterly exhausted. "It only repeated once every seven hours, so it took a few weeks to memorize."

Directly behind her were Halvdan and Meldun, and they too looked an inch away from death. "I know it doesn't seem like it to you," Meldun said as he paused next to Alrin, his monstrous arms hanging lifeless at his sides, "but for me it was months ago. I hope that you have forgiven me by now."

Alrin nodded, but he didn't really answer. It didn't surprise him to learn someone like Meldun wouldn't be able to bring himself to make an actual apology, and he knew it was the closest thing to one that he would get.

Alrin turned and followed them silently out of Brugden. When they passed through the Bone Gate, the eyes of the wraiths appeared as Trishna stepped over the glowing boundary across the floor, but stayed around only long enough to see Alrin and then quickly vanished.

The remainder of the day was filled mostly with silence, and had it not been for Moltrix, the journey would've been dreadfully uncomfortable.

She was so wonderfully oblivious to the tension in the air, bouncing back and forth among all of them and trying her best to lift their spirits. Every time a bird flew overhead, she would disappear into the trees, only to return a few minutes later, panting heavily and scanning everyone's faces for a reaction. If anyone so much as cracked a smile, she would bolt into the trees again and return a few minutes later expecting to see an even bigger one. She repeated this again and again until she was too tired to move. And then she would do it all over.

Watching her brought Alrin a bit of peace. There were very few things he could stare at for hours without noticing how painfully quiet it was. A campfire…the stars…and Moltrix. With his eyes on her, the silence was bearable.

It was all a game. She didn't even want to catch the birds, Alrin eventually realized. Even when one flew low enough that she could have easily snatched it up with her monstrous claws, she only pounced to the ground and wagged her fiery tails back and forth, hoping it would dive at her again. She only wanted someone to play with.

"Don't go too far, Moltrix!" Halvdan yelled, finally breaking the silence as she dashed into the trees after a blue jay.

But watching her didn't distract Alrin as long as he'd hoped. His mind eventually found its way back to the questions he was trying to avoid. He hadn't forgotten about the mysterious bow across his back and how Sagittari had magically come to possess it. He couldn't shake the desire to find out just how far back Meldun and he actually went. It wouldn't surprise him to learn that Sagittari had once been a member of the Verindi as well. But what would it mean if he had been? There were still too many questions to ask, too many stones unturned, and the list of people he could trust to answer them only seemed to be growing smaller.

It wasn't until the smoke rising from Mount Dorgundul looked like a distant rain cloud that Alrin knew what he needed to do. Some way, he had to speak with Darius again. The only way to do that, however, was by scrying...and that would mean removing the only thing that was protecting him from the eyes of the king. The Dinivus bracelet.

Now that he thought of it, Alrin wasn't even sure how to scry. Scrying was the one skill Halvdan had avoided during their weeks of training, despite how glaringly useful it was. The only way to practice it would've been by risking being found by the one person they were doing everything in their power to avoid, so perhaps that was the reason Halvdan had skipped it.

Alrin thought it might be best to try it on someone close first. Trishna was the obvious choice. He tucked his arm inside his shirt, making sure no one was watching him, and slowly slid the bracelet off his wrist.

As luck would have it, scrying was a lot easier than he'd imagined. It was almost like reaching out with his voice and tapping her on the shoulder. She nearly jumped when she heard his voice inside her mind.

"*It's OK,*" Alrin said. "*It's me.*"

"What are you doing?" she whispered, flinging a horrendous glare at the hand tucked inside his shirt. "Put that back on!"

"*I can't. There's something I have to do. I just needed to test it out first.*"

Trishna pleaded with her eyes. "Alrin. Don't."

"*Don't worry, it's not Thrain,*" he said, rolling his eyes. Then, despite Trishna's silent objections and arm flailing, he closed their connection and began searching for Darius.

It didn't take long to find out that scrying someone farther away was much more difficult. The greater the distance, the more magic required. He glanced up at Halvdan, secretly wishing he still had the Dinivus stone, but not able to conjure up a good-enough reason to ask for it. He reached into the Void and focused harder. He pictured the gently rolling hills surrounding Darius's house, and the little vegetable garden by the river.

And that's where he found him. It was like trying to find a certain star in the sky. Hard to spot at first, but obvious once he found it. He didn't know how, but Alrin knew it was he.

His mind was blocked at first, but after several attempts, Darius finally let him in.

"*Master Glade,*" Alrin called out to him. "*Err...I mean Enoch. Can you hear me?*"

"Mr. Frills? Is that you?" Darius said, quite surprised. "I told you not to drink from that potion! I knew something like this would happen."

"*No, it's not your cat.*" Alrin shook his head. Just what was he getting himself into? "*It's Alrin.*"

"Oh…yes, Alrin. That makes much more sense. So how did the second test go? Did you find a good use for that silver coin of yours?"

The way he said it, Alrin could tell he was smiling. "*You knew,*" Alrin said. "*When you said keep it close, you were talking about the coin.*"

"Of course I was," he said. "Surely you didn't think the Dinivus stone or that whirling waste of time had anything to do with the actual test, did you?"

"*Then why didn't you just tell me if you knew all along?*"

Darius took a deep breath. "Footprints," he said cryptically. "Because all footprints are important. If you were lost in the woods and came across your own set of tracks, what would you do?"

"*Umm…probably go a different way the next time,*" Alrin answered.

"Precisely. A question that you must ask yourself is if you had known how the story ended at the beginning, would you have gone the same direction? If I had told you where to step, then you may have been distracted by your own two feet— just as the others were."

"*So it's true, then, about the tests. They are just distractions.*"

"Not entirely," said Darius. "They are still most definitely part of the real test, just not the part that many can see. When I first heard that a Trace had appeared in Brugden, I went there to see for myself. I watched countless numbers enter the chamber to try to solve it, and every time, a child followed them in. Never the same one, mind you, but without fail, a child always came."

"*So you passed the test too, then? The real test?*"

"I likely could have," Darius answered. "But as I said before, I was never the one meant to pass them."

Alrin felt very lost. Was he the one the prophecy spoke of, or wasn't he? If Darius could pass the tests, then that would mean that anyone likely could have.

Darius chuckled to himself. "Quite right."

"*Sorry?*" said Alrin. "*Right about what?*"

"The first thing you should know about scrying," Darius said, "is that it isn't too much different from thinking."

"*Oh,*" said Alrin bashfully. "*I guess you heard all of that, didn't you?*" Although he was slightly embarrassed, it could have been a lot worse. At least he was learning it now rather than when he'd been talking to Trishna. There was no telling what could have slipped out of his mind by mistake.

Darius laughed again.

"*Oops.*" Alrin cringed. This was going to take some getting used to.

"I sense there was something else you wished to ask me," said Darius.

"*Yes,*" Alrin answered. "*The Trace. You had it too. I guess my question is…How? And if you can pass the tests—then why aren't you the one destined to find the Dorekstone? You're a lot stronger than I am.*"

Darius sighed. "You still don't get it. The Dinivus brothers were the most powerful beings to have ever walked the earth, this much is certain. But they cared nothing for it. I am but an old man with far too many yesterdays and too few tomorrows. I have nothing to gain in searching for this power other than the power itself. The Trace comes to those who possess what the brothers deemed to be true power—the same power you possess—but the instant you desire it for yourself, the Trace will disappear."

"*Power that I have?*" Alrin asked quite skeptically. "*What power is that?*"

"The answer will come to you in time," Darius answered. "As it came to me. The king has taken much from you, Alrin, but what he has given you in return is something invaluable. A purpose. He gave you a reason to find the Dorekstone for something greater than yourself."

Trishna nudged him in the side, bringing him out of his dreamlike conversation. She was growing more and more impatient by the second.

"*Just one more thing,*" Alrin said. He had been saving this question for the very end. His only hope was that he would get a straight answer. "*How were you able to get past my bracelet?*"

There was a very long pause. "That," Darius answered, "is the question I hoped you would ask..."

Then, suddenly, Alrin felt the wall of his mind return.

"*Darius...Darius!*" But there was no answer. The star was gone. No matter how hard he tried, he couldn't reach him.

Trishna gave him another hard jab to the ribs. "What's going on?" she whispered.

Alrin nodded. He was about to tell her everything, but first he thought of something. It was a terrible suspicion that he couldn't deny any longer. He simply had to know if it was true. Keeping his hand hidden under his shirt, he clasped the bracelet back around his wrist. "*Can you hear me?*" Alrin scried.

"Yes," Trishna whispered. "Now can you tell me what happened?"

Alrin nearly stopped breathing.

He looked at Meldun and was suddenly very afraid of the man he was following. The bracelet wasn't real.

"Who were you talking to?" Trishna asked.

Alrin was deadly stiff. "*Nobody…Don't worry about it.*"

"Tell me!" she barked, this time loud enough that everyone heard.

Alrin looked up to see Meldun watching him very carefully, and that's when the realization hit him. The person Thrain had warned him about—the reason not to trust anyone. It had to be Meldun.

It had always been he. He'd had his hand in everything. From the first moment Alrin saw the dragon on his arm, he should've known. Once a Verindi—always a Verindi.

Meldun glanced back again. "What's on your mind, Son?"

Alrin clenched his jaw and watched his feet as he walked. There was no use holding back. If he was playing into a trap, then he was going to be utterly certain that it was coming. In the bravest voice he could muster, he said, "I was just wondering what Halvdan was planning to sacrifice at the final test."

Meldun stopped walking. "How do you know about the third test?" he asked nervously.

"It's obvious, isn't it? You broke the mirror, Veda solved the wheels in Brugden…so that leaves Halvdan. What's the first rule of magic, remember? All magic requires sacrifice."

Veda turned to him proudly. "It's good to see your training is finally paying off. But to your question, it can't be just anything. You have to sacrifice the thing you cherish the most."

Alrin fell silent. He couldn't help but think that in some way, the sacrifice was meant to be he.

"It is something we will certainly dread to part with," Meldun said, "but a necessary sacrifice nonetheless."

Veda explained that the final test was located near the town of Luleá, only one day away if they could somehow find the correct path through the Ashvale Mountains. Besides the Great Northern Road, which was normally the safest route into the city, apparently there was but a single trail that could lead them through the snowcapped terrain—the treacherous Shimmering Pass.

Finding any other way through was far too dangerous, for the Ashvale mountains were home to the strongest creatures in all of Dalroth. There were ice giants—towering beasts that would use their magic to freeze anyone they came across and smash them into frozen bits. There were blephonite golems, with bodies tougher than diamonds, that could shoot daggerlike shards straight through you and any armor you wore like bolts from an unstoppable crossbow.

These monsters were deadly, yes, but at least you could see them from a long way off. If by some miracle you managed to avoid them, then there were always shadow wraiths, phantom wisps, and mountain specters to contend with. And they could see you long before you saw them—so by then it was far too late.

Needless to say, everyone gave Veda as much time as she needed to find the correct road.

"Your grandfather never led you through the pass?" Halvdan asked nervously, as she studied the mountains with far too much uncertainty.

"Of course not," she snapped. "Can't really maintain a reputation for wisdom leading children through the Shimmering Pass."

Trishna snickered. Veda had an excellent point.

"He did, however, carve a map into a piece of bark and had me trace it every single day for two months to memorize it." She knelt down and, with her eyes closed, began to trace her finger through the dirt. "But I was young and had far fewer Aerean lines then. Those memories are foggy at best. He only brought me to the libraries of Luleá."

"I thought you had to be level seventy to get into the city?" Trishna whispered as Veda continued to draw in the dirt.

"To get into the underwater portion where the guilds are, yes. But not to the libraries."

Alrin felt a ray of excitement. Ever since the symbols of the Trace had been burned into Meldun's table, he had secretly hoped they would be going to Luleá. He'd heard that part of the city was hidden under a lake and had always wanted to see it for himself. To get to the main part of the city, you had to go through huge tunnels with high, arched ceilings made entirely out of glass. He heard that if you looked up through the lake at the right time of day, you could see monstrous shadows circling nearby and then disappearing back into the depths.

But Alrin knew they couldn't risk being seen on the main road, or even in Luleá. With a level requirement that high, they would surely encounter the Verindi at every turn. So the Shimmering Pass was their only option.

"Aha! Here we are." Veda rose, erased what she had drawn, and began walking. "The Trace that marks the third test is said to have been where the Dinivus brothers forged the items of Triem. This land has been scoured for centuries, but none have ever found it. If it was truly where it all began, then it would make perfect sense to be where it all would end. Follow close," she instructed. "I can only imagine that it will be very well hidden—and guarded even better."

The entrance to the pass was nothing more than a large crack through the face of the mountain. It was so narrow, in fact, that everyone had to walk in single file—a reality that no one was particularly fond of because no matter how they arranged it, someone had to be at the back. Every so often the path would fork off in a different direction, and each time Veda would bend down and draw the same memorized line into the dirt.

This continued for hours until, as Veda stopped at another fork and knelt, Meldun finally had enough. "Now I know we're going in circles!" he said, looking toward the sky. "If you're supposed to be leading us north, then why is the sun setting behind us?"

"You can't trust your senses in here," whispered Veda, erasing the map she had drawn and then leading them down another turn. "There are things in these mountains that play tricks on your eyes. You begin to see things that were never there, and miss things that were there all along."

"Can't trust my senses," he huffed. "You're the one drawing a map completely from memory! Who's to say we can trust yours?"

Veda ignored him. "Sometimes it doesn't matter where you are," she said softly. "Only what direction you're going. This way."

Alrin looked as far as he could down the path that Veda hadn't taken, and for a second he could've sworn he saw someone standing in the middle of the path watching them.

Moltrix saw it too. A thin line of fire ignited across her body.

"Uh…Veda?" Alrin stammered. "Did you just see—"

"It's a mountain specter," she interrupted. "Just keep moving."

Alrin looked for it again but couldn't find it. He could've sworn it was a little girl. "They're not any worse than shadow wraiths, are they?"

"Well, they're actually quite similar," she answered. "But unlike wraiths, specters can't actually touch you."

Alrin let out a nervous laugh. "From the way you said it, you made it seem like that was a bad thing."

She glanced at him as if Alrin were missing something obvious. "It is," she said blankly. "They can't touch you, but they can make things appear that aren't there. And, as you can imagine, that can be much worse."

Trishna laughed. "There's no way that can be worse!"

Veda paused at another fork, and once she finished what looked like nothing more than a coin toss in her head, she led them down another narrow split in the mountain. "They can see your deepest memories," she said, "and are masters of finding ways to twist them against you. Once you realize what you're seeing isn't real, they've lured you straight off a cliff or into the den of something that *is* capable of touching you— and won't hesitate to do so. Specters can be very tricky beasts indeed, and very dangerous."

The next fork they came to split in six different directions. As Veda stooped down to draw her path into the sand, Alrin looked around nervously for the specter.

But Trishna found her first.

"*Alrin,*" she gasped. "Look."

When he turned toward the path Trishna was facing, he saw it. A little girl was sitting on the ground and drawing with her finger in the dirt. She had thick black curls draped across her face, and in her hand was a tiny bow. She began to sing a soft little tune, her voice echoing off the canyon walls, and every hair rose on end when Alrin heard what it was.

Under the willow where the grass shines green;
Beyond the veil of golden gleam.
Twinkling bright, shine their candlelight,
To all below in sleepless dream.
Under the willow where the grass shines green…

"Sirena!" Trishna screamed. "It's me…it's Trishna!"

Alrin immediately grabbed her wrist. He knew that at any moment she was going to sprint toward the ghost of her little sister. "Trishna, it's not her," he urged.

"It is too! *Let me go!*" Tears began streaming down her face as she lunged forward. "Sirena!"

Alrin pulled her in against his chest as tight as he could. Trishna wailed and sobbed and pounded against him as hard as she could, but Alrin only held her tighter. "I miss her too," he whispered, rocking back and forth as she fought against him. When he glanced back up, the girl wasn't sitting anymore. She was standing only a few feet away and staring directly at him with the most unnervingly blank expression. Then, as fast as she had appeared, she turned and disappeared through the wall beside her.

Alrin felt Trishna's body go limp as she sank to the ground and buried her face deep into her knees.

Moltrix rushed over and leaned in against her cheek, wiping away a tear with her wet nose, and all Alrin could do was just sit down beside her. He knew nothing he could say would make anything better.

"That's the phoenix in her," Meldun said consolingly. "Always eager to help."

It took everything for Alrin not to explode. He couldn't stand to even hear his voice. Every bone in his body wanted to lash out at him for even trying to comfort her. But by some miracle, he didn't. He needed Meldun to think he still trusted him. If only he could wait a little while longer. Somehow he was going to do whatever it took to control the Trace, and then he would have all the power he needed. Then nothing could stop him—not the king and most certainly not Meldun.

"Maybe we should camp here for the night," Halvdan suggested. "We could all use some rest."

"No," said Veda. "Not in here. Besides, it's not much further now."

"Just wait," Alrin demanded. "One more minute. You go ahead, we'll be right there."

Veda nodded. "We'll be down this way." She pointed down one of the six long corridors. "Don't be too long."

Alrin stared at the ground because he knew that if he let himself look anywhere else, he would be burning holes through Meldun. Once he finally got himself back under control, he turned his attention back to Trishna.

She was resting her chin on her arm and staring down the path where her little sister had been. "Can you tell me who you were talking to now?" she said. She took a deep breath and wiped her face with an arm.

"It was Darius."

"I figured." She sniffled softly. "What did he say?"

Alrin looked up and saw Meldun watching them from around the corner. He knew that his every move was being watched (and that it likely had been this entire time). He reached out and grabbed Trishna by the hand, making it seem as if he were simply comforting her, but also making sure that his bracelet was in clear view.

"*We have to stick together,*" he scried into her mind.

She didn't fully grasp what he was telling her until she noticed that the bracelet was still clasped around his wrist. Her eyes nearly doubled in size, and she came to the same conclusion as he, a lot faster than Alrin had expected. "Meldun?" she whispered.

Alrin nodded and motioned down the path. As she glanced over, she caught Meldun looking at them, then immediately started patting Moltrix on the head.

Trishna rested her head on Alrin's shoulder, which would have meant the world to him if she hadn't been shaking. "But if the bracelet isn't real," she whispered, "then why did it light up all those times?"

It was something Alrin hadn't given much thought to. When he figured out what had likely happened, a sickening sense of betrayal coursed through his body. "*It doesn't take a 99 in magic to light something up,*" he said. "*Illumination is only level thirty-two…That was probably Meldun as well.*"

"Then he's leading us into a trap. We have to tell Halvdan!"

"*We can't,*" Alrin scried.

Trishna looked at him as though he'd lost his mind. "Why not? We can trust Halvdan!"

Alrin shook his head. "*If he knew about the bracelet, then he's in on it. For now we have to pretend like we don't know anything.*" Alrin got to his feet and then reached out to help her up. *"Trust me, I know what I'm doing."*

She looked at his hand but didn't take it. "Whether you like it or not, Alrin Turner," she whispered as she got to her feet and brushed off her pants, "those ensignis are changing you."

Alrin turned after her with something very clever to say, but it vanished as soon as his he saw what surrounded them.

Everything was different. Each path had changed entirely and they now stretched ahead for miles in every direction, each perfectly identical to the next. But the worst part was that someone was walking down one of the paths directly toward them.

"Alrin...?" Trishna gasped and grabbed his arm. "Is that...?"

Alrin stared at the approaching figure, and he couldn't believe what he was seeing. It had to be another specter, or at least he prayed that it was.

It was a man covered from head to toe in black, razor-sharp armor. The armor was dented and gashed and there was a symbol of a black dragon across the breastplate. The only parts of the body left uncovered were the face, which pointed toward the ground, and the right hand.

The hand would tell Alrin everything. He wouldn't know for sure until he saw the ensignis—but before he caught a glimpse of them, Trishna pointed him down a different path.

It was he again—the same warrior, equally fierce and frightening, approaching from a different direction.

Then there was another. Then another. They whirled around to find that each of the six corridors held the same dark nightmare. It was Trishna who saw the ensignis first. "They're all ninety-nines," she muttered.

Alrin could feel her try to move behind him, but it was no use. They were completely surrounded.

He couldn't take his eyes off the ensignis. Seeing three 99s next to one another was even more unnatural than he'd always imagined it would be.

"Is it him?" Trishna asked. "Is it Abaddon?"

"No…" Alrin trembled. He wasn't sure why, but he felt he would immediately have known if it were Abaddon. That brand of evil would be easy to recognize. This was someone different entirely.

"No…," he said again. The name hurt to even say out loud. "It's Thrain…"

CHAPTER TWENTY-ONE

STAY

Alrin searched every lesson Halvdan had ever given him. Every spell on Glade's list flashed through his mind as perfectly as if it were there in front of him, but nothing he'd learned had ever prepared him for this. All he knew for certain was that specters were masters of pitting your deepest fears against you, so it surprised him to see the image of his brother barreling toward him instead of the king. He would've guessed that his greatest fear, the one thing that the specters could've forced him to confront before he was ready, would be the man responsible for making him face everything he feared most. After all, it was Abaddon who had catapulted him into this world of power. It was Abaddon who had made him not only peek over the fence of the unknown, but jump over blindly, forcing him to abandon everything about himself that he recognized.

Yet it wasn't Abaddon that he feared the most. And even the specters saw that. There was something much deeper, something that he'd buried too far down to even admit to himself. From the first night he'd dreamed of seeing Thrain through the iron bars of the Verindi's cage, it had been steadily growing inside. Even after the countless sleepless nights, the constant replaying of it in his mind, it took staring at it face-to-face for him to realize that what he feared the most had never been Abaddon. It had been—after all he'd gone through, after everything he'd done in order to reach his brother—that there wouldn't be anything left to save by the time Alrin found him.

The person standing in front of him was nothing more than an empty shell. Blind obedience dancing at the ends of strings of an invisible puppeteer. Yet no matter how completely unrecognizable the rest of him looked, it was Thrain's ensignis that made it feel as if this wasn't his brother.

"What do we do?" Trishna whispered.

"I don't know," Alrin said. "Did Halvdan ever teach you how to dispel a specter?"

"No," she uttered hopelessly.

"All I know is that they will try and lure us into danger. If we just figure out which way they want us to go, we simply go the opposite way."

"OK, but which way is that?" Trishna said. "There's no way out!"

And she was right. The specters didn't seem to be luring them anywhere. Alrin looked down each of the paths, searching for anything that would make it seem as if he and Trishna were being pulled in one direction or another. Maybe they could at least rule one direction out. Surely one of the paths was more enticing than the others. Maybe something about Thrain was different, maybe one of deep gashes across his body wasn't there, or, if Alrin managed to look hard enough, he might find even the smallest glimmer of hope that a piece of his brother remained.

But there was nothing. All the specters and every mirage they'd created were identical. They weren't luring them anywhere. They stood there, cold, emotionless, unflinching, unblinking, glaring them down from every direction. It almost seemed as though they didn't want the two of them to move.

Alrin gasped when the idea hit him. Maybe that was it.

"Which way did everyone go?" he asked frantically.

Trishna raised an arm and pointed down one of the paths. "That way, I think."

"You have to be sure!"

Trishna paused and thought it over very carefully. "Yes, I'm sure of it," she said. "We came from over there, so they had to have gone that way," she said, continuing to point down the path.

"Good," Alrin muttered. "You may want to close your eyes for this."

"Close my eyes for what?" she asked, but before she had the chance to object, Alrin wrapped his arms around her and forced her down the path she'd chosen. "*No, wait!*" she pleaded, digging her heels into the dirt, but it was useless. Trishna's strength ensigni was no match for his.

Alrin continued to fight her toward the hollow, locust-shell remnants of his brother, and not more than a few steps away, the specter began to shift into something else. It rose high into the air and every inch molded itself into black, pearlescent scales. It breathed in deep, fanning its perfectly impassible armor over its body like daggerlike reeds bowing in the wind, as a gurgling breath prepared to engulf them in flames.

"It's not real," Alrin whispered again and again to himself. "It's not real." But no matter how much he wanted to stop, he simply couldn't. The urge to run in the opposite direction only further confirmed he was right.

Alrin closed his eyes and held his breath, wrapping his arms around Trishna as if he were about to carry her through a burning building. As soon as they barged through the dragon, the specter disappeared and the mirage it had created dissolved with it. They looked up to see Halvdan, Veda, and Meldun, all with the same mix of relief and terror spread across their faces. All together, almost as if in slow motion, the three of them lunged toward Trishna and Alrin and yanked them out of the way. Not a moment later, a large portion of the mountain above them folded in on itself like the crest of a wave and crashed to the ground right where they had been standing.

The ground shook beneath their feet as clouds of dust rose into the air and filled their lungs. Alrin coughed and gagged and tasted blood in the back of his throat as fragments of rock rained against his back like a hailstorm. But the only thing running through his mind, as he held his arms between Trishna and the hurtling debris, was whether he was managing to block enough of it from reaching her.

Once enough of the dust had settled, Alrin saw Trishna peek back through the cloud of dust covering her face. "See. I told you I wouldn't let anything happen to you," he said, smiling, trying his best to pretend that his back wasn't throbbing as much as it actually was. Apparently his arms failed to notice they were out of danger, because they were still bolstered resolutely against either wall beside her head.

He could still barely see her, but he felt the warmth of her body move in closer and he instantly forgot all about how close they'd just come to death. She whispered a shaky "Thank you," and then, after brushing her hand gently across his face to move the hair away from his eyes, she reached up and pressed her lips against his.

"I'm sorry...I couldn't get through," Halvdan stammered, almost as though he felt responsible for what had just happened. "They were too strong."

Veda silenced him. "The rockslide could've made more of the mountain unstable," she said, coughing through every other word. "We need to move quickly." Everyone filed in line behind her and followed her away from the settling debris. All except for Meldun, who continued to stare deadpan, his face pale and beading with sweat.

"What's wrong?" Alrin said as he passed. "Looks like you've seen a ghost."

Seeing the look of worry across Meldun's face made his blood boil. He had spent every ounce of patience on his father's perfectly rehearsed act of parental concern, and he was having a difficult time not letting it show. He knew that this uncharacteristic burst of courage had only been fueled by the swelling invulnerability from Trishna's kiss, so he quickly wrestled the anger back down before anything else could slip. He looked down at his bracelet and reminded himself of what Meldun was capable of. Somehow he was going to have to find a way to play the part of clueless just awhile longer.

The mountain pass continued for several more miles in the same incoherent weblike way, Veda drawing her map in the sand at every fork, until finally they turned and saw trees up ahead. Far off in the distance, Alrin could hear birds and crickets playing their welcoming songs, which sounded more like a symphony to him because they likely meant one spectacular thing…running water.

They pushed through several rows of pines and thick brush until they eventually gave way to a large, open clearing. Walls of stone rose up behind the trees in every direction, creating a perfect circular cutout in the mountain. Roaring waterfalls flowed over the ledge and down into crystal-clear pools bordering the dizzyingly high walls of rock. Alrin felt a wave of nostalgia, as if he were back at Batara again, staring up the walls of the cliff where he had somehow miraculously survived, and he knew at once that Veda was right. It made perfect sense that where it had all begun would be where it all ended.

Alrin wanted nothing more than to rush over and plunge his head into one of the sparkling pools. He could almost feel the coolness of the water soothe the constant ache at the back of his throat. He pictured himself lying at the water's edge, drinking as much as his stomach could possibly hold and then flopping over like a fish and basking in the sun until he fell asleep. Even Moltrix, who hated water nearly as much as she hated the dark, had all but dived in, which made a sound like cracking an egg into a red-hot skillet as the water rushed over her scorching body. But Alrin didn't budge. He was still much too nervous and too nauseated to think about anything other than what his eyes had locked on in front of him—a narrow path leading to a small island at the center of the clearing.

"Is it a dead end?" he asked no one in particular. He already knew the answer, of course, but his nerves were simply begging for someone to break the silence. He could feel each butterfly slowly wake inside his stomach, each one bringing a new wave of nausea with it. He had known the instant he saw the trees up ahead—this was the location of the final test.

At the center of the island were three stone pillars arranged in a triangle, and inside them was a small area of sand raised up about a foot taller than the grass surrounding it. As Alrin looked closer at the pillars, he saw exactly what he'd expected to see. Halvdan approached them first, raising a hand and brushing it over the Trace and the cryptic markings of the ancient language. "What do they say?" he asked cautiously.

Veda circled them, studying each one as silently and intently as she would one of the many books that she kept in her mind, and once she made it back to where she'd begun, she confirmed what they needed to do. "'True power is bought with sacrifice,'" she said quietly.

Halvdan was first to step toward the triangle, and when he did, Moltrix immediately jumped to her feet and started to follow him in.

"No, girl," he said firmly. "Stay."

She let out a very annoyed grunt but obediently plopped back down to the ground. Alrin thought that he actually saw her roll her eyes for a second, and enjoyed the possibility that she may have learned that from him.

"Whatever is inside the triangle once he leaves is what will be sacrificed," Veda explained. "No one can follow him in."

Alrin looked at the sand inside the triangle and realized he'd seen that color before. It was the same lifeless hue that had been left after the king's curse had drained every last bit of life from their cabin. And from the looks of the small mountain inside the pillars, there was no telling how many sacrifices had already been paid. He stared at each pile of whatever had entered before them, and he prayed that none of them had been Thrain—and then prayed even harder that he wasn't about to be one.

"I'm starting to think someone has a thing for triangles," Alrin scryed Trishna flirtatiously, and unsurprisingly, she didn't respond. She didn't have to; Alrin rolled his eyes for her. Even on a normal day, Alrin usually came across as awkward or uncomfortable when he tried to talk to her, but ever since the unsuspected kiss, he'd become a bumbling calamity of gracelessness. It felt as if he were learning to speak all over again. He was just glad they didn't have to go much farther, because it was very likely that he would've quite literally tripped over himself just walking beside her. He still could feel the soft tingle where her lips had pressed against his, the absence of them now even stronger than the sensation when they'd actually been there, and he couldn't stop his mind from overthinking everything she was doing. Every look held endless meanings that he couldn't interpret; every consecutive moment of silence was filled with the increasing torment of wondering what she was thinking. She was a book of a thousand languages, and Alrin was illiterate in all of them.

Of course her silence might simply be due to the fact that his being able to scry someone while still wearing the bracelet was a glaring reminder that they were in very real danger, but that explanation was only number four of seventy-two, and his mind never slowed down long enough to land on it.

"You're sure this will work?" Halvdan suddenly asked, interrupting Alrin during *She probably hates me and is never going to speak to me again,* of which his mind had firmly convinced itself at this point.

"It has to," Veda answered. "There is nothing stronger."

That's when Halvdan reached into his pocket and took out the Dinivus stone. When Alrin saw it, he let out a sigh of relief so loud that he was sure everyone must've heard it.

Great, now she thinks I'm a coward. His mind raced again. *Well, she's probably right…Maybe I should actually do something about it for once. What if I entered the pillars first to see what happens? That just might…Yes, that would do it.* But thankfully, seeing Halvdan move closer silenced the voices in his head before Alrin had fully convinced himself that the only way to redeem a slightly audible exhalation was to sacrifice himself and become a lifeless, yet courageous, pile of sand.

Before stepping into the triangle, Halvdan looked back one last time to make sure Moltrix wasn't behind him, then, with a brisk turn, extended a foot cautiously beyond the pillars and pressed it into the sand. He wasted very little time, meandering around several knee-high mounds, which made Alrin grimace once he allowed himself to dwell on their implications too long, and knelt down to place the stone directly at the center of the triangle. He stayed there for a while, staring down at it as it rested in the sand. Alrin couldn't tell whether he was having second thoughts or simply saying good-bye, but it was obvious that parting with the stone was the hardest thing Halvdan had ever had to do.

What a waste, Alrin thought to himself. It was all just a distraction. Though he didn't have the slightest idea how to pass the test—the *real* test—he knew it would mean leaving behind something more than just some dumb rock. Of course, to everyone else standing there, the Dinivus stone was more than enough—probably even too much.

But even with its unlimited power, it still wouldn't be enough to pass the real test, and Alrin knew it. Halvdan's only reason for parting with it was to find the Dorekstone and wield even more power, so if anything, it felt hypocritical. Whatever sacrifice would be worthy in the eyes of the Dinivus brothers, this most certainly wasn't going to be it.

Eventually Halvdan stood up, brushed the sand off his knees, and then slowly began to walk back toward the others. Before he reached the pillars, however, he stopped and looked back up at something behind Alrin. Alrin followed his gaze just in time to see a shadowy figure duck back behind a tree, and not a second later, it emerged again as something else.

The realization hit everyone at exactly the same time: a specter had followed them in.

But it didn't turn into a person this time. It wasn't Sirena, or Thrain, or a hellish, fiery dragon, or anything that would strike fear into the heart of anyone, for that matter. Of all things, it shrank into a tiny bird and went about hopping along the ground, stopping every so often to scratch its twiglike feet in the dirt as if it was searching for something to eat.

Everyone stopped and stared, curious as to whom it was trying to lure into danger…everyone but Halvdan.

"*Moltrix,*" Halvdan screamed. "*Stay!*" He raised his hands in the air, motioning for her to sit, but of course she didn't listen. Her rear end rose excitedly into the air, and her fiery tails began flicking back and forth.

The bird suddenly rose into the air and made a hard dive toward her, narrowly escaping her grasp; then, at the exact same time that Alrin realized what the specter was about to do, it headed straight toward the pillars. Halvdan moved faster than he ever had before. "*Stay!*" he screamed again, sprinting as fast as he could to get out of the triangle before Moltrix got lured in.

The bird continued to flutter teasingly out of Moltrix's reach, flying high enough to stay out of her grasp, but low enough to keep her blissfully entertained. Halvdan reached the edge first, but just as he tried to dash out of it, his body slammed into an invisible wall and he stumbled back, dazed by the incredible impact. He looked back to the stone, which still rested perfectly at the center of the triangle, and as he turned back again, Alrin saw the painful realization of what he'd known all along spread over his face.

The test was going to require more than just a stone.

Moltrix paused and sank low to the ground, wagging her body stalkingly from side to side as she watched the bird fly straight into the triangle and land directly on top of the Dinivus stone. A thin curl of a grin appeared over one side of her whiskers and her body locked into position like the bolt of a crossbow.

"Moltrix," Halvdan begged again. "Stay…"

But it was no use. In a single explosive jolt, she soared straight over Halvdan and landed right on top of the bird just as it vanished into thin air. She lifted her paws excitedly, but after seeing the bird was gone, began to pace curiously back and forth trying her best to find it again. It wasn't until she glanced up at Halvdan that she finally stopped.

Tears were streaming down his face. His knees dropped into the sand and he wrapped his arms around her, tightly grasping the fur over her back. Moltrix immediately knew something was wrong but she didn't have a clue as to what it could be. Once Halvdan finally relaxed his grip, her big orange eyes darted back and forth against his, searching for some way to help him.

Tears continued pouring down his cheeks and into his scraggly gray beard as he brushed his thumb through the hair on top of her head. Moltrix leaned in and gave him a big lick across his face.

"Stay," Halvdan whispered.

Alrin suddenly felt a drop of rain hit his arm. *Of course it's starting to rain,* he thought to himself, annoyed at how terribly clichéd the weather was behaving, but as he turned up toward a cloudless sky, he noticed the tears running down his own face. He watched Halvdan reach down and pick up the mana stone lying on the ground and turn to leave. "Stay," he whispered again.

Without a bird to chase this time, Moltrix quickly obeyed. She sank down into the sand, twisted her head curiously to the side, and whimpered loudly, but didn't follow him.

Halvdan continued walking, each step more painful than the last, until finally he stood at the edge of the sand. But even then he didn't look back. He slowly reached his foot out to make sure the boundary was gone, and with the last step across, Moltrix turned as solid as a statue. She didn't blink…her sides stopped expanding with every breath…her flame was gone. Then, very slowly, she turned the same lifeless hue as the ground around her and crumbled away until she was nothing more than another pile of sand among the rest.

Halvdan stared off into the distance, his eyes welling with what the world thought to be weakness. Without a word he walked over to Veda and extended his arm…and in his hand was the final piece of the Triclave.

"*Nooo!*" Trishna yelled, still staring at the ground inside the triangle. "She'll come back! It's the phoenix in her, remember? Just wait…she'll come back!" She turned and looked at

Halvdan and then to Meldun, who had to clench his jaw in order to maintain his unflinching stoicism. He looked to the ground and subtly shook his head.

Veda reached an arm out and rested it on Halvdan's arm. "The stone wasn't enough," she said, trying to console him, "one of us would've had to…"

"I know," Halvdan interrupted, trying to stop his words from shaking as badly as his jaw. He glared up at her almost as though everything were her fault. "Let's get this over with."

Meldun and Veda reached into their pockets and took out their pieces of the key, and together they walked over to Alrin. "Hold out your hand, Alrin," said Veda blankly.

Alrin was very confused as to why she would think he had any part to play, but when he finally did as she asked, they dropped their pieces of the Triclave into his hand. "What do I do?" he started to ask, staring down at the strange hunks of metal, but as he did, the pieces started to move. Tiny interlocking pieces began flipping and twisting together as in one of Jorund's intricate puzzle boxes, and it felt so much like a bug squirming in his hand that he nearly dropped the pieces to the ground. Once each piece had finally clicked into place, an intricate key lay in the palm of his hand.

"It is time," said Veda. "The legend says that the Dorekstone will only be revealed when the one who is worthy rises to possess it. That person is you."

Meldun suddenly raised his arm and placed it on Alrin's shoulder. "This is it, Son. It's time to claim your destiny."

Alrin looked at each of them and saw nothing but anticipation in their eyes. Even Halvdan, who had just lost one of his dearest friends in the world, looked as though he were poised at a starting line, ready to charge the stone as soon as it revealed itself.

So this is it, Alrin thought to himself. This was what they all were waiting for. This was the reason they'd brought him along in the first place—so that he could reveal the stone and they could have it all for themselves.

"This is your only chance to save Thrain and your mother," Veda said impatiently.

Alrin gripped his hand tightly around the key. There was no use holding back now. He took a deep breath and reminded himself of the only thing he knew to be true…*Nothing but distractions.*

"It's not going to work," Alrin whispered as he looked up at them and slowly opened his hand. As his fingers uncurled themselves from the strange metal, the key withered into dust and blew away into the breeze. "I haven't passed the third test yet."

"*Noooo!*" Halvdan cried. "What have you done?"

Before anyone else could say a word, a deep and terrible laugh came from behind them.

At first Alrin thought it was another specter. Standing there, staring blankly ahead of him in the same shredded armor as before, was his brother, the three 99s clearly visible across his hand. But the laugh wasn't coming from him. It came from someone behind him—and it was the same voice Alrin had heard flowing through the Verindi camp countless times in his nightmare. The same voice that would command Thrain to engulf Alrin in flames just before he woke up drenched in sweat. The figure wore black armor that glistened like thousands of sharp, tiny scales. A black helmet covered his face and muffled his evil laugh, but even from across the clearing,

Alrin could see his eyes, deep and piercing, staring daggers straight through him. Everything about him demanded fear.

Meldun's voice cracked as it formed the words Alrin had wished never to hear again.

"King Abaddon…"

CHAPTER TWENTY-TWO

HIDDEN POWER

Y ou've done well," said the king, staring at Alrin. "You would've made an excellent Verindi." He slowly removed his helmet and revealed his face. "Perhaps in another life," he muttered.

He looked just as Alrin had always imagined he would; eyes sharp blue and beard black as night. He looked more like one of the wraiths Alrin had encountered in Brugden than an actual man. "Our infamous light of distinction," he said, a lifeless grin playing at the corner of his mouth. "I've been watching you for quite some time, Alrin Turner." He peered down at the helmet in his hand. "I knew it was wise to let you live."

It was the helmet—the last item of Triem. The king had had his eyes on him every step of the way.

"Of course, you never would have made it this far on your own," he said, turning his gaze to those standing next to him. "We have someone else to thank for that, now don't we?"

Alrin closed his eyes and waited for Meldun to say the words that he'd anticipated for quite some time. That he had been behind everything; that every word from his lips and every act of devotion had been for the dragon on his arm, and not to protect his own flesh and blood. Once a Verindi—always a Verindi.

But what came from him instead was something far different.

"If you knew I took the Talismans, then why let me live all this time?" he asked.

Another deep and terrible laugh rumbled off the canyon walls. "Because you are so perfectly oblivious," the king roared. "He was so convinced you were the one betraying him that it kept him blind to those who actually were. I barely had to lift a finger to make you look like his enemy."

Meldun suddenly seemed even more frightened than Alrin did.

"Although…I must give credit where it is due. The person we should really be thanking is someone standing right beside you," the king smiled. "If it wasn't for their idea to switch out the bracelet in the very beginning, you indeed would've been dead a long time ago." The king eerily reached out his hand, as though he were welcoming home a long-lost child, and said, "Come forward, my brilliant web-weaver."

Alrin heard someone behind him gradually start to move, and he suddenly couldn't breathe. It was as if something had burst inside him and every last bit of air was rushing to escape. He opened his eyes just as the blue tattoos running down Veda's hand rested in the king's hand, and at that exact moment, the Verindi dragon appeared over her forearm.

"Wear it proudly," said the king. "You've earned it."

"No…" Meldun shuddered. "What about your grandfather? Abaddon murdered him!"

As Veda turned back around, it was as if a mask had been lifted. Her eyes went narrow and dead as if there were no longer a person behind them. "Not everyone can embrace death so easily," she said. "My grandfather was given the same choice as I, but instead of power, he chose a different path."

Meldun's fists shook wildly as he glanced down at Alrin's bracelet. "It's not possible. You never had the chance to switch it," he whispered. "I didn't give it to you." Meldun's eyes went to Halvdan, who was doing everything in his power to avoid making eye contact with him. "I gave it to…"

The same feeling that Alrin had had when Halvdan broke into his memory suddenly returned. "No…," Alrin whispered. "Not you…"

Halvdan continued to stare nervously at the ground, but in barely a whisper, he said, "Forgive me, Alrin. He knew everything. Even before you told me about Batara, he already knew."

Alrin stumbled back, tore off the bracelet, and threw it to the ground. "It can't be," he stammered. "What about Iarund's memory…and the Verindi camp? He didn't even know about Everglen until then. What about Veda's son?"

As he turned to Veda, the monster within her continued to emerge. A terrifying grin appeared across her face as though she eagerly anticipated the amount of pain she was about to inflict. "I never had a son," she said, smiling. "You saw what you were supposed to see…exactly what Abaddon wanted you to see. Don't tell me you honestly believed there was a chance to hide from the most powerful being to ever live," she hissed. "Let me guess, I suppose you thought the memory of your mother wiping the hair out of your eyes and kissing your forehead was actually protecting you from someone breaking into your Void, didn't you?" Her laugh grew even louder. "I was listening to every thought you ever had. Every night when you lay awake thinking of all the ways you were going to get your brother back. You even figured out the bracelet was fake and you still did nothing! Who did you think was lighting up those useless rocks around your wrist each time? Meldun? You're even more pathetic than he is."

"Coward," said Meldun. "Both of you!"

Halvdan continued staring at the ground, too disgusted with himself to even look up.

"So," Abaddon interrupted. "I will give you the same choice I gave them. "Swear yourself as a Verindi once more, or join so many of those who have gone before you," he said, motioning toward the sand inside the triangle.

At first it seemed as if Meldun didn't hear him. He continued to stare back and forth between Halvdan and Veda as if he were expecting to wake up at any moment, a fervent delusion Alrin most certainly shared. "You're only a man," Meldun finally whispered. "You can't live forever."

The king chuckled. "That's the other thing…" He turned and raised his hand toward Veda, and the Soul Gem rose from her pocket and floated straight toward him. "You were wondering who had struck so much fear into the wraiths of Brugden?" he said as the gem landed in the palm of his hand. Then, with the slightest effort, he shattered it in his grip and tendrils of light shot up his arm and into his neck. "The wraiths are among the few remaining who know me by my true name. One that has long been forgotten."

A wave of terror spread over Meldun as he opened his mouth to utter the name that Alrin had heard only once or twice before. The name that could rarely be spoken without the mention of things equally impossible.

"Beswic..."

"I've waited an eternity for this." The king smiled. "Not killing me when they had the chance was the most foolish thing the Dinivus brothers could have done. You have no idea what I've sacrificed. How many thousands of wraiths I've hunted down to see this day." He began to pace slowly back and forth behind Thrain, who was still staring straight ahead of him like a statue. "Although...I suppose I was equally foolish back then. I only wanted what was rightfully mine—to be honored and feared just as they were." He suddenly raised an arm and struck Thrain hard across the face with the back of his hand. A thin red line appeared across Thrain's cheek and dripped from his chin, but he still didn't budge. It was as if even pain had been beaten out of him. "Why I wasted so much time wanting to be praised by something so insignificant, I'll never know." He turned his attention back to Meldun. "Last chance, Meldun. What will it be?"

"Let Thrain and Alrin go," Meldun said, "and I'll do whatever you want."

Another deep laugh echoed through the clearing. "You think I went to all this trouble just to let them go? No, even a hundred of your lives aren't worth a single one of theirs."

Meldun lowered his head. In whatever way, his mind had been made up. He turned and looked at Alrin out of the corner of his eye, and suddenly his voice entered Alrin's mind. "*I wasn't honest before,*" he scried, "*when I told you why I left. I think I even convinced myself it was to protect you and Thrain, but I knew in my heart that wasn't true.*" His eyes grew very heavy. "*I hoped that in searching for power, my awareness of it would begin to fade, but it seems that the emptiness inside is even larger than when it first began. And now, even in all my strength, you've achieved a power I could never reach. Every day since the day I left has been filled with regret, but the one thing I regret the most is never having the strength to say this until now...*" His eyes welled up with pain. "*I am proud to call you my Son.*"

"What will it be?" the king roared again.

As Meldun looked back up, the fierceness in his eyes made it abundantly clear that if Abaddon wanted to get to Alrin, he was going to have to go through him.

The evil grin on the king's face returned. "So be it," he said softly. He turned his gaze to Thrain, who instantly winced as his arm slowly began to move. It looked as if with every movement he made, he was pleading with his own body to fight what the king was forcing him to do, but inch by inch his arm slowly rose toward Meldun.

"I'm so sorry, Thrain," Meldun whispered, and after a few moments of Meldun's looking at him, the bracelet around Thrain's wrist lit up.

A sadistic grin fought its way onto Thrain's face as he opened his mouth to speak. "It's too late," he muttered, but instead of his voice coming out, it was the king's. "Thrain is mine!" he roared, as a beam of light burst from his hand and shot straight through Meldun's chest.

Alrin dove just in time to push Trishna out of the way as the beam shot past, narrowly missing them both, and exploded into the wall behind them. Deafening sounds of splitting rock continued through the mountains for miles, echoing off the walls around them, before the beam of light finally dissipated.

When Alrin turned back, Meldun had collapsed to the ground, and Thrain's face turned blank again.

That's when Alrin felt it. The same feeling as when you can't tell whether you're sleeping or awake. As much as he fought against it, the flickering Trace appeared over his hand, lighting up the clearing around him like bolts of lightning.

With blurry, tear-soaked eyes, Alrin turned to his brother and knew that his greatest fear had come true. He suddenly wished he'd just died at the very beginning. He wished the Trace had never saved him in the first place. Everyone he had ever cared about would be much better off if he had—Thrain most of all. Alrin barely recognized him now. Even after having been forced to kill his own father, he seemed completely unaffected, as if he were nothing more than a puppet taken from a shelf only to be returned once the king was finished with him. Everything that had once made Thrain Alrin's brother was gone.

Everything inside Alrin burned as his power pleaded to come out. It was on the tips of his fingertips and crawling under his skin. It felt as if the power were guarded by nothing more than a bubble, and if he but simply reached out and touched it, he would be granted the unlimited power of the Dinivus brothers.

"Good," the king blurted out. "Let it consume you."

"No," Alrin cried. He could tell that this was exactly what the king wanted. "This was your plan all along, wasn't it? You've seen each time the Trace has appeared. You needed me to summon the Dorekstone, and you knew I wouldn't be able to control it. That's why you took Thrain instead of me. You knew I needed a reason to pass the tests and summon it for something other than myself."

The king glared at him with his empty blue eyes. "Too clever for your own good," he said, raising his arm toward him and clenching his fist.

Suddenly Alrin felt his entire body lock into place and lift high into the air.

"Perhaps we trained him a little too well," the king said, looking over at Veda. "Not to worry, though. This changes nothing."

Alrin gasped for breath as the king's magic gripped him even tighter, and just before his eyes started to darken, the king released him and he toppled to the ground. Alrin clenched the ground between his fingers. He didn't even need to open his eyes to know where the king had dropped him. Inside the pillars.

When he finally found the courage to open his eyes, the first thing he saw was the pile of sand where Moltrix had been moments before. He scrambled away from it, but didn't get more than a few feet before his back slammed into the invisible wall.

The king laughed again. "Not so fast. You still haven't passed the final test, remember?"

"There's nothing left to sacrifice." Alrin trembled. "You've already taken everything."

"Oh, I strongly disagree." He turned his head to Trishna, and not a second later she was grasping her neck, kicking and screaming through the air until she fell to the ground right next to Thrain. "I'm a gracious king," he said, walking up to them and placing a hand on each of their shoulders. "I'll even let you choose. He leaned in closer to Trishna, nearly pressing his cheek against hers. "The girl that you've loved since the very first time you laid eyes upon her. The girl who brushes the hair out of your eyes the same way your mother did."

Trishna lowered her head to the ground, but the king raised it again, forcing her to look at him. "Or," he said, turning to Thrain, "the one you would travel the entire world to save. And ironically, the one who would burn an entire city in order to save you."

"That wasn't him," Alrin said, gritting his teeth. "Thrain wouldn't hurt anyone."

"What...you mean Brugden?" The king chuckled. "He did that all by himself—murdered all those innocent woman and children, and I didn't even have to lift a finger."

"That's a lie," Alrin snapped.

The king's eyes turned even darker. "Oh, I wouldn't lie about this. Not when the truth is far too great. You see, I used to think the best way to control someone was to torture them until they broke. Not too pleasant, I admit, but effective nevertheless. Then, one day, I stumbled upon something even better. Do you know what that thing was?" He looked at Alrin as if he actually expected a guess. "It was love," he said viciously. "You see, controlling your brother was easy; I simply gave him a choice. Kill all those people...or...I kill you instead. After that, I just had to sit back and watch him destroy every piece of himself until there was nothing left to fight me."

"You're a monster," Alrin cried. "You can never force me to choose."

The king let out a heavy sigh. "I suppose you're right," he said, "So I suppose I'll choose for you." He raised his hand above Trishna's head, and with a snap of his fingers turned her to stone.

Blades of pain coursed throughout Alrin's body as the Trace flickered over his ensignis.

"You're making this harder than it needs to be, Alrin. You've held back your entire life, and look where it's gotten you. Just let go already. Give in just this once, and it will all go away."

Alrin's body shook as he struggled to hold on. Waves of energy pulsed over him and spread across the sand and up the pillars. He focused on the ground as tears dropped from his eyes and wetted the sand clenched in his shaking hands. But he was forced to look up when he heard footsteps enter the pillars and sink deep into the sand next to him. Then his heart sank even further when he saw whom they belonged to.

"You should feel honored," said the king, as Thrain crept deeper into the sand and stood over him. "You're quite literally standing on the sacrifice of thousands before you. Let it go, Alrin, and I will release everyone I've cursed—Aurora, Trishna…and even Thrain. But if you don't, they will all be lost."

As Alrin searched for an answer, the only words that echoed in his mind were those that Darius Glade had once given him. "'Stay true to the path that lays ahead, for it is far too narrow to stray…,'" he whispered.

The king shook his head. "Useless words from a useless man," he said, disappointed. "There's no telling how many times I've dreamed of this. And yet it feels like something is missing. I had always hoped a lot more people would be around to see me pry those pathetic brothers out of that stone." The king shot him a terrible look. "Speaking of dreams," he said snidely, "you're going to love how it ends." He raised his arm high into the air and then smiled as if he'd been waiting centuries for what he was about to do. A strong breeze floated into the clearing, and with it came a terrifying whisper.

"*This is why you were chosen…,*" came his voice over the wind.

The words ignited Thrain into an obedient fury and he looked at Alrin with pure malice in his eyes.

It was the final piece of his nightmare—and this time there was no waking from it. This cage was real.

"Thrain, it's me!" Alrin cried, half expecting to see his brother turn into a dragon and engulf him in flames. But what happened instead was something far worse. He opened his mouth and the same spell that Halvdan had used against the wraiths roared out of it.

"*ADHUC MORTEM!*"

By the time Alrin recognized the words, it was already too late. He shielded his face with an arm just as the magic struck him, and immediately he felt his energy leaving him.

"Now or never," the king yelled. "Release it."

With each passing second, he felt himself growing weaker. It was like being in his cabin all over again in the grips of the Myoclonus curse. It felt as if the spell had punctured a hole, and, like grains of sand, his energy was pouring out of it. He dropped to his knees, breathing heavily, and just as his vision started to fade, Halvdan's voice entered his mind.

"*Alrin! CATCH!*"

Alrin reached out and snatched whatever Halvdan had thrown him out of the air.

"*Noooo!*" roared the king. "*You fool!*"

Before Alrin even knew what was happening, Halvdan had lifted high into the air and was launched the entire length of the clearing. His body slammed against the far wall and then crumpled to the ground and laid rigidly still.

For a moment Alrin felt a glimmer of hope as he opened his hand to find the Dinivus stone. He felt his power returning in waves, but as the magic shooting from Thrain's outstretched hand started to fade, whatever hope he'd originally felt quickly faded with it.

The stone was useless, he realized. Even with unlimited magic, the spell couldn't be broken. One of them still had to die.

To Alrin, it had never been a choice…He opened his hand and the Dinivus stone rolled from his fingers and dropped to the ground.

As he felt the grains of sand start to pour out once more, he reached into the Void and found a memory of Everglen. He pictured himself sitting on the old moss-covered tree stump next to their cabin, breathing in the serenity of the mountains as he had nearly every morning growing up. It was nearly spring now. Creatures of every kind would soon return to the valley and begin nosing their way through the snow for the first sprouts of fresh grass. The lake beside their cabin would melt any day now to once again paint the Tatra mountain backdrop atop its still, glassy canvas. The snowcapped peaks were already starting to shed their thick winter blankets, and the Narew River would be born once again to bring new life back to the valley.

But it wasn't home anymore. There was nothing left of home to return to. Home was before he'd ever cared about his ensignis…before power had sunk its teeth into every part of his life and robbed him of everyone he held dear. The home he knew had disappeared long ago.

He opened his eyes and dropped to his knees as the beam of light disappeared from Thrain's outstretched hand. It felt as if a door closed inside him, and all at once there was nothing left. But as the darkness closed in around him, Alrin looked up to his brother and could see tears pouring from his face.

Somehow, despite the king's attempt to bury it under countless layers of darkness, something must have remained. Somewhere deep down, a tiny piece of him must have been able to survive. Thrain shook violently as everything in him struggled to move. Very slowly, as if every inch he moved broke another bone in his body, he forced his hand over his armor and, with a single finger, lightly tapped against it.

Thump-thump. Thump-thump.

It always came in twos. Like a heartbeat.

It was the constant reminder that he was still there. Still awake.

And that's when Alrin felt it—the last grain of sand.

CHAPTER TWENTY-THREE

THE DOREKSTONE

Falling.

The last thing he remembered was falling.

They say your life flashes before your eyes when you die. You look for the light at the end of the tunnel, or you reach out and a loved one grabs you by the arm and pulls you out of the darkness.

But there was no tunnel. No light.

It couldn't even be called darkness, for darkness in itself is still something. This was emptiness.

It was bigger than boundless and farther than forever. There was no beginning, no end, no point of reference, or unit of measure. It just was. Then out of the emptiness came a voice. And with it unapproachable light.

"*Well done, faithful warrior.*" It was one voice—and three voices. Just as the three triangles of the Trace overlapped to form one line, each voice was perfectly aligned and indistinguishable from the next. With each word they spoke, light wrapped around him in brilliant bursts of color. It was like being born in a sunrise or bathing in the stars. Every word awakened truth and unmistakable clarity. The exact moment that the question entered his mind, he already knew the answer.

"You're the Dinivus brothers, aren't you? Gondor...Oswyn...and Draegan."

"*I am,*" the voices answered.

"What is this place?"

"*More important than what...is where,*" the voices answered. "*It has been called many things since the beginning. You know it as the Void, but in a different age, it went by another name. It was first known as the Dorekstone.*"

"I...I don't understand."

"*It lives in everyone. It was once a gateway—a bridge that allowed anyone to tap into the power that we three possess. But since the dawn of the ensignis, the world has chosen to praise itself and remained blind to what was truly important. Once greed found a foothold, it funneled here until nothing was left but a bottomless and unfillable void. Our power was never meant to dwell with such darkness, so it stayed hidden. When you gave your life for Thrain, you broke the seal that Beswic's curse had over it, and you were no longer bound by its power.*"

"So does this mean...I'm dead?" Alrin asked.

"*Far from it, Alrin. You are the dawn—the first light after the darkest of nights. But now the burden rests on you to bring this light to the rest of the world.*"

"But why me?" Alrin asked. "Who am I to bear this burden?"

The colors that circled him turned soft and warm. "*That is why it must be you,*" they said. "*Start by showing them the hole in their puzzle box.*"

There it was again—the puzzle box. It had always been just another riddle he could never figure out. The hidden meaning within its hidden meaning. "Jorund never told me why it was really there," Alrin said. "He only said it would mean something different to everybody."

"*And what does it mean to you?*" the voices asked.

"I know it's supposed to symbolize the emptiness we feel within that drives us," he answered. "But...to me it seemed like he just enjoyed telling children that sand story. Honestly, I think it was just so they would come back and ask him why it was there."

"*Yes,*" answered the voices. "*The hole in the box serves the same purpose as the Dorekstone. They were placed for no other reason than to point you back to those who placed them. For those who truly search for their meaning must inevitably return to their maker.*"

"It was you, wasn't it? You made all of this. The Dorekstone...Dalroth...everything."

"*Yes,*" they answered. "*But that is something that no one can be forced to see. Like the meaning of the puzzle box, all must find it for themselves. Even those who are blind to it can never deny it—there is a void that lives inside them that power can never fill or satisfy. It is there that you must shine your light. Though the world seems as though it has never cared, it has been searching since the beginning.*"

"Then I was right," Alrin said. "I wasn't chosen for anything. There was never a stone to begin with. It was just another answer for those who were asking the wrong questions—just like the Triclaves."

"*Oh, Alrin...we chose everyone. But the secret to our power was never hidden in a stone, and it most certainly was never found in our strength, magic, or wisdom. It is found in anyone who chooses to see it. For it takes true strength to be humble...the wisest in the world are but fools if they are without compassion…and the truest of magic is found only within a sacrificial heart. This was why you passed the tests when no one else could. This is why the Trace felt further away the more your ensignis grew. You must be the light, Alrin, the light of distinction in the endless sea of similarity. If you awaken but one to this truth, then you will have shown them something far greater than their ensignis ever could.*

"*Now go,*" said the brothers, "*and rid the world of this shadow. Be the light of distinction…to end all distinction.*"

And that's when it finally came—the light at the end of the tunnel. The same door that had closed when his power ran out was suddenly wide open, and behind it was pure, unfathomable power.

It was like when the Trace had taken over, only now it was constant. There was a perfect harmony between him and everything around him. He could feel the movement of the trees, the beat of every bird's wing as it sat perched in the swaying branches above him, even the divergent paths of insects as they relinquished their trails to fallen leaves. Everything was connected. It all had a place. It all had a purpose.

Without even opening his eyes…he already knew. He could sense the 12-1-4 of Thrain's ensignis and the gash in Thrain's arm where the rock had pinned him atop the cliff just before Alrin had fallen. He sensed Thrain standing above him, the panic of his breathing growing steadily as he stared down at the emptiness of Alrin's hand.

They were gone. Like a heaviness upon your chest you can recognize only once it's lifted. The curse of his ensignis was gone. As he slowly opened his eyes, he found himself staring up at a familiar sky—the same sky he'd seen so many times before—the one at Batara.

Thrain leaned in over him. "Alrin!" he gasped. "How are you alive? You just fell off the cliff!"

Alrin sat up and looked around. The arrow he'd shot from the top of the cliff was stuck in the ground beside him, and he saw the fresh tracks of the deer after it had scampered off when he fell. He couldn't believe it. He was home.

As he followed the tracks away from the falls and into the woods, it reminded him of something and he finally started to understand. *Footprints*, he thought to himself, smiling. *Because all footprints are important.* Darius once asked if Alrin had only known how the story would end from the very beginning, would he have done anything differently? Alrin wasn't entirely certain if he'd simply been sent back, or in that first flash of unlimited power, everything that had happened was just a glimpse of one possible set of footprints. But one thing he did know for certain was now that everyone he loved the most was still very much alive, the possibility alone was a gift—one that he intended to take full advantage of.

"Alrin," Thrain said again. "Are you OK?"

With a crooked grin, Alrin looked up to his brother and repeated the words he'd said at the very beginning. "The sun rises and the sun falls, then hurries back to where it rises."